Wedding plans had come together much faster than Mia had anticipated. Not in the month that Damien had first given her, but in a little under two months, and that, she thought, had been a miracle. Between finalizing plans, working, and going to classes, she found little time for going to listen to Damien sing or spending time with her brother. In only two weeks she would be married to the man who made her shiver with desire. Just the thought of it made her wet. She could hardly wait.

MISTY BLUE

DYANNE DAVIS

Genesis Press, Inc.

Indigo Love Stories

An imprint of Genesis Press, Inc.
Publishing Company

Genesis Press, Inc.
P.O. Box 101
Columbus, MS 39703

All characters in this book have no existence outside the imagination of the author and have no relation whatsoever to anyone bearing the same name or names. They are not even distantly inspired by any individual known or unknown to the author and all incidents are pure invention.

ISBN: 1-58571-186-1
Manufactured in the United States of America

First Edition

Visit us at www.genesis-press.com
or call at 1-888-Indigo-1

DEDICATION

This book is dedicated to my editor, Sidney Rickman. Without you this story would have never been told. Thank you for hearing Mia's voice clearly when she attempted to steal Ashleigh and Keefe's story in *The Wedding Gown*, and for your wise counsel that perhaps Mia needed her own book. I am truly grateful for the psychic connection, and for your phenomenal editing. You belong in the editors' hall of fame. Thanks, Sidney.

ACKNOWLEDGMENTS

All Glory, Honor, Praise and Thanks go first and foremost to God—without whom I could do nothing.

I want to thank Dr. Goodman, for his support. You are the best, most gentle dentist in the world, but I'm glad you live in Bolingbrook and that you specialize in treating cowards.

To all of the staff at Dr. Summers, Goodman and Sulke office, you're all terrific.

I would like to thank all of the readers who have waited so patiently for this book to come out. You're the greatest. I appreciate your support. Thank you for your letters and emails this entire time.

I would like to thank the entire Genesis family, with special thanks to Angelique and Heather for always being there. And to Jennetta, I will always have a fondness for you. To the Genesis authors, I'm glad we're in this together.

Special thanks to Stephanie Geter Pansy, and congratulations on your marriage to George.

And God's blessings to Alvena McNeil. You're the best. Thanks for your daily emails.

To all the RWA Windy City Members, you are the most talented and supportive group of women on the planet. Thanks to Sherry Weddle, for being our official cheerleader.

To my critique partners: Wendy Byrne, Barb Deane and Lauren Ford. You three are terrific writers and told me in the first three chapters of *The Wedding Gown* that Mia was attempting to steal the book. Thank God, Sidney wouldn't allow it or Mia would not have had a chance to tell her story.

As always I begin with thanking God, and end with thanking the two most important people in my life. My husband Bill and my son Bill Jr. Bill, thank you for just being you, for never wavering, for going with me all over the place, for being so well known in the group that the women ask about you when you're not there, for not making me dust off my driver's license and for never mentioning that you taught me how to drive several decades ago. I love you. Billy, you're the greatest gift God ever gave to two parents. I love you with all my heart.

CHAPTER ONE

Mia's heart stopped. A tiny shiver began at her toes and traveled upward. "Damien," she whispered. She'd reluctantly accompanied Keefe and Ashleigh to the nightclub and had not really been paying attention when the emcee called his name. Nothing could have prepared her for seeing the man she loved living out his dream. And to think she'd almost missed it.

She turned to look at her brother and Ashleigh. "You knew he'd be here, didn't you, Keefe?" For an answer her brother kissed her forehead and held his hand out to Ashleigh, leaving Mia to deal with Damien on her on. He was right to do that. It was about time. A surge of pride filled her as she listened to Damien singing.

"I told you he was good," she murmured as her brother and Ashleigh walked away. Though she spoke to them, her eyes remained fastened on the stage. On Damien.

As the background music played on, Damien began crossing the stage toward her, his eyes never leaving her face. She held her breath. It had been so long, and his face was unreadable. He was giving no indication that he was happy to see her.

Then it happened. On the stage he stopped directly in front of her and smiled, first a tiny little smile that could have been missed. Then the smile took over his entire face until he was grinning broadly. His eyes closed briefly and when they opened, the look he gave her was the same as the one he'd given her the first time she'd seen him and had fallen in love with him—just from the look in his eyes.

As it had been the first time, the look mesmerized her, embraced her, and filled her with things she'd felt for only one man in her entire life—him. Her love was for him. Passion, lust and love tumbled through Mia and again her breath caught in her throat.

Right in front of her, suddenly Damien stopped singing and simply stared at her. Soon the entire audience was looking in her direction, no doubt wondering why the entertainer had stopped singing even though the music continued to play.

"Mia," Damien whispered, for the first time admitting to himself that he'd been afraid she wouldn't come. He'd almost called a dozen times to ask her, but hadn't. He'd been determined not to give in to his feelings for her. Yet he had hoped that she would be there to witness his success. And now she was. And all he wanted in the world was to climb down off that stage, take her in his arms and kiss her, and never let her out of his sight.

As he continued to stare at her, wanting to tell her those things, it finally registered that he wasn't singing. He smiled again at Mia and waited for an answering smile before he resumed singing and turned to walk toward the other end of the stage.

This was it—his moment in the sun. He glanced into the crowd of smiling faces, listened to the women screaming his name. Though it was just as he'd always imagined, the truth of the situation hit him as he sang two more numbers.

None of the attention meant what he'd thought it would. As much as he'd dreamed of a singing career, he wanted something else more. He wanted Mia in his arms. Now, not when the show was over. Now. He smiled at the audience, hoping they would forgive him for what he was about to do. If they didn't…well…so be it.

Damien walked back toward Mia, hardly able to continue singing over the sudden lump constricting his vocal cords.

Mia's attention was riveted on Damien. She didn't want to miss a note. As he sang, her heart soared with love for him. Conflicted, she both wanted the show to go on forever and also to end—so that she could throw herself into his arms, beg him to forgive her, and assure him that she would trust him forever.

When Damien turned and smiled at her again, her heart fluttered erratically and a sudden, intense heat speared her and pooled in her belly. She wanted nothing more than to be in Damien's arms. She needed to warn him not to come any closer but it was too late. He was coming closer and closer, and she was doing everything in her power to remain seated. She didn't want to ruin Damien's opening but God how she wanted to kiss him. He must have had the same thought because a moment before she could whisper, "No," he walked off the stage and stood directly in front of her. In his eyes she saw a question.

"Mia, I love you." Damien said hoarsely. "Can we try again?"

Her eyes shifted automatically to the door her brother had exited through and Damien shifted his body to block her view.

"I don't want Keefe, Mia, I want you."

Her heart soared. She didn't need Keefe's opinion on this one. She'd been given a second chance at loving Damien and she was darn well going to take it.

She flung herself into Damien's arms. "I love you," she murmured into his ear. "Can you ever forgive me?"

He pulled back a little to look at her. "I will if you'll answer my question. You didn't say," he smiled. "Can we start over?" He held her tighter, not wanting to let her go.

"Yes, yes, and yes!" she answered and gave him her entire heart in that moment, without hesitation, without reservation. His lips claimed hers and as the kiss deepened, loud clapping exploded, bringing both of them back to planet Earth. Damien smiled down at her.

"Come on," he urged, taking her hand and pulling her onstage with him. His arm firmly around her, he whispered directions to the band.

He began singing a ballad with music so sweet that each note wrapped around Mia like a warm hug. Then she heard the words, "*Mia, I love you.*" In that instant she realized he'd written the song for her and about her. She was holding back tears as he sang to her as if no one else in the world existed. When he was done, he pulled her to the center of the stage.

"This is Mia," Damien said by way of introduction. "Isn't she beautiful?" Everyone clapped and Damien grinned. "I guess you can all tell that I'm in love with her." Again, the audience went wild.

As much as she wanted to be in Damien's arms, Mia wasn't keen about doing it with an audience. She gave his hand a squeeze and started to walk away, a little afraid that he wouldn't let her off the stage. He followed, kissed her one last time, and released her to return to his singing. She couldn't believe it. She'd almost ruined things, but somehow it had all turned out fine. She smiled as she listened to Damien's deep sultry voice belting out song after song. He'd made it.

"Hi, honey, mind if we join you?"

"Introduce yourself to the girl. She doesn't know us."

Startled, Mia pulled herself together enough to smile at the woman and man who'd just approached her table. She knew instantly who they were. Damien's parents.

"Sure," she answered. She stuck her hand out. "I'm Mia," she said and immediately felt like an idiot. There was not one person in the club that didn't know her name.

"Yes, we know that, Mia," the man answered. "My name's Charles. Charles Terrell. Most everyone calls me Chuck. I'm Damien's old man and this is Kathy, Damien's old lady."

"Damien's mother," Kathy corrected.

"So you're the little piece of…"

"Chuck," Kathy warned.

"That wasn't what I was going to say. So, Mia, you're the little piece of fluff that's been driving Damien crazy all these months? I'd sure like to know what you've got. My son's nose is wide open. And honestly, you don't look at all like what I expected."

Mia felt the smile slipping from her face. Instant compassion for Damien flooded her. For months he'd put up with crap from her brother who until recently had despised him and had done everything in his power to keep her away from him, and at the same time he must have been taking crap at home.

"I beg your pardon," Mia said. "I have no idea what you're talking about."

"Don't listen to Chuck. He's just trying to start trouble. He's only playing with you. Don't take him seriously."

Mia studied them both as she listened to the lilting notes of Damien's song, praying that he would be at her side soon to deal with his parents. She smiled at Kathy but didn't answer.

"Damien told me that you thought you were better than him." Charles continued his attack.

"I never said that, and I never thought it," Mia defended. "There were other things going on in my life that had nothing to do with Damien."

"Yeah, we heard. While you were stringing our son along, you were engaged. We know all of that."

Mia's head snapped toward Charles and she wondered why she was being attacked. This man was almost an exact replica of the man she loved, broad shoulders, beautiful chestnut complexion, a mouth full of white teeth and a killer smile. He didn't, however, have Damien's deep sexy voice, though his own wasn't bad. And he definitely didn't inspire love in her the way his son did. No, on the contrary, what she was feeling for the older man was distaste. There was something slimy about him. While his mouth spoke of her hurting Damien, he'd used his eyes to undress her. She'd felt it as surely as if he'd used his hands and she was disgusted.

"Leave her alone, Chuck."

"I'm just saying I don't see what all the fuss is about. She's just a little slip of a thing. I don't see how she got the boy all twisted up like she did. I want to know her secret. What's the harm in asking her that?"

"It's none of your business."

Mia turned grateful eyes to Kathy before scanning the stage for Damien, praying he would hurry. The show was over but there were still three or four women hanging around him, wanting his autograph, and he was obliging.

"Damien," she whispered, knowing he couldn't possibly hear her. But at that instant he turned and caught her eye and his eyes widened in alarm. She could tell he was rushing through the next autograph.

Then he literally jumped from the stage and came toward her. A sigh of relief escaped Mia. This was one time she was grateful to be rescued. She stood and so did Kathy and Charles.

"Hey, you came. I didn't see you," Damien said to his parents.

"No, I suppose you didn't. Not when you kept looking over this way, at this little girl here."

Again Mia felt dirty. There wasn't anything wrong with the man's words, not even with the way he'd said them. But her skin was crawling all the same.

Damien's arm slid around her and she could almost swear that he was trying to push her behind him.

Damien answered his father's unasked question. "I didn't know Mia was going to be here."

"Then how did she rate a special seat right here in the front while your mother and I were stuck in some funky little corner? And by the way, hot shot, we had to pay to get in."

Charles was poking Damien in the chest with his finger as he punctuated each word. Kathy was biting her lip and Damien looked extremely uncomfortable. Mia was embarrassed for him. She could understand family humiliation. It was her specialty. Her mother had given her a lifetime's worth. Suddenly she noticed something she should have noticed before. Charles was feeling no pain. It was obvious he'd had more than a few drinks.

"How come she rates and we don't? We've been the ones supporting you. She had her ass off somewhere doing God knows what, with whoever. But we know it wasn't you. So why did you reserve a front row seat for her and not us?"

Now it was definitely not her imagination. Damien was positioning his body in front of hers. He was trying to protect her. Instead of feeling the intense annoyance and aversion for his father she had felt a moment before, Mia felt a surge of love for Damien.

"I'll pay for your admission and your drinks. Just tell me what you spent."

The emotion in Damien's voice was pure exasperation. Mia was extremely familiar with that tone.

"Fifty dollars, admission and drinks." Kathy looked at her son and smiled weakly.

Mia watched as Damien's hand went to his pocket.

"How the hell would you know? Did you pay for anything?" Charles interrupted. "It was a hundred."

Observing this family situation from behind Damien, Mia saw Damien tighten his jaw. She also saw as he counted out the money and handed it to his father that he didn't have anything left in his wallet.

"Now that you have your money, can I please give the two of you a proper introduction? Mia, my parents, my mother, Kathy Morrison, and my father, Charles Terrell." He continued before anyone else got the chance to speak, "No, they're not divorced. They were never married. Sorry, Pop, I just thought I'd beat you to it."

He kissed his mother's cheek and Mia watched the woman's eyes as they became veiled. Damien had never spoken a lot about his parents, just that he'd moved back home with his mother. His father, he hadn't mentioned.

"I told her to call me Chuck."

"You hate it when anyone calls you Chuck." For a moment Damien stared at his father in disbelief, then recovered. "Come on, everyone, let's sit down," Damien said.

"I still want to know how she rates a front row table," Charles said as he crumpled Damien's money and put it in his pocket.

"Ashleigh asked me to reserve a table. I did."

"You're banging them both?"

Damien leaned over and whispered to his father and when he pulled away, the man looked Mia over, a slight sneer on his face.

"I'm sorry, Mia. It seems my son thinks I've offended you. Perhaps I was wrong in my assessment of you. Maybe you didn't think you were too good for Damien."

He turned from Mia to glare at his son. "Maybe it's my son who's gotten weak since he moved back home with his mama." A huge scowl replaced the sneer. "Man, this woman's got you whipped. I warned you about that." He then turned his glare on Kathy. "So you finally got your way. You managed to turn my son into a freaking mama's boy. Well, if I have any say about it and you know I always have," he laughed crudely, "I'm going to see to it that he changes back."

Charles laughed at Mia. "Enjoy this while you can because I'm going to go find my son's balls. And when I do, I'm going to give them back to him and he's going to start acting like a man again, no more pulling some woman on the stage and singing to her, telling the whole damn audience that he's in love with her." He glared at Damien. "Do you think I ever did that with your mother? Hell, no!"

Mia watched as Kathy winced noticeably, as though she'd been hit. "I don't—

"I agree with Mia," Damien said, interrupting her, turning to look at her, pleading with his eyes. "I don't think now's the time for this."

"Makes me no never mind," Charles retorted. "I'm outta here."

"Chuck," Kathy stood. "How am I supposed to get home?"

The look he gave her turned what before had been only dislike into something worse for Mia.

"Don't worry, Kathy, I'll take you home," Mia volunteered, ignoring the fact that her brother Keefe had brought her and she was herself without a ride home. Still, Damien's father needed someone to wipe that look off his face and Damien's mother needed an ally.

"Don't worry, Mom, I'll take you home." Damien kissed his mother's cheek and pulled Mia into his arms. "I'm so sorry. My pops had a few drinks. Will you please wait for me? I have another show."

"I'll wait." Mia smiled at his look of doubt. "I don't have a ride home either." She watched as he grinned, then retook the stage.

She sat down, barely glancing at Kathy. "Would you like something to…to…eat," she asked, changing her mind about asking the woman if she could buy her a drink. She didn't think she wanted to talk to anyone else tonight who'd been drinking.

"Thanks, Mia, but I'm fine."

Mia looked up and found Kathy studying her, a strange look on her face. "Is something wrong?" she asked, praying she was not opening herself up to attack by another of Damien's parents.

"I love my son," Kathy began, "but I'm wondering why you're with him. I can understand why you broke it off but to do it again…" She tsked. "He's going to hurt you, Mia. He can't help it. He's just like his father."

Like father like son. Like mother like daughter. Mia had more in common with Damien than she'd ever realized. It was in that moment that her heart broke for him and it was also in that moment that she determined that she would mend both their hearts, attend their hurts. Damien was nothing like his father and she was nothing like her mother.

"Kathy, don't worry. Damien is not Charles. He loves me."

"He's my son, but he's a dog just like his father. He couldn't be true to you if you paid him."

"But he has been."

"That's because he didn't have you. You confused him. He didn't know how to react."

"Why are you saying this?" Mia asked, puzzled.

"Because I don't want you to get hurt." Kathy's eyes wandered toward the door. "I'm not doing this to be mean."

"You don't believe Damien loves me?"

"He does for now, until he gets what he wants, then…" She shrugged her shoulders. "I think his love will fade and you'll be all alone and heartsick. With luck maybe you'll have one thing to remember him by. A baby, a blessing and a curse."

Mia took Kathy's hand. "It's not going to happen, not to us. Damien loves me and I love him. You have no idea of the obstacles we've overcome to get here."

"I know."

Mia watched as Kathy laughed softly. She was getting a sick feeling in the pit of her stomach and wished that the woman would just stop talking. But by the intense look on her face, Mia knew that wasn't likely to happen.

"I know him a hell of a lot better than you and I've known him for a whole lot longer. I birthed him. When he gets what he wants, I promise you he will throw you to the side. The two of them are just alike. They're two peas in a pod. That might be a cliché, but it's true " She nodded again toward the door. "That's Damien in twenty more years. Look at me and you'll see yourself in twenty years if you stay with him."

Mia stared at Kathy, then shook her head and looked toward the stage. Kathy was wrong. *Ignore her*, she ordered her mind. Her future with Damien would be whatever they made it.

CHAPTER TWO

"I'll bet you wish you hadn't chosen tonight to make up," Damien said as he climbed back into the car and shut the door. He glanced again at his house and saw the lights being turned off in the kitchen. That meant his mother was going to bed. He sighed, wishing as always that she had more in her life. He had tried for years to dissect his parents' relationship to understand why they remained in each other's life, but there was a missing piece he'd yet to find.

Another quick look and Damien could drive away. All was safe; he knew that. He'd walked his mother into the house and checked it, making sure. An old habit, one he'd adopted when he was fourteen. He wished he could stop worrying about her and pretending that he didn't. Besides, his worrying had not changed things for either of them.

Mia smiled. "How's your mother?"

"Fine. She's used to this. I wish I could tell you that I don't know what happened, that this was the first time I ever saw them behave that way. But it would be a lie and I think you know that." He pressed his lips together and rolled his eyes. He didn't want to talk about his mother right now, not when he was feeling ashamed of his parents and feeling guilty for doing so.

"She made a choice. She doesn't have to put up with this; she never did. Apparently she wants to."

"And your father doesn't have to treat her the way that he does." Damien turned slightly to frown at her and Mia stopped. "It's your family. I'm sorry."

"No, I am. I had no idea that you would be there tonight. And I didn't think they were coming. They said they weren't." He tried for a smile. "It looks like everyone chose tonight to surprise me."

Mia leaned her head on his shoulder. "Are you sorry that I came?"

"Are you crazy?" he asked. "What do you think? Did I look sorry to you?" He tried for a smile. "The only thing I'm unhappy about is that your first impression of my family is the one you got tonight. My pops is really charming, especially when he tries. I guess it might be my fault that he was so rude to you."

He gave a half smile. "I guess after I told him everything that had been happening with us he just formed a negative opinion of you. I would have liked the chance to explain to him that I didn't mean everything I said."

"Your mother was nice."

"Yeah, a nice doormat."

"Damien!"

He glared then at no one in particular. "Tell me you didn't think that, that you didn't wonder why the hell she was putting up with that crap from a man who wasn't even her husband, a man she still holds out hope will marry her? God, what a fool. Tell me something, Mia. Why didn't you ever tell me?" he asked, shifting the focus of the conversation from his parents, not wanting Mia to play psychologist and scrutinize his emotions. Hell, he'd done enough of that to last him through eternity.

"Tell you what?"

"You know what I'm talking about."

"Not really."

Damien sighed. "Why didn't you ever tell me that you were a virgin?" he said softly. "Didn't you think I should know that?"

"Who told you?"

"Your brother."

"My brother?" Heat flamed to her face. "He doesn't know."

"Well, he does now. He came to talk to me with Ashleigh and they both told me."

"Why?"

"I don't know. I guess they were trying to help." He pulled into the driveway of Mia's building and turned to look at her. "That doesn't matter. Why didn't you tell me?"

"It didn't seem important."

"That's a lie, Mia. It's important to you or you wouldn't still be a virgin. Didn't you think it would make a difference to me knowing your refusal to make love with me was because you were...what? Afraid? Now it all makes sense."

He kissed her eyelids. "Don't worry, baby girl, now that I know, there's no need for you to be afraid. I knew you wanted me as much as I wanted you."

Damien pressed Mia against the door with one hand, relieving her of the key to her apartment with the other.

"I wasn't afraid." She watched as surprise filled his eyes. She waited until he opened the door and followed her in before saying more.

"You mean it was me?" Damien asked, his voice tinged with hurt.

"No, of course it wasn't you."

"Then what?"

"I'm not a slut."

"A slut?" Damien frowned. "What are you talking about? Making love doesn't make you a slut."

"That's what you think."

"That's what I know."

"And you know this because? Damien, you've slept with so many women you don't even get a vote on this. You're the equivalent of a male slut." To Mia's surprise, Damien burst out laughing.

"Tell me something, Mia. Didn't you ever want to know what it was like to make love? Didn't you ever come close to giving in?" He grinned.

"Yes to both questions." She was also grinning, not telling Damien anything that he wasn't asking.

He was standing in front of her now, his eyes capturing her and his hands wandering over her body. "Tell me when you were tempted."

"The first time?" she asked.

"That and every time after."

Mia kissed him on the lips. "The first time I was tempted was the day I met you. And every time after has been whenever I was in a room with you."

"Like now?"

"Like now."

"Then why haven't we?"

"I plan on being with only one man, Damien, and that man will be my husband."

"Ahh," he said and released her. "But you were engaged to James. Why didn't you ever make love with him?"

"There's a difference between being engaged and being married. We both know what happened to the engagement. I met you, and he married someone else, so…"

"So you're not taking any chances?"

"I never thought of it like that. I just thought whoever I married would be glad I waited." She smiled at him, then went past him to sit on the sofa.

"Are you sure some of this doesn't have to do with your brother?"

"Why would my being a virgin matter to Keefe?"

"I can think of a good reason. The guy thinks he's your father instead of your brother and you act like it too. You don't want to do anything he would disapprove of. So I think it has something to do with your not wanting to disappoint him."

Mia lifted her face so she could better glare at Damien, who was still standing. "Why are you trying so hard to pick a fight?" To her surprise he smiled before answering.

"Is it that obvious?"

"Yeah, it's that obvious. "Come on, are you really so anxious to fight with me that you don't want to make up?" She bowed her head. "I mean, make up more fully," she finished.

"Are you saying what I think you're saying?" He was at her side in two easy strides. "You mean finally you're going to let me make love to you?"

"My God, Damien, you have a one track mind and you don't listen," she said, shoving him aside. "You're like those e-mail jokes I keep getting that say, 'Tell a man to pick up his clothes off the floor and he hears, blah, blah, blah, on the floor, you and me, right now, oh baby come on.'"

Damien couldn't help laughing. "Men are not like that."

"Oh no?" Mia replied. "I told you not less than two minutes ago I wasn't going to…that I was staying a virgin until I married. And what did you just ask me? '*Oh baby, are you ready?*'"

"That wasn't what I said."

"That's what I heard."

"And you say men don't hear well." He pulled her into his arms and kissed her thoroughly. "In that case, Mia Black, will you marry me?"

"That's not much of a proposal."

"I should have known." He grinned. "Girl, you do believe in working my nerve, don't you?" He dropped from the sofa onto one knee and held Mia's hand. "Mia Black, will you marry me?"

"Why?" she asked.

He smiled and a sound escaped his lips. "That wasn't quite what I was expecting. Shouldn't your answer be yes?"

"It will be as soon as you answer the question."

"Because I love you. Is that good enough?"

"Not when you say it like that."

"Mia!"

"Damien?"

He groaned. "I must truly love you because you have tried every nerve I possess." He got up and walked to the refrigerator for a soda. He popped the top, took a swig and walked back over to where Mia sat waiting expectantly. He once again got on one knee, held out the metal ring from the soda can and said, "Mia, I love you with all my heart. You're all I think about, all I've thought about since the moment I met you. I can't see my life without you in it. Will you marry me and make me the happiest man on the face of the planet?"

She smiled and he slipped the metal circle on her finger. She looked at it. "It's beautiful," she laughed, "and that, my darling, was the perfect proposal for the start of our perfect life together."

"Now can I have some?" Damien asked as he took her in his arms.

"We're getting married," Mia shouted into the phone.

"When?" Keefe asked.

"I don't know. We haven't talked about it yet, but we're going to. I just wanted to tell you. I wanted you to be the first person to know. I wanted to make sure." She glanced at the sofa, at Damien. She had been about to say she hoped Keefe approved, but changed her mind. "I wanted to make sure you knew how happy I am."

"I'm glad, Mia, Keefe replied. "I really am. Damien does love you."

"What about you?" she asked her brother. "Anything you want to tell me about your plans with Ashleigh?"

"Well, we were in the process of, shall we say, talking about our own future when you called."

"I'm sorry…oh Kee, I'm sorry…," she stammered, finally realizing what it was she'd interrupted.

"Don't be," he laughed. "I'll talk to you in the morning."

Mia grinned at Damien. "Looks like I caught them at a bad moment."

"At least he has the right idea. I'm glad that at least somebody is getting some action tonight."

"Is that the only reason you want to get married?"

"No, but I can tell you this: I won't wait for you to plan a wedding a year from now. I don't even want a wedding in months. I want to get married as soon as possible, because I am tired of waiting." She sat on his lap. "Aren't you?" he asked as he eased his hand under her bra and began caressing her.

His arousal pushed into her thigh. "Tell me you're not curious to know what I feel like, what I look like? I can show you, you know, right now."

"Will you stop teasing me?"

"You think I'm teasing?" He bent his head and pushed it under her sweater, shoving her bra upward in the process. "Set a date, Mia, and make it quick."

"No, Damien, stop." Damien's hands were all over her and Mia was having the same feelings she always got when he touched her. Dangerous feelings. She was doing everything in her power to keep her vow. She wouldn't become like her mother. She moaned low. She heard Damien's muttered curse but he stopped and moved away, looking angrily at her.

"Mia, we're not kids. I'm getting tired of this."

"So am I. Why can't you take no for an answer and stop trying?"

"Because I love you and I want you. Damn, there's nothing wrong with that. Or do you need permission from big brother?"

"I told you my brother has nothing to do with my decision. Don't blame Keefe because you're frustrated."

"Horny, Mia, that's what I am, not some nice little word. I'm horny. And do you want to know why? You are the culprit, my dear, sweet, innocent virgin. I haven't had any since I met you."

"Damien…"

"Not only haven't I had any," he continued, ignoring her wish to clean up his conversation, "but I haven't even come close to getting any. I'm thinking, okay, we're engaged, at least a little sample."

"I'm not a deli and I don't give samples. You have to…"

"What? I have to buy the merchandise?"

"I don't like the sound of that."

"Then how do you want to say it? You're talking about me but you're the one that's making it sound like a bribe."

"You know something, Damien, it's like we have two things going for us, passion or anger. As much as I love you, it makes me wonder if we're not moving too fast. What happens when the passion dies?"

"Oh, baby girl, you won't have to worry about that. When I make love to you, you're going to be begging for more. I can hear you right now screaming my name. '*Damien, Damien, please don't stop, please.*'"

Mia laughed. "You're awfully sure of yourself and very cocky I might add. I hope this isn't all boast. I do hope you can fulfill that promise."

"I can show you right now if you want. There are a couple of things I know for a fact that I'm good at, and making love is one of them."

"And you think that's a ringing endorsement?"

"I'm just telling you the facts so you'll know what to expect on our wedding night and every night of our married life."

"Promises, promises." Mia sashayed past him, laughing when he caught her, going breathless when he kissed her.

"Go ahead, feel me, Mia," he said, placing Mia's hand over his constant arousal. "It won't bite and there really isn't a good reason to keep putting it off."

"Not a good reason? Are you kidding me? We have to be careful, make sure everything's perfect. We've been through so much. Just a few months ago you were living with the woman my brother fell in love with."

"So what? That's in the past."

"The not-so-distant past. I met you when I went to buy her wedding gown. A gown, I might add, she made to marry you."

"We were never really in love. Even if we had been, it's over. Keefe is with Ashleigh and I'm with you. Let it go," Damien urged, pulling Mia close.

She moved her body a little ways from Damien, shrugging her shoulder. "I suppose if I were Ashleigh, things would be different right now. She probably wouldn't hold out on you."

Damien was glaring, "Damn it, Mia. Is this some kind of test? I'm in love with you. You, Mia, not Ashleigh. What is it that you want? I can honestly say for the first time in my life, I'm truly in love. You're all I think about, all that I want… Well, maybe not all that I think about." He smiled then, his voice becoming more gentle.

"I'm not going to tell you that I don't want to make love to you. I've wanted to make love to you from the moment I saw you standing there in that wedding gown. That hasn't changed. Hell no, if anything it's intensified."

Damien exhaled noisily. This was not altogether an unfamiliar role, comforting someone he loved. He'd always done it with his mother but never with a woman he'd wanted to bed. But Mia was not a woman he just wanted to bed. He wanted her in his life forever. That was the one crucial point that made all the difference.

"Mia, I was true to you even when I didn't have to be. The entire time you wouldn't see me because you were waiting for your boyfriend to come home, because your brother disapproved, I was true."

"So was I."

"But you didn't have outside forces working against you. I did. Even when Keefe got me the worst job that he could, I hung in there. What did I do? I'd shovel manure all day at the zoo, come here and you'd get me horny as hell, then push me away. You were still the only woman that I wanted."

"That's the reason you believe you love me?"

"It's love, Mia. I've never denied myself anything, especially loving. And like I told you before, I hadn't touched Ashleigh in months even before I broke up with her."

"You didn't break up with her, Damien, she dumped you. And you were definitely not faithful to her. You used her charge card to take another woman to a hotel, remember?"

His grin was wide. "True, but I'm trying to tell you that although I've been a dog most of my life and proud of it, I've changed. Loving you has made me see the light."

"I'll bet."

"Seriously, Mia, you're going to have to trust me. I'm too old to continue playing games. You're going to have to stop testing me."

"I wasn't testing you." She saw the disbelief on Damien's face and smiled. "Maybe just a little. I was just wondering if you had the chance,

19

if you would go back to Ashleigh. I mean, after all, you didn't leave Ashleigh because it was your choice."

"You don't have to keep saying that."

"But it's true." She felt herself getting hot in the face. "I'm not doing the things for you that she did so…"

"Sex isn't everything." He saw her look and grinned again. "I repeat, sex isn't everything. You want to know what you do for me, Mia? You make me feel proud of myself. I never would have believed I could be in a relationship where I wasn't getting laid. Hell, I bragged about that.

"And me working at a zoo? That is just so unbelievable. I walk through the gates everyday amazed that I work there. I love it. It doesn't matter what my job is."

"When I asked Keefe to help get you a job, I didn't know he would get you one at the zoo. I'm sorry that he got you the worst job he could find."

"Don't be. Sure, I know your brother got me this job to make me look bad in front of you. And at first I took it just to prove him wrong. I wasn't going to allow him to win. Now it seems this was just what I needed."

"To shovel—"

"Not that, being out in nature, working with the animals. There's something so spiritually rewarding about that." He shook his head. "I have a knack for it. The animals are comfortable around me. Your brother did me a big favor, trust me. I wouldn't mind working with the animals on a full-time basis."

"Should I tell him that?" Mia grinned.

"No, he'd probably talk them into giving me an inside job, something where I would have to wear a suit and tie, be more like him. No, baby, don't tell him." He pulled Mia closer, his lips finding hers, kissing her into submission. "No more talking about Keefe."

Her kisses matched his for hunger. When he touched her face she'd melted, and he'd known from the way she closed her eyes and the easy way her body swayed into him. She wanted him. This he knew with a certainty. Damien thought he would come right there in his pants.

This was getting to be a hell of a lot harder than he'd thought. He'd started out teasing Mia, knowing that she wouldn't give in, but her moan of pleasure had sent him over the edge, wanting to take the kidding to a new level, wanting to make it real. She wanted it too. He'd made love with enough women to know that Mia was craving his touch. She might be a virgin but it didn't matter. She wanted him and he knew it. The thought of making love to her on their wedding night was all that was getting him though this.

He groaned as his flesh jerked against the coarse fabric of his jeans. He backed off just a little. He had to wait, and then he would keep his promise to her. He would make her beg for more.

"Damien."

"Yes, baby."

"Your lips are so soft."

"What?"

"I like the feel of your lips." Mia was trying as hard as she could to bring some control back to both of them. Her statement startled Damien and made him smile, giving her a chance to catch her breath.

While Damien was kissing her Mia had wanted to cry out from the joy she felt in her heart. She wanted to give in to all the feelings, but thoughts of her mother's many men kept her from it.

Still, it was hard. She'd never felt this way about anyone except Damien. As much as she hated hearing him tease her about what a great lover he was, she'd known it anyway. She wished that she could be his first. But then again, at least one of them needed to know what to do. If she didn't know how very much he loved her she would worry. But he was teasing and she knew it.

"One month, Mia, and not one day longer," Damien insisted.

"I have to find a hall. I have to call my mother. I have to send out invitations. I need more time. One month isn't enough, no way." Mia stared at Damien in amusement, thinking there was no possible way she could do as he was asking.

"We could just elope. We could get married tonight."

"You're kidding, right?"

"Why? A marriage only needs two people. We're both here."

"Damien, I want a wedding."

"Okay, then take your month." Damien groaned loudly, rolling his eyes.

"It's impossible to have a wedding in a month."

"I suggest that you make it be enough because I'm not waiting longer than that." He got the calendar and pointed at a date. There, one month. Start making your calls. I don't need a wedding. All I need is you, a justice of the peace and a nearby bed."

"If you don't stop that I'm going to believe that you're marrying me for one reason only. Help me, Damien." Mia was trembling and turned watery eyes on him. "Please help me keep my vow. I don't have the will to resist you anymore. I'm tired of fighting. All I want is to lie next to you in bed. I want to have your hands all over my body."

"Then why don't you give in to those thoughts?" he grinned. "I wouldn't mind and I wouldn't tell anyone."

"Will you help me?" Mia insisted. "Will you turn the power down at least halfway?"

"My pops was right," Damien moaned as he leaned back against the sofa and pulled her head onto his chest, "I am whipped. Yes, Mia, I'll help you keep your vow. I won't pressure you until after the wedding. I promise, but after that, baby girl, look out. And I'd advise you not to choose a place for our honeymoon that you really want to visit. I don't plan on letting you out of bed long enough for sight-seeing."

Mia was right. He had to stop. He would have never gone so far if his father's words hadn't been nagging at him. He was close to his father, almost as close as Mia was to her brother, and the thought of his father thinking he was a punk didn't sit well with Damien. Add to that the knowledge that Mia and his father didn't like each other. It had sparked something in him which had gone a little out of control, making him touch her in forbidden places.

22

"I love you," Mia's voice whispered soft and sweet, bringing Damien back to what was important. For a moment he'd forgotten how much Mia meant to him.

"I love you too, baby." He hugged Mia to him. Just like that the worries about what his father thought ceased for the moment. He wanted Mia and he would do whatever it took to be with her. Even if that meant that to his father he was being punked. Damien knew that he wasn't.

CHAPTER THREE

Ten seconds after Damien left Mia's apartment she was on the phone calling her mother. She had no idea what time it was in Phoenix. She didn't care. This was one of the few times in her life that she had a number where she could actually reach her mother. As she dialed the number, Mia couldn't help recalling the pain her mother's nomadic life had caused both her and Keefe. But she refused to dwell on that. She was getting married to Damien and she wanted her mother to know.

"Who is this?" her mother's sleepy, angry voice barked.

"It's me, Mom, Mia."

"Mia, why on earth are you calling me at this time of morning?"

Mia swallowed her hurt. Sure it was early, but shouldn't her mother's first comment have been to ask if there were any problems, not to indicate that she was being inconvenienced? She ignored her pain at her mother's coldness and answered.

"Damien and I made up." Mia was bubbling over with joy, so much so that she almost missed the silence on the other line. "Did you go to sleep on me, Mom?"

"No."

"Is there something wrong?"

"I was sleeping."

"I know. I guess I should have waited," Mia said, hoping her mother would say that it wasn't necessary, that she was just grumpy in the morning when she was first awakened, that she was happy Mia had called. Mia waited for a full minute but her mother didn't say another word.

"Damien asked me to marry him. I wanted to tell you."

Silence.

"I'm really sorry I woke you up. You're right, this could have waited."

"Thank you."

Mia was feeling like a fool. She wanted to cry like a little girl. Keefe had warned her over and over, but she'd dared to hope that things had changed. A month ago when she'd broken up with Damien, her mother had been there for her. She'd held Mia and allowed her to cry. She'd been wise, all knowing, and had given both Keefe and her good advice. For the first time in their lives, she'd been a mother, something she'd never been before.

Mia tamped down her feelings. She shouldn't have gotten her hopes up that things would remain that way. Her brother had warned her to be grateful that someone had put their mother in a giving mood. She blew out a breath; she would deal with this later.

"Do you want me to call you later with the details? I mean, do you want to come?"

"Of course I'll come, Mia. Your brother would never stop yakking about it if I didn't. Besides, with the size of that last check he wrote me, he probably thinks I owe it to you."

There was so much vehemence in her mother's voice, something that wasn't normally there. Usually she had more of a pleading, whinny quality. *That's when she wants money.* The thought came to her in a flash and she attempted to push it away. But it was too late. Another came on its heel. *She doesn't need you at the moment. She doesn't need you to beg Keefe to give her money.* He already had and he'd done it as he'd done most things in his life. To make Mia happy.

"Is there something wrong? You sound angry."

"I was sleeping."

Push it way, Mia, don't think about it. It doesn't matter, don't let her know she's hurting you. "I'll let you get back to sleep," Mia managed to say. "I'll call you later."

"Why? You woke me up. Give me the details now, then you won't be tempted to wake me again."

"I'm sorry," Mia repeated, biting her lips to keep away the tears.

"You've said that already. Just give me the details and don't get so dramatic. I don't have time for this."

That was just it. Mia didn't really have any details. She was just happy and for some foolish reason she'd thought her mother, who hadn't given a damn about them their entire lives, would this one time be happy for her.

A picture of the foster home she'd been forced into after her mother abandoned them came to her mind but as usual she pushed it away. She wasn't going to revisit that. She was beyond that. She was a counselor; she would counsel herself through it. She had a master's in psychology and in another year she would have her doctorate. She could deal with this. She could and she would.

"We're getting married in a month. Keefe is—

"A month! Are you pregnant?" Her mother interrupted.

"No, I'm not pregnant."

"I can't believe you would be stupid enough to get yourself pregnant before you got a ring on your finger. He could change his mind, you know."

"Mom, you're not listening to me. I'm not pregnant."

"I don't believe you. Why the hell would you plan a wedding in a month? That's the only thing that makes sense. You're lying, Mia."

"I'm not pregnant. I'm still a virgin," Mia blurted, not meaning to, yet not wanting her mother to think she was either stupid or, God forbid, a slut.

"Damien is just anxious to get married. He said he won't wait longer than a month."

Loud laughter greeted Mia's explanation and for the first time in her life she felt a spark of hatred for her mother and vowed to harden her heart as Keefe had always done. She didn't care how many books said not to allow hate to consume her. Right this moment, hate was the only thing she could feel, because she could tell from the harsh sound of her mother's laughter that she wouldn't like the words that would come when the sound stopped. *Later, Mia,* she scolded herself. *Deal with this afterward.*

"All of those months you were sneaking around with him, lying to your brother, and you're a virgin?" She laughed again. "And the infamous Damien, the dog, wants you? My God, Mia, he's going to be so disappointed. You have no idea what to do. Your brother told me about all the women Damien's been with. Do you really think you can make a man like that happy? You want some advice, Mia? Find a man and get some experience before you marry Damien or he's going to kick you out on your ass so fast it won't be funny. A virgin." She laughed again. "In this day and age."

Mia's face was burning. She knew she should just hang up. She didn't have to listen to this. It didn't matter that it was coming from her mother. She was an adult. She didn't have to take this. But she found herself unable to let go of the phone.

"Okay, Mia, I suppose your pompous ass brother is still going to give you away?"

That did it. No way was Mia going to remain mute and allow her mother to attack the only true parent she'd ever had. "What's wrong with you, Mom? Why are you acting so nasty? Why are you back to attacking Keefe?" *Why the change? A little over a month ago you were kissing Keefe's behind.* That's what Mia wanted to say but didn't. She counted to ten. *Push it away. Don't let her get to you.*

"I was only making a true statement." Her mother laughed.

"Keefe is not pompous. And of course he's giving me away."

"Keefe's your brother, not your father. Even if he thinks he is. He isn't. I ought to know. Why don't you ask someone else?"

"Why don't you tell me who my father is? Maybe I'll ask him."

"How the hell would I know? Pick one, I gave you enough choices."

"Keefe's giving me away. He may be my brother but he also played the role of father for me," Mia paused, "and he was also my mother."

"Do you think that's going to hurt me? You're both adults. Do you think I'm going to beat myself up over every little thing I did wrong in my life? No, Mia, I'll tell you, I'm not."

"Little thing? You abandoned us. We went to foster care."

"And you got out. It's over, let it go. God, you're the one who's going to be a psychologist. Didn't any of your teachers ever teach you that?"

Mia couldn't believe the conversation she was having with her mother. She shook her head. It felt as if she'd just dropped down in the middle of some horror flick. Her mother had never talked to her in that manner before. *Because I gave her money.*

Keefe was right. He'd always been right. Their mother was a narcissistic, self-centered woman who didn't care. In a rare moment she'd reached out a helping hand and Mia had allowed that to make her think there might yet be hope. Probably the best thing her mother had ever done for them was to ditch them.

"Listen," Mia said, intending to end the conversation. "I'll let you know when everything's settled." She wondered if she really would bother calling her mother again.

"When are you going to stop taking advantage of your brother?"

Wham! That came out of nowhere. The moment when Mia had been able to disconnect the phone vanished. "What are you talking about?"

"You. It's time you let him go. Start now. You're making a new life for yourself. Start with that. Pick someone else to walk you down the aisle."

"Why? Keefe wants to…"

"How do you know that? Have you ever given him a choice? I'll bet if you did he'd take it."

She knew she should hang up the phone and not allow her mother to get to her, but she had to ask. "What makes you think Keefe doesn't want to walk me down the aisle?"

"Mia, you're either stupid or truly naive. Your brother is in love with Ashleigh. Get the picture?"

"What does that have to do with him giving me away?"

"Duhhh. You're marrying the man who was engaged to the woman your brother is now in love with. Use your brain, girl. Do you really think your brother will be comfortable doing that? No. You're taking advantage of him, just like you always have."

Mia winced. "Keefe loves me. He wants to do it," she repeated, hating the fact that her mother had reduced her to feeling as if she were still a little girl. Mia could feel the pressure building in her. She shook her head, ordering herself to not allow the words inside.

"That's just it, Mia. He's not your father and you've asked too much of him already. He's given up everything for you. Now you want to put him in a position where he's bound to be uncomfortable. Why don't you ask him? Tell him you're going to ask someone else. See if he puts up a fight or if he's relieved."

"I can't do that to Keefe. He's looking forward to this."

"Is he? Are you sure?"

"Yes, I'm sure," Mia answered, not feeling sure at all. "I want him to…"

"See? There it is. It's what *you* want. And you two have the nerve to call me selfish. I'm realistic, Mia, I don't use rose-colored glasses to look at the world as you do. I see very well without them. I was there. I heard Keefe tell you it was time the two of you let each other go."

"He didn't mean it like that. He just thought we depended on each other too much. He would be hurt if I asked someone else. You don't know him and you don't know what you're talking about."

"Ahh, you're getting angry." Her mother laughed at her. "Are you afraid to know that your brother has gotten tired of you? Wake up, Mia, and grow up. It's time you let your brother get on with his life. If I'm wrong, he'll tell you. But for heaven's sake, you owe him that much. Just tell him you're going to ask someone else. You'll see how relieved he is."

"I'll talk to you later, Mom," Mia said, this time more than ready to hang up.

"Mia," her mother called out before she could hang up. "About that other thing. I wasn't kidding you. You'd better get some experience before your wedding night or Damien's going back to his old ways real quick. Hell, the first woman that he sees he's going to want to screw if you don't know what you're doing."

"You're wrong."

"Am I? Hey, I just thought of something. I know why Damien wants to marry you in such an all-fired hurry. You won't give it up and he wants the drawers. God, how I wish I could be in the room with you on your wedding night. What a joke that's going to be."

Mia hung up the phone, her mother's vulgar words and cruel laughter ringing inside her head. All of the joy she'd felt when she'd called her mother was now gone. She looked down at her hands. They were trembling. She wanted to talk to her brother, tell Keefe what their mother had said to her. She wanted to hear him tell her that the whole thing was ridiculous, that of course he wanted to walk her down the aisle, that she was not being selfish in asking him, that he loved her. But she didn't call him. She'd deal with this as she had every problem in her life, only not right now. She didn't want to relive the conversation so soon. Her process would work when she was ready. It always had.

As for Damien, a lump formed in her throat. He'd been teasing her about giving it up. That wasn't why he wanted to marry her. She refused to entertain that thought. Mia hated her mother for planting the seeds of doubts. She knew her life with Damien would be what they made it. It still remained in her control. She was determined not to allow the seeds to take root.

Mia fell asleep knowing that her mother might be right about Keefe. He would do anything to make her happy, even if it made him miserable. He'd proven that over and over. God, she prayed, let her mother be wrong. She wanted him to be the one to give her away.

CHAPTER FOUR

Mia's hand shook as she applied her lipstick. Three days had passed since she'd talked to her mother. At the oddest times her mother's words would jump out at Mia, making her doubt, reminding her of things she'd rather keep hidden. Her mother's words had restarted the prickly sensation that crawled over Mia's skin when she'd been hurt.

She chewed on her lips, hating the way her mother always threw her a little off kilter. Every time she took two steps forward, boom, her mother would do or say something, and Mia would be back at the beginning. She hated the power her mother had over her; she hated the fact that in spite of all the woman had done she still wanted her mother to love her and Keefe.

Give Keefe a chance to say no. Tell him you're going to ask someone else to walk you down the aisle. Are you afraid?

A shiver traveled from the crown of her head to her back and hovered around her hips. Mia blew out a breath, determined to let go of her mother's hateful words. It had always been Mia and Keefe against the world. Nothing had changed. Her emotions began to thunder through her faster than she could keep pace, faster than even her deep breathing could handle. *Later*, she thought. *I'll deal with it later.*

With an even shakier hand Mia finished applying her makeup rushing out to answer the door when she heard Damien calling her name. Tonight they would meet with Keefe and Ashleigh. The four of them would mend their fences and attempt to become a family. She would forget her past; she would forget everything but her future happiness.

Keefe sat next to Ashleigh, smiling at his baby sister. She was beaming and he was happy for her, thrilled that she was getting what she wanted. Still, there was doubt that clawed at him, fear that she was rushing things.

"A month, Mia? Why the rush?" he asked at last, watching as Mia's face became red.

"Damien and I talked. It's going to be closer to two months."

"That's still a very short time. What's the rush?" Keefe turned as he heard a snicker from Ashleigh and glanced at her, then at Damien before he understood. "Oh, I get it," he said softly, not wanting to carry that part of the conversation farther. "Okay, tell me what you want me to do and I'll do it."

"When are you going to stop taking advantage of your brother? He's not your father and you've asked too much of him already." Her mother's words were hammering away at her. *Not now*, she thought, balling her hand in her lap and wishing she'd examined her feelings earlier.

She shook her head slightly before looking at the way Keefe was holding Ashleigh's hand. Could her mother be right? She didn't want to think it, but the notion refused to budge. Maybe she should offer him an out and see if he'd take it.

"Mia, snap out of it. There's a lot to be done in two months, but between the two of us I'm sure we can handle it. Now what do you want me to do?"

"Nothing."

"Nothing?" Keefe laughed and shook his head, grinning at his sister. She was kidding, she had to be. This was Mia. Not want him to do anything? No way was that possible. "Mia, come on, we don't have time for us to pretend you don't need my help. I'm willing to give it. Now tell me what you need."

"I'm serious. I don't need you to do anything. I'm going to handle everything on my own."

"I can help," Damien offered.

"So can I," Ashleigh chimed in. "Four people working will take a lot of the pressure off you, Mia."

"Thanks," Mia said slowly, "but I don't need any help. I want to do this, Keefe. Alone," she said for emphasis.

Keefe tried smiling but he couldn't, so he licked his lips instead. "You don't need me?" he asked.

"I don't need you." Mia answered.

A lump was forming in his throat. He must be saying it wrong. He decided to try again. He smiled, trying not to show that he was hurt. "You need me to walk you down the aisle," he said, hoping that by repeating the word '*need*' Mia would look up at him and realize what she'd said. Instead, she smiled at Damien before answering him.

"I was thinking of asking someone else to walk me." 'Give him a choice, leave it up to Keefe.' Heat flooded her face and her palms turned sweaty. *This is crazy*, Mia thought. Why should she even think about the nonsense her mother had said? She should not doubt her brother. If she were going to doubt anyone, it should be her mother, not Keefe.

"Who's going to walk you down the aisle?" Keefe was pissed. It wasn't like Mia to shut him out of the most important day of her life.

"I was thinking of asking Jerry."

Keefe swallowed and rubbed his chin, wondering what was going on. When he finally looked up, Damien was staring at him with that damn compassion in his eyes, making Keefe forget that he'd decided to bury the hatchet. He felt the fingers of Ashleigh's hand gently caress his thigh, trying to offer him comfort.

This was too much. He'd planed forever to walk Mia down the aisle. Just in the past year he had been the one who was going to give her away when she was supposed to marry James. What had changed? He glared at Damien, returning his look of compassion with one of anger. He didn't want compassion from the man. Suddenly he knew what was different. It had to be Damien who didn't want him involved in Mia's life.

Keefe didn't answer Mia. He couldn't. How could she sit there so casually talking about shutting him out of her life? He couldn't believe it.

"Did he put you up to this?" Keefe hissed between clenched teeth, jerking his thumb in Damien's direction. "Is this some kind of payback for my initial reaction to your being with Mia? Is it the job," he asked, turning toward Damien.

"I had nothing to do with this," Damien said, defending himself.

"Leave him alone, Keefe. This was my decision. It's what I want to do."

"Then by all means do it," Keefe sputtered. "I wouldn't dream of stopping you. In fact that should be one of the first things you take care of. You want to make sure he's not busy."

"I know what I need to do and when I need to do it. You're not my father, Kee. Stop acting like you are."

Suddenly Keefe was finding it difficult to breathe. He put his hand on his chest and saw the concern in Ashleigh's eyes. She handed him a glass of water and he took a sip, knowing that it would take a lot more than water to get past the hurt.

"I just want Jerry's number." Inside she was praying, *Please, Kee, just tell me, no way, no how, is Jerry going to walk you down the aisle. Tell me that you want to do it. Tell me that Mom's wrong. Please, Keefe.*

Keefe stood and reached in his back pocket for his wallet. He rifled angrily through the assorted cards, then threw one down on the table.

Mia watched her brother, her vision clouded by memories of not being wanted by her aunts, her cousins, and her mother. But she could only continue on the path she'd started.

"Do you think he'll want to do it?" Mia forced the words from her mouth, trying to give her brother one more chance. Her throat was so dry she didn't know how any words could come out.

"Why shouldn't he?" Keefe answered, wanting to ask her instead, *Why do you want him?* Jerry wasn't the one who'd raised her. He was. Sure, Jerry had given them a helping hand but if she was looking for a father, she should be looking at him, not Jerry.

Damien watched the look of pain cross Keefe's face and knew that despite his denial and Mia's, Keefe blamed him for Mia's decision. Hell, he didn't even have a clue who Jerry was. He almost laughed. Talk about bad timing… If only Mia had told him of her intention, at least they would have been on the same page.

But Mia appeared to be unaware of Keefe's pain and Damien was left to bear the brunt of the hate-filled glances. *Not this time*, he thought. He was not getting in the middle between brother and sister. He'd had enough of being in the middle of family. He'd done it almost his entire life with his parents. He didn't want to be in the middle of Mia's relationship with her brother. Whatever she said, he would do. He just needed to make sure she was doing what she wanted.

"Mia, are you sure?" For a long moment only silence greeted him. Mia was staring at him, a puzzled look on her face, while Ashleigh appeared to be holding her breath. And Keefe…if possible, he was even angrier than before. Yet they all waited for Mia's answer.

"I think I need a father for this." Her glance took in her brother and she smiled. "Keefe doesn't care. You don't mind do you, Keefe?" Again she prayed, *Please Kee, tell me that you do mind, tell me you want to walk me down the aisle.*

"No, Mia, I don't mind," Keefe lied. "You're an adult, it's your wedding. Do whatever you want. You want to handle it alone, go ahead."

"Good. Then that's settled," Mia answered around the lump in her throat. *For once their mother had been right. She'd given Keefe a choice and he'd chosen not to do it.*

Mia didn't notice that her brother had stopped talking, nor did she notice that he was staring at her with a shocked expression on his face. She was too busy trying not to cry, too busy stuffing her emotions into her psyche for examination later.

If only he'd tried harder to talk her out of it. Mia bit her lip, holding back the tears that were threatening to come. Since Keefe had fallen in love with Ashleigh, things had slowly changed. It wasn't that she wasn't happy for her brother to have someone, she was. It also wasn't because she wasn't ready to learn to stand on her own. She just wasn't ready to let go of her brother.

She glanced at Ashleigh, noticing Ashleigh's total attention was focused on Keefe. She'd accused her brother months before when she was still engaged to James, of wanting her to get married so his obligations to her would be over. As her gaze moved from Ashleigh to Keefe, Mia now knew she'd been correct. Keefe was relieved not to have to worry about her. Despite all the nasty things she'd said, their mother had been right. A shudder touched her soul.

"Just a thought, and I'm asking only out of curiosity. What about money, Mia?" Keefe asked.

"Don't worry about the money," she answered. "I'm going to keep it simple."

"You don't have to."

"I don't need your money, Kee," she said a bit more sharply than she'd intended. And she didn't need his money. She needed to know that her brother wasn't as happy as he seemed to be about getting rid of her. It wasn't ever about his money, it was about him. But now, now that he had Ashleigh… Mia bit her lip as she tried to stop the thought, but it came anyway. Keefe didn't need her. The offer of money was all that he had left to give her.

Mia's began to rock back and forth so slowly that no one noticed but her. *Stop it*, she ordered herself angrily, tamping down the need to be alone.

"If you can do it without me, then I'll stop asking." Keefe's voice was also sharp. What the hell was happening? How had a couple of days made that much difference in his sister's feelings for him? So be it. Whatever the hell she wanted. If she wanted him to stay out of her life he didn't care. *Like hell he didn't care. It was tearing him apart.*

A tense silence followed the brother and sister outbursts. Everyone shifted positions, moving their food around on their plates, doing anything to bring back normalcy.

"Not having to shop for a gown will save time," Damien said, hoping that the change of topic would bring some needed relief.

"I don't think so." Mia glanced in Ashleigh's direction. "I think I'll get a new one."

"A new wedding gown? You paid three thousand dollars for that gown and now you don't want to wear it?" The words were out before Keefe had a chance to think about his new vow to himself to stay out of Mia's wedding plans.

"Mia, have you suddenly come into money that I know nothing of? Where the hell are you going to get enough money to pay for a wedding and buy a new gown on your own?" Keefe was fuming. If she so much as hinted that she was going to charge it, he was going to paddle her behind. There was just so much staying out of her business that he was willing to put up with. And allowing her to throw away good money was not one of them.

Mia inclined her head toward Ashleigh and glared at her brother, not answering him.

"Oh, I almost forgot. Sorry," Keefe answered, subdued.

"Mia, it's your gown. You paid for it. If you want to wear it, I really don't mind."

Mia looked from Ashleigh to her brother, then turned her attention to Damien. "What do you think?" she asked.

"You did look beautiful in that gown, baby girl."

He kissed her lightly and she smiled. "Thanks."

That more than anything Mia had said during the course of the evening pissed Keefe off royally. Who the hell did Mia think Damien was? Oh yeah, he'd almost forgot—the man she was going to marry.

And to think he'd played a part in getting Mia back with Damien. Damn. *I should have left well enough alone.* The moment he thought it Keefe knew he was wrong. He'd done the right thing. Mia had been unhappy without Damien. She'd broken up with Damien because she was trying to protect Keefe under the mistaken idea that Damien was trying to use him, take him for money.

Keefe glanced at Damien, then at Mia. She was happy. That alone was worth him getting her back with Damien. Besides, Damien said he had nothing to do with Mia's kicking him out of the wedding. If they were going to be family, he had to forget Damien's past.

Just as he had to forget that Damien had been the man before him in Ashleigh's life, that they'd lived together for two years and that Ashleigh had been planning to marry him. It would probably be better for all of them if Mia didn't wear the gown Ashleigh had made for her own marriage to Damien.

Keefe felt the pressure of Ashleigh's hand squeezing his thigh. He would have to forget all of that, just as Mia would. Ashleigh loved him now, just as Damien loved Mia.

Keefe wouldn't deny that a couple of times when he'd made love to Ashleigh he'd had thoughts of her making love with Damien. But he'd quickly banished those thoughts. And when Ashleigh screamed out his name as she came, Keefe knew he was the one on her mind, not Damien.

He hated thinking about his sister's private life but he hoped that when the time came, she would be able to put it out of her mind as he'd done. He hoped that the fact that Mia was still a virgin would help her.

Keefe drummed his fingers on the table, then took in a deep breath. He didn't want to think any longer about that part of his sister's life. That would be up to her to work out with the man she was going to marry. He glared once more at Damien. That was a problem for the two of them.

Right now, all Keefe was concerned about was finishing dinner and getting the hell out of there. He'd had enough of the new family bonding.

No sooner had they entered Mia's apartment than Damien plopped down on the sofa, pulling Mia with him. "What the hell was that all about? Why didn't you tell me that you were going to hit your brother with news like that?"

"What?"

"Come on, Mia, you know what I'm talking about. You know Keefe thought he was going to give you away."

"He doesn't want to."

"He does. You didn't see the look on his face. And you know what else? He still thinks it's my fault. He was just barely tolerating me, and that little stunt you pulled voided all of that. Tell the truth. Don't you want Keefe to give you away?"

"Of course I do.

"Then why did you tell him you were asking someone else?"

"Because he told me that he wanted me to stop depending on him so much. He's right. I figured now is as good a time as any. I want to do this myself without having my brother come in to save the day." She shrugged her shoulders. "Besides, you heard him say he didn't care."

"Are you sure that's what your brother meant?"

"Are you calling me crazy?"

"No, but I am asking if you're jumping to conclusions." He lifted her chin and looked into her eyes. "I love you, baby girl, and I don't want to hurt you, but you do have a tendency to jump to conclusions."

Mia attempted to pull away but he held fast to her, not letting her leave his arms. "I'm not trying to piss you off, baby, but come on. We both know how your brother feels about you. Hell, he's threatened me enough times. I'm just saying I think you're making a mistake."

"You think you know my brother better than I do?"

"No. But I saw his face. You were looking down."

"I asked him if he minded and he said no. He even gave me Jerry's number."

"That's not quite the way it happened, Mia. You asked him for it. What choice did he have?"

"He could have not given it to me. He could have said no, so it's the same as his not caring."

"No, it's not. Think about it. Keefe has always been willing to do anything in the world to make you happy, even if it kills him, and I don't think he's changed that much in a couple of days."

"But he has Ashleigh now."

"I don't think that makes a difference, Mia."

"I wanted him to tell me no, that he wouldn't allow it, but he didn't object. If he'd really wanted to do it, he would have said something, but he didn't. He said nothing. He doesn't care. He wants me to learn to be independent, to get along without him, and that's what I'm trying to do."

"Mia, I think you're wrong but if you're sure, I'll shut up. Now, let's talk about the wedding. I'll help with all the expenses. I'll even buy you a new gown if you want it, but not for three thousand dollars."

"No, like I told Keefe, this is my wedding and I'll pay for it."

"Your wedding?" Damien moved away so he could get a good look at Mia. "This is not '*your wedding.*' It's *our* wedding! And we will pay for it together."

"But…"

"No buts. I'm not your brother and I'm damn sure not your father, but I am going to be your husband. We're going to be a team so you might as well get used to that right now."

Mia looked at Damien, thinking, *Why didn't Keefe put up more of a fight, like Damien.* She knew she was being childish. She'd had no business testing her brother in the first place but as long as she could remember, when Keefe had really wanted her to do something he found a way. He'd given up way too easily.

"Mia."

"Yes."

"Are you listening to me?"

"Yes."

"And?"

"Okay, we'll do it together."

"Good. Now I want to hear more about this Jerry. Are you close with him? I mean, do you really think of him as a father?"

"No."

"Then why on earth…"

"Because he's the only person I could think of that Keefe would believe I was even seriously considering. Anyone else and he would have seen through it."

"Why won't he see through Jerry?"

"Jerry helped us. Our mother took off and we were sent to foster care." Mia's voice lowered. "It wasn't the first time she'd taken off, just the first time she didn't come back. We, well, I called around to our relatives, searching for her. Keefe warned me not to, told me what would happen if I did. I did it anyway. One of my cousins called social services and they found out we were alone. Keefe was taking good care of me, like always, but they said he couldn't. They put us in separate homes."

Mia closed her eyes, shivering at the unpleasant memory. "I couldn't believe it when they came to take us. I was screaming and hollering, kicking everyone in sight. I couldn't believe it. It was all my fault and poor Keefe…"

Mia's voice broke and she sobbed. "He was fighting with them, trying to stop them from taking me. But it was no use. They took me anyway. The last thing I heard was him promising to come and get me."

"How long were you in foster care?" Damien asked.

"We were separated for a couple of months. But it seemed like forever. They wouldn't tell me where my brother was, wouldn't let me see him. I almost went crazy. They put me in the hospital because I refused to eat until they let me see my brother. When he came, I begged him not to let them take me away again. I promised him I would be good, that I would listen if he saved me."

"Save you? Save you from what, Mia?" Damien asked gently. Did someone…"

"I don't know. I just knew that I needed him to save me. Still, they took me back to the home. But within a couple of days I heard Keefe's voice screaming for me. I was hiding in a closet, had been for a very long time. At first I thought someone was playing a joke. Then I ran out. He was with Jerry. Keefe told me not to worry, that he'd come to get me and he'd never let anyone hurt me again."

"Jerry became your foster father?"

"Sort of. He pretended. We could call him if we needed him, if social workers were coming, things like that. He kept some clothes at our apartment."

"He just left two kids alone?"

"Damien, he helped us. No one else would."

"Why didn't he let you live with him?"

"He had a girlfriend who didn't want us there. But it didn't matter. We didn't want to be there. Keefe made a deal with Jerry that he would take care of me. They both warned me not to say anything to kids at school or to any relatives."

"You didn't?"

"Only once. I almost told one of my friends. Luckily Keefe was around. He looked at me, and I remembered that I wasn't supposed to tell anyone that we lived alone. I think my almost slipping up worried Keefe. He called Jerry and asked him to come over.

"Jerry warned me that if I told, he would go to jail and I would go back into foster care and I would never see my brother again, ever. After that, I stopped having friends. I couldn't take a chance of forgetting, of telling anyone."

"Your brother didn't want you having friends?"

"He didn't mind. He just told me I had to be careful. It was my own decision. Besides, Keefe didn't have friends anymore. I felt bad for him. He stopped going anywhere with them. He took me everywhere with him."

"What about your relatives?"

"They hardly ever came over. They'd invite me to my cousins' birthday parties but Keefe got mad because they didn't invite me to more things, like the pajama parties my cousins had, so he told me I wasn't going anymore. Anytime they had a party, Keefe would take me some place fun so I wouldn't miss it.

"Did it work?"

"No. But I pretended. My brother wanted me to be happy. I knew that so I pretended that I was."

"I can't believe no one ever came to check up on you."

"Believe it. No one cared. After a couple of visits the social worker assigned to us mostly called and asked if we were doing okay. If some miracle happened and a relative stopped by, Keefe would call Jerry and he would either come by or call back and it seemed like he was taking care of us."

"I can see why Keefe acts like he thinks he's your father and why you love him so much. Sounds like he gave up his whole childhood for you."

"He did and that's why I can't ask him to do something that could make him uncomfortable."

"Mia, I still think that you're wrong."

Mia closed her eyes for a second, opened them and blinked several times. She'd just told Damien of the things in her life that had caused her the most pain and she'd done it in a matter- of-fact manner, as though none of it mattered. That was the farthest thing from the truth.

"Don't worry," Mia assured Damien. "Jerry is a good guy. And if it's not Keefe, he's my second choice. Like I said, he did a lot for us. He took a big risk giving us an apartment, putting all of the utilities in his own name. He helped Keefe get a car, took him for his license, and even put Keefe's car under his insurance."

Damien wasn't buying it. He was staring at her with a funny expression on his face. Mia sighed. She shouldn't have to be trying to sell Jerry to Damien. But somehow she felt that was exactly what she was doing. When she could take his staring no longer, she rolled her eyes and asked, "What?"

"I still don't get that an adult would just leave two kids to fend for themselves. He expected a lot of Keefe. I'll have to give your brother his props."

Mia smiled. "I'll tell him that."

"Don't you dare." He looked over Mia's head, then grinned. "I'm not trying to take anything away from Jerry but I know that people get money from the state to take in foster kids. It looks to me like the guy got money for the two of you without having to actually take care of you. I don't think that's right."

"Is that what's bothering you? When Keefe graduated from high school, Jerry gave him all the money he'd taken out over the years for the rent on the apartment and he taught him about investing."

"Okay, so he's not a bad guy. I always thought I had the worst family life imaginable." He paused as he remembered, then quickly brought his attention back to Mia. "I guess I'm thankful that both of my parents stuck around. What about your mother?"

"She actually came here a month ago."

Mia barely looked up as she answered Damien's question. She didn't want to see his eyes for she knew what would be there. Pity. She didn't want Damien's pity, only his love.

She anticipated what was coming next. Any sane person would have a hard time believing that a mother would just walk out and abandon her two kids. After all these years, she still couldn't believe it herself.

"Your mother never came back until recently?"

Damien had surprised her. He hadn't asked how her mother could do such a horrible thing. She could kiss him for not asking, for providing her a way to give an answer that was factual. She didn't want to deal with the emotional side of their mother leaving them, not now.

"She started popping up right after Keefe graduated," Mia explained. "She'd found out where we were. When she saw how well we were doing she'd come by needing money every few months. I wanted her to move in with us. Keefe didn't. He hated her."

"Why didn't you?"

"I don't know. I loved her, she was my mother."

"Did she ever say why she took off?"

"Yeah, she said the situation was too hard on her, that she was only one person and she couldn't take care of two kids. She said it was hard for her to have a life, that men left her because of us. She said she was only trying to be happy and that if we weren't so selfish we'd see that and want that for her."

Damien's glance slid over her and in spite of the pain, she felt the warmth of his love. Besides Keefe and her therapist, Mia had never told anyone the things her mother had said to her.

"Baby girl, I wish I had been there for you." Damien hugged her to his heart. "I guess you can be grateful that your mother never told anyone the truth, that your brother was taking care of you alone."

Mia smiled sadly. "She threatened. She told me once when Keefe got angry and wouldn't give her money that she could make one phone call and I'd be back in foster care. By that time they couldn't do anything to Keefe. But there was no way I wanted to go back, so I badgered him to give her what she wanted. I always did. It became a routine even after I'd graduated from high school and knew there was nothing she could do. I still got money from him to give to her."

"She never apologized for abandoning you and your brother?"

Mia cringed. Even now she hated to use that word. She didn't like people knowing or saying that her mother had abandoned them."

"No, she never believed she had anything to apologize for."

"I guess I'll have to cut Keefe some slack. He did a good job of taking over after your mom left. I'll give him that."

Mia smiled at Damien. "Actually he's taken care of me my entire life. From the age of three, I can remember Keefe combing my hair, washing my clothes, getting my breakfast, making me say my prayers and letting me play with the big kids."

Her eyes suddenly felt gritty, burning with the torrent of tears just waiting to be released. She didn't want to cry but all this talking about Keefe was enough to make her resolve crumble. He was her rock, the one person she'd counted on her entire life. The thought that he would abandon her as their mother had done was more than Mia could bear. She felt she was losing something precious and she wanted very much to hold on to it.

"I don't know what would have happened to me had it not been for Keefe."

"What about your father? Didn't he ever try and help?" Damien asked, disbelief coloring his voice.

"We have no idea who he is. Our mother won't say. Once one of our aunts told us that when Mom was a teenager she took off and disappeared for several years and no one heard a word from her. When she returned she had us in tow. She never told anyone where she'd been or anything about our father. And it didn't matter how many times we asked. Keefe said our father knew we existed and if he really wanted to, he could find us. So he told me to just forget about him. It was bad enough worrying about one absent parent. Neither of us had the energy or desire to worry about two of them.

"You never wondered about him?"

"Sometimes, but Keefe was always there. He was my father all the time and my mother most of the time," she added, then closed her eyes and looked away.

"Come here, baby girl." Damien's arms circled Mia and he crooned to her. "Looks like parents can really mess a kid up. We're going to have to make sure we don't do that to our kids. I promise you, Mia, I'm going to be a good husband and a good father."

"I know that." She opened her eyes and looked at him. "I never had a doubt that you would. So do you want to tell me about your parents?"

"Next time, baby, but just so you know, a good chunk of my life has been spent trying to figure those two out." He laughed, "Maybe that's the reason I fell in love with you. We both had hellish childhoods and lived through it."

CHAPTER FIVE

Keefe couldn't keep still. He paced the rooms of his apartment glaring at Ashleigh, though he wasn't angry at her. "Can you believe that?" he asked for perhaps the hundredth time. "I helped her get back with Damien and now she's shoving me out of her life. I don't believe it."

"Tell her," Ashleigh said.

To this he only glared more. "She should know this already. Jerry hasn't earned the right to be thought of as her father. You don't just give that job to anyone. That's an honor and Jerry didn't earn it. I did."

Keefe sat down, finally out of steam. "What's happening?" he asked Ashleigh, knowing she wouldn't be able to answer.

"I know you want to blame Damien but I think you're off base. He wouldn't care. He's grateful to you. I know he is."

"Then I don't know what to do. There is no way in hell I'm allowing Jerry to walk Mia down the aisle."

"I thought you liked him."

"I do and if I were dead, I wouldn't mind Mia asking him. But I'm not dead. I'm very much alive. And if you think I'm letting him give my sister away, you're as crazy as she is." Keefe blinked, and blinked again, wincing at his words. He'd not meant to call Mia crazy. But still he had no intention of having Jerry step in after he'd done all the work.

"What are you going to do? Call him up and tell him not to come? What if he tells her no?"

"I'll do as I've always done. *I'll save her*," he muttered so softly that he knew Ashleigh couldn't hear him. "I'll do it myself."

"Why do you and your sister go through so many obstacles to avoid talking? You're always second guessing each other and you're always wrong. Why don't you just tell her you want to walk her down the aisle? She worships you, Keefe. I'm sure she would say yes."

"I shouldn't have to ask her. It should be a done deal. It was a done deal."

"You're still trying to blame Damien. I agree that something is going on with your sister, but I don't really know her that well. I did notice that she wouldn't look at you when she said she wanted Jerry to walk her down the aisle."

"I wouldn't know if she looked at me or not," Keefe growled.

"I know. You didn't look at her either. I swear, I don't get the two of you."

Keefe couldn't prevent the scowl. Ashleigh didn't understand that he didn't want Mia doing him a favor by saying yes. He wanted her to want him, to need him as she always had.

"Why do you treat her as if she's so delicate? She's probably much stronger than you think."

Keefe stared for a few seconds in Ashleigh's general direction. "Mia is strong. I know just how strong she is, but I also know that inside she's still a little girl. I know she has demons, Ashleigh. And I haven't been able to help her get rid of them."

"I know that your mother abandoned you and that you raised her. But that's in the past, isn't it? If there's something more going on, why don't you tell me? Maybe I'll be able to help."

"I don't like talking about it."

"Not even to me?"

He smiled wanly. He didn't tell many people about his experiences or Mia's in foster care. He'd always wondered about the things that had happened to his sister when he'd not been there to protect her and he felt guilty as hell for whatever might have occurred.

"You know most of it already," Keefe offered as he attempted to smile at Ashleigh, not quite pulling it off.

"I want to know it all," Ashleigh countered. "I love you, Keefe, trust me to understand."

He sat beside her, sighing, and took her in his arms. He loved her; it was time to share his life with her.

"Mia and I were put in foster care," he began, "for a short time, but it seemed like forever. It was the first time I'd ever failed my sister."

"Keefe, you're taking responsibility for things that weren't in your control. It was your mother's fault, not yours. If anyone failed Mia she did, not you."

"Mia never expected our mother to protect her. I was the one she trusted." He sighed again. "Maybe she's…I don't know. Maybe she doesn't think I deserve to walk her down the aisle."

"Snap out of it, Keefe, and stop feeling sorry for yourself. Yes, Mia was a little girl and had a hard life. So did you. She had you, Keefe. Who did you have? You've got to stop beating yourself up. This thing with your sister could be fixed so easily. I'll bet if I talked to her…"

"No."

A shudder of revulsion ripped through Keefe at the thought of Ashleigh questioning Mia. If she didn't already feel betrayed, she surely would after talking with Ashleigh. "This is between my sister and me, Ashleigh. No offense but I don't want you talking to her."

He watched as Ashleigh wrestled with her own feelings of betrayal. He couldn't help it. He would protect Mia at all costs. Still, he didn't want to hurt Ashleigh. "I'm sorry, baby," he whispered to her. "I told you it was hard for me to talk about."

"I understand," Ashleigh said, still sounding a bit miffed, especially when she continued.

"I'm sorry that your sister and you were put into foster care, but that happens. Besides, you got out and you're both okay."

"It's what Mia went through while she was in foster care. She was just a little girl. They wouldn't allow us to be together and at first they wouldn't even let me call her or check on her. That is, until she landed in the hospital."

Keefe shuddered, then shook his head to dispel the image of his baby sister when he'd first seen her in the hospital, her eyes wide and frightened, her arms thinner than they'd ever been—the look of total terror on her face.

He could still remember how he'd stood there for an eternity staring at his baby sister before rushing forward to hug her. She'd pushed him away, her look piercing his heart. *She didn't know who he was.*

Keefe had looked into her eyes, but Mia wasn't there. Fear had raced through him and he'd grabbed her shoulders. *"Mia, look at me, it's Keefe."* He'd had to shake her several times to make her focus. When she concentrated on his face and finally recognized him, she'd screamed his name. Then she'd held on to him for dear life. *'He hurt me, Kee. Save me!'* It was her words, *'He hurt me,'* that had haunted Keefe every day of his life since. It was those words that he'd shoved away and not examined, fearing what they meant. It was what made him so determined that no one would ever hurt Mia again.

He closed his eyes, hugging Ashleigh close. Ashleigh couldn't possibly identify with what had happened to Mia. He thought about dropping the matter but found he wanted her to know, so that she could at least try to understand. "She was in bad shape," Keefe finished.

"Keefe."

"The only person I could think to call was Jerry. I pleaded with him to get us out of foster care. I promised him that he wouldn't have to be responsible for either of us. His girlfriend didn't want him to, but he'd never known me to cry. He agreed to help us, to pretend that he was taking care of us, that he was our foster father. He rented us an apartment in his building and gave me the money that was left over from the check the state sent to help us out. And I worked. I worked my ass off."

"And it paid off. Look at both of you, all that you've accomplished. Your sister's not yet twenty-four and she's working on her Ph.D. I'd say you've done wonderful job." Ashleigh smiled her acknowledgement.

"That's now. A lot happened before we got here. You weren't there, Ashleigh. You don't know the nightmares Mia had when we were finally back together. She blamed herself for everything, for our mother being what she was and for our being thrown into foster care."

Ashleigh looked at him with a question in her eyes. He knew what she wanted to ask, the same thing he'd wondered about many times. He had asked the social workers the question, the people at the home where Mia had lived, but he'd never asked his sister. *Had she been abused?* No, that was one question he'd never ask her. He'd instead made it his mission to insure that she would never be hurt again. Mia had never mentioned that she'd been hurt after they were reunited. It was probably the one thing that had kept Keefe sane.

"When our mother left...when she abandoned us, I warned Mia not to call anyone. We were used to her taking off for weeks at a time. Only this time she took all of her clothes and personal possessions. I knew it was different. I knew she wasn't coming back. Mia was usually such a good little girl. I told her what could happen, but she didn't understand what I was trying to tell her. She called a cousin and asked if she'd seen our mother and the cousin called the department of children and family services.

"After we got out of foster care, Mia barely let me out of her sight. She never got in trouble, never really played with other kids, except once in a blue moon. She just wanted to stay near me. She was so afraid that something would happen, that I would leave her, that..."

Keefe remembered once when Mia was about fifteen and he'd yelled at her because he'd caught her kissing a boy. He didn't remember the exact words he'd spoken, but he did remember her tears. He vaguely recalled saying something about how she was acting like their mother, that he wasn't going to let her be a slut.

The force of the memory pounded itself into him and he knew he was as much to blame as their mother for some of Mia's demons. He was the reason Mia was still a virgin. She'd not wanted to disappoint him. He would bet money on that.

"Keefe?"

Caught up in past memories, he'd not even been aware that Ashleigh was talking to him. "Let's just say I have good reasons to worry about her."

"Are you worried that Jerry will hurt her?"

"No."

"But you want him to say no to Mia."

Keefe smiled.

"Isn't Jerry a good guy?"

"Yes."

"I think maybe you're just jealous. You made her stop seeing Damien to wait for James and look what happened. James married someone else. Keefe, you've got to stop trying to control your sister's life."

"You're wrong about my motives. It's not like when I didn't want her seeing Damien. I thought he would hurt Mia. It's not like that with Jerry. Jerry would love to see Mia get married. I know he would jump at the chance to do this…it's not that. It's just…I want to do it."

"Then tell her."

He kissed Ashleigh. She didn't know how much he'd worried about Mia, how he still worried about her. And he couldn't tell her, so he kissed her instead. He would not be responsible for causing his sister any more stress than was necessary, not if he could help it. He knew that in the end he would give in to Mia's wishes. But he could hope, couldn't he?

CHAPTER SIX

Exhaustion was Mia's constant companion. For weeks every moment of her time had been taken until it got to the point that she even had to schedule time to be with the man she loved. Wedding plans had come together much faster than Mia had anticipated. Not in the month that Damien had first given her, but in a little under two months, and that, she thought, had been a miracle. Between finalizing plans, working, and going to classes, she found little time for going to listen to Damien sing or spending time with her brother. In only two weeks she would be married to the man who made her shiver with desire. Just the thought of it made her wet. She could hardly wait.

Admittedly, she had Keefe to thank for everything coming together so quickly. She'd called Stavros, a business associate and friend of Keefe, who owned Boomerang's, a small exclusive hotel that boasted one of the state's best banquet halls. Stavros had agreed to allow Mia and Damien not only to have the reception there but he'd told them they could get married there as well. He was setting up a makeshift chapel with a grape arbor covered in lilies and white roses. Damien had even managed to secure a minister for them. It was all well within their budget, especially since she'd decided to wear the gown she'd bought from Ashleigh. Mia was proud of all they'd accomplished and of her steps toward staking a claim on her independence.

The only thing Mia hadn't done was call Jerry. She shuddered, knowing she couldn't keep putting it off. Keefe was not going to ride in and save her from being an adult. She'd made her choice and now she would have to live with it.

"Mia, it's getting really hard to help you with your vow. I want you so bad," Damien moaned into her ear. "Tell you what. Just touch me once and I'll go home." He leered at her. "You know you never have. Don't you want to?"

Mia looked slyly at the bulge in his pants and ran her hand down the ridges, pausing to cup him for a few seconds. She giggled and dodged as Damien lunged for her.

"You're a tease, Mia."

"We have only a couple of weeks."

"Yeah, but if you count all the time we haven't made love, that's a lifetime. Did I ever tell you that a man could go insane if he doesn't have release on a regular basis?"

"Only about a million times."

"You think I'm making this stuff up." Damien adopted an indignant scowl. "If you don't believe me, check it out on the web, visit any mental institution in the country and talk to the doctors, talk to the patients. You'll see that I'm right."

Really getting into his story, he turned away from Mia. If he saw her face as he spun his web, he'd laugh. "Have you heard of the Terrell clinic in Sweden?"

"No, but since it bears your name I'm sure it has to be a sex clinic."

"Well, the name's only a coincidence. But you are right about the type of clinic that it is. They've been taking patients from the mental hospital, men mostly, and making sure that they get plenty of sex. So far they've had a ninety-nine percent success rate. All the patients except one were returned to society to work and pay taxes and all because of good sex."

"What happened to the one patient?" Mia asked, laughing.

"Oh, he liked sex a little too much. He wouldn't leave the clinic because, let's face it, he got to have sex twenty-four hours a day. So they're waiting for him to tire of it. Like that's ever going to happen." Damien laughed and joined Mia on the sofa.

"I love your stories," she said as she kissed him.

"And I love you, baby girl. And if I can't have you for a few more days, I guess I might as well feed both of our fantasies. Now come on and give me a kiss. I have to get home before I'm no longer able to help you keep your vow."

After several more kisses they walked to the door and Mia slid her hand down the center of his arousal and smiled.

"Like I said, you're a tease, baby girl."

She laughed and closed the door, wondering how in the world either of them had been able to resist giving in to the instincts that were bowling her over. She tingled from the contact with Damien's body, from touching him through the fabric of his pants, from his touching her and she wanted so much more.

She wanted to forget her vow, forget everything but the wonder of having Damien make love to her. They would be so happy, she knew that they would. As for the vow, the only reason she was keeping it was to prove to her brother that she wasn't a slut. She wouldn't ever be that. She would marry Damien and she would spend the rest of her life making him deliriously happy. She would never be like her mother, moving from one man to another.

Mia shivered. She'd not called her mother again. She didn't know if she really wanted her at the wedding or not. She had a bad feeling about her coming, something that she'd never had before. Always she'd been too busy keeping the peace between her mother and Keefe, trying to make her mother see that both she and her brother had done things that any mother should be proud of. Of course she knew at her age it was unhealthy to worry about the approval of a parent. She would be getting her Ph.D. in psychology in a little over a year, give or take a few months. She would open her own practice and she would counsel people just like herself. Still, she recognized that she too had failings.

In a couple of weeks she would no longer have to fight the sexual urges she had. She would freely and gladly make love with her husband, day and night. A delicious tingle filled her and she danced around the room before heading to the window to wave one last time at Damien.

Her face flushed at the thought of finally touching and being touched in all the ways she'd never allowed, but in all the ways she'd wanted to since meeting and falling in love with Damien. So many times they'd come so close, each time going a little farther. She knew it was more of a miracle than will power that they hadn't gone all the way. God, she wanted to. They both wanted to.

Damien smiled as he looked up toward Mia's apartment, searching for her to appear in the window. When she appeared, his heart swelled with love for her. He didn't care that his father thought he was whipped. He had Mia.

Of course all of his friends assumed that the deed had been done months ago. He'd never bothered to tell them any better. It wasn't really any of their business. He'd only told his parents, and only then because he wanted to show them just how special Mia was. It had backfired with both.

"You're going to marry her without first hitting that? Man, you're a fool. You don't even know if she can give good head. Hell, you don't even know if she'll be willing. You're taking an awful risk marrying a virgin. Don't do it. Make her give up the drawers, or tell her to take a hike. Besides, she could just be leading you on. How the hell do you know she hasn't been had? Man, you could look up on your wedding night and just fall into a massive hole that's been used by more men than you thought. This is a stupid move you're making."

That had been his father. And his mother had not been much better.

"Mia must be a fool to be planning on marrying you. Damien, you've had so many women that she should be afraid your little thang is going to fall off. That girl is too good for you. She's not going to understand your perverted ways. Don't you hurt that girl, Damien." Then she'd changed direction and had thought of another way to taunt him.

"Why should I warn you? You're just like your no good ass father. How can I expect you to know how to treat a woman?

"You know what?" His mother had laughed then. *"It would serve you right if you marry the one woman in the world that you want, that you think you want and she doesn't get turned on by your ass. God, what a joke if you can't even get it up. That would be your punishment for whoring around, for not listening to me. You deserve to not be able to satisfy her. You and your father both deserve to have that happen."*

Damien had not bothered answering his mother. She was bitter and the thought that Damien was finally getting married didn't seem to matter. Although she'd told him his fate for years, he'd thought she'd at least be happy that he was changing. Well, she wasn't and neither was his father. One thought Mia was too good for him. The other thought if she wasn't putting out she wasn't good enough.

Damien laughed to himself. Neither of them took into consideration how much he loved Mia, that for him it wasn't just about the sex. True, he could barely wait to make love to her. She kept him in a constant state of arousal and he was forever walking around with at least a semi-erection.

But that wasn't why he was in love with Mia. Even he couldn't explain why the moment he saw her he knew she was the one. Somehow he'd known in his heart. After their first time together when she'd walked away from Ashleigh's after purchasing a wedding gown to marry James, he'd known she was the one. They'd sat in McDonald's, of all places, for five hours.

She'd smiled at him and listened to every word he had to say with real interest. It hadn't bothered her in the least that he didn't have a job. Damien laughed to himself at his musings. The job thing *had* bothered her. She'd told him to get one. But still, the fact that he didn't have one hadn't stopped her from falling in love with him.

Damien was grinning widely, glad no one was around to see him. It seemed like all he ever did was think about Mia. How could he not? She amazed him. And the most amazing thing of all was it hadn't even bothered her that he was a dog. He'd never forget the words she'd said to him when he let her out at her apartment after their first meeting. "Damien, I'm glad that I met you. You have a very good heart and a good soul." He'd been taken aback and had teased her. "That's not what my mother says."

"Then she should look into your eyes," Mia had said. "You're very special."

He hadn't known how to answer her and she'd gotten out of his car without kissing him and shoved him away, laughing.

"I think you behave as a dog so that no one will know how truly wonderful you really are."

He'd never heard these words spoken about himself before. He'd wanted to run after Mia, beg her to tell him how she knew he was special. But he'd only sat in his car thinking, *Wow she thinks I'm special. I must be.* He knew without a doubt that she was special. And if she thought he was also, it had to be true. Damien had set about trying for all these months to prove her right and his parents wrong.

During the months they'd been separated, his mother had laughed every time she saw him, repeatedly reminding him that she'd warned him. But he hadn't given up on them. If some other woman had told him to wait around for her, Damien would have had a different woman the moment the words left her mouth. But not with Mia. With Mia he'd not wanted anyone but her. And he'd waited for her, the wait tearing him apart, his mother's taunts piercing him afresh each night and day. Still, he'd waited.

And now, he thought with a smile, she was going to marry him. He grinned. He had to be special for her to marry him. He couldn't wait to touch her in all the ways he'd wanted, to kiss her body from bottom to top, to make her scream out his name. The one thing he'd listened to his mother about was how he would need to be patient. He would remember that Mia was a virgin. He would take his time. She was inexperienced but she wanted him, she always had. That much he knew. He could hardly wait until the day they became man and wife.

"Are you ashamed of us? Who in the hell do you think you are? You think because someone's letting you get your ass up on stage and sing that you're a hot shot now? You're still Damien Terrell, my son, my blood, and you can stop this act. We both know as soon as you hit *it*, you're going to be back in the streets looking. God hasn't made the woman who can take care of us the way we need."

Charles leered across the table. "There is not one woman that can keep men like us satisfied. I ought to know, you're my son. Hell, it's in your blood."

Damien glanced at his mother, wishing for more times than he cared to remember, that his father wouldn't just say whatever the hell he thought. But the man had no moral filter. And it didn't help that his mother had been content to play his door mat since way before Damien was born. Still, he wished that his father didn't constantly throw it in her face that she'd not been enough for him.

"Okay, I'll set it up with Mia. She'd love to see you again," Damien lied. "Dinner tomorrow night."

He got a sick feeling in the pit of his stomach and hoped that Mia would still think him special after spending an evening with his parents. How he'd kept them apart all this time had taken a bit of ingenuity. Now he'd been called on it. He didn't have a choice, for despite his misgivings, he did love his parents.

CHAPTER SEVEN

Damien was nervous as he closed the door of the car and walked around to the driver's side. His father was bringing his mother and meeting them at The Pasta Place, a new trendy restaurant with great food, reasonable prices, and a dance floor. He was hoping all of that would make for a fun evening.

"It's going to be okay." Mia stroked his arm. "We should have done this already. Keefe's been after me to meet your parents."

"Can you just imagine what would happen if the six of us got together, Keefe and Ashleigh joining us? Naw, Mia, I think it's going to be hard enough with the four of us."

"Who are you avoiding, Ashleigh or Keefe?"

She was teasing and he knew that but he glanced over at her just to make sure. "Baby, you know that I don't…that it doesn't bother me being around Ashleigh. Does it bother you when we're all together?"

Mia squirmed. She'd only been kidding and now he was asking her a direct question and they'd promised not to lie. "Maybe a little. I'm working on it."

"You have nothing to worry about. Believe me, if I didn't look at another woman once while I waited for you I'm definitely not going to look now."

An unwelcome thought flashed across Damien's mind and he remembered his father saying that he would. Well, he wouldn't. He didn't want anyone but Mia.

"I know. I just think that as we get closer to the day it gets a little scary and I worry."

"Do you worry that you're making a mistake?" He held his breath waiting for an answer.

"Of course not. But I suppose I worry that you might think you're making one." She laid her head on his shoulder. "Damien, I want to be married for keeps," Mia whispered. "I have no plans on ever getting divorced."

"Divorced, Mia? Damn baby. Where did that come from? We're not even married yet."

"Come on, I'm serious," Mia insisted. "I hate the word *divorce*. My mother was divorced so many times that…I…I just want you to be sure I'm who you want. Am I?"

He glanced sideways at her, then pulled into the drive of the restaurant and parked. "Come here, Mia. He looked into her eyes, took her hand and placed it over his heart. "What do you think? I love you, Mia. I promise you that that will never change, no matter what."

"Mia, it's good to see you again. We've been asking Damien to bring you over." Kathy smiled at her.

"What are you talking about, *we*? The way you sound Mia will think we live together or something." Charles cocked his head in Kathy's direction. "That's not true. We get together and kick it every once in a while, nothing more, just a little sex. No big deal."

Mia glanced at Damien and saw that he was trying to behave normally. The only thing that gave him away was the tenseness she detected in his jaw. *Okay Mia*, she thought to herself, *this is going to be your new family. You're going to be an expert at familial relationships.* She laughed to herself. Oh yeah, she was an expert alright. The only thing she knew for sure was how to get good grades and give the right answers—enough to earn a degree. She doubted if anyone could ever really understand people. Still, she had to do something.

"Kathy, that's a beautiful necklace that you have on," Mia remarked, attempting to change the conversation. "It's very unusual."

She saw the grateful smile Damien gave her and the sneer that Charles cast her way. Him, she didn't care about. The man was continuing to be unpleasant and this time he didn't even have the excuse of too much to drink.

Kathy fingered her necklace. "Damien gave it to me several years ago for Mother's Day."

There was a pleased look on Damien's face. His gaze fell on his mother and he smiled warmly at her until he caught his father's glance and looked hurriedly away. Mia took a bite of her salad, wondering if by changing the conversation she'd inadvertently made it worse.

"Why would your mother need jewelry? She doesn't go anywhere but to work."

"Lay off, Pop," Damien muttered. "I think it looks nice on her and so does Mia." He turned to smile at her. "I'm glad you like it." He leaned in closer, kissing Mia's ear. "Be nice and for your first Mother's Day, I'll buy you one." he whispered low, so that only Mia heard.

Mia felt the inevitable heat sear her as surely as if Damien had caressed her. Smiling at him, she wanted to tell him to stop his wicked looks but she loved them and she loved him. And in time she would learn to at least tolerate his father.

"Kathy, I was wondering if you'd like to get together with me one day next week, just the two of us, so we can get to know each other better, maybe take in a movie or something?"

"I'm sure you have a thousand things to do before the wedding. You don't have time to spend with me," Kathy answered.

"Of course I do. You're going to be my mother-in-law. I'll make time."

"And what about me?" Charles asked. "Are you going to make time for me also?"

Mia knew he was baiting her, and her mouth dropped just a little. She took a sip of her water, her eyes searching out Damien's.

"Why are you looking at him? Can't you answer for yourself?" Charles insisted.

"Of course I would like to get to know you better, but next week I want to spend time getting to know Kathy a little better."

"I don't understand why I can't be included."

"Chuck?"

"Don't Chuck me." Damien's father turned to Kathy. "What? He's my son as well as yours, probably more so. He's more like me than you. He has balls. Or at least he used to until about a year ago." He sat back in his seat and glared first at Mia, then Damien.

"Pop, stop picking at Mia. You're spoiling for a fight and you're not going to get one. Not tonight anyway. Mia asked Mom out for a movie, not you. Leave it at that. God, I don't get it, if you and Mom hate being around each other so much, why do you bother?" He shook his head. "I pray before I die I can figure it out," he said disgustedly.

"Come on, Mia, let's dance." Damien said as he stood and held his hand out.

She gladly accepted. She was literally trembling with anger. On the dance floor she asked, "What in the world does your father have against me?"

"It's not you, baby. He's just being ornery. Usually he charms women. I don't know why he's not trying to charm you."

"He couldn't if he tried." Mia spoke without thinking and her words sounded harsh. She looked away when Damien stared at her.

"Mia, I don't blame you for being pissed. I'm just asking you to try, okay?" Damien sighed. "I've taken a lot more from your brother," he said in a firmer voice.

"So is this payback?" Her eyes filled quickly with tears and she blinked them away. "Did you put your father up to this?"

Damien pulled away an inch or two to study Mia. "I knew getting together wasn't going to be good. We're fighting, and I don't know why. If anyone other than my father was treating you like that I would have slugged them already."

"So your father can do what he wants?"

"Mia, think about what you're saying. Let's not go there. No family feuds. It's only going to escalate. We both come with people that the other may not like but we have to try and get along. I'm not trying to continue the fight, but at least my father talked to you. Your brother has only glared at me for the past month and we both know the reason for that."

"You're changing the subject."

"Don't you think we should?"

Mia saw Charles heading for them and knew what was coming. "Yeah, I think we should." She held Damien tighter. "I don't want to dance with him," she whispered as Damien looked in the direction of his father.

"Please, baby, one dance. I'll make it up to you. I promise."

Mia gritted her teeth and held on to Damien. She loved him, surely she could dance once with his father.

"I want to cut in," Charles said with a swagger in his voice as well as his step. "Maybe that's how we should get to know each other, Mia. If you like Damien's moves, you'll love mine. I taught him everything he knows."

Mia shivered and glanced at Damien who had a pleading look in his eyes. "Of course." She attempted to smile. "If Damien doesn't mind." She looked at Damien and he nodded his head. She went into his father's arms thinking she would have her revenge when and if her mother arrived. She was worst than Charles. She would be all over Damien. A sobering thought hit Mia. She didn't want her mother's hands all over Damien.

She looked at Damien watching them dance from the sidelines and she knew. He didn't want her dancing with his father. That thought made the dance easier. She and Damien had even more in common than they'd discussed.

Damien stood for a few more seconds watching Mia, knowing that his mere presence would only make things worse. His father would not release her until he left. It was as if he were trying to prove something to him and using Mia to do it.

Looking toward the table, he saw the sad look on his mother's face as she sat there alone. He walked toward her and sat down. "Why is he being so nasty to Mia?"

"Because he's about to lose his playmate," his mother answered.

"What are you talking about?"

"You and him. You've been following in his footsteps from the time you were born. He's your hero. He knows that. He hasn't grown up and he never thought that you would. He never thought this day would come."

"What, me getting married?"

"Charles doesn't care about you getting married. He can't stand the fact that you're in love with Mia."

"Mom, that makes no sense." Damien stared at her, then at the dance floor. When he caught Mia's gaze he looked away. "He's treating her like that because I love her?"

"Yes. When you were with Ashleigh, he knew you didn't love her. My God, Damien, you were with anything that moved when you were with that girl. But Mia, she goes against everything that he's taught you to not want. It's almost like you're rejecting him."

"That's stupid," Damien muttered.

"That's your father."

Before Damien could answer Mia came stomping back to the table. She was angry and looked as if she were going to either cry or pitch a fit. Damien groaned, wondering what had happened. He looked at Mia first and she refused to meet his gaze, so he turned to stare at his father. "What happened?" he asked.

"I told her a couple of jokes," Charles answered, shrugging. "And she thought I was too close on her. That's the problem with virgins. They always imagine things."

Damien closed his eyes and counted to ten. When he opened them he ignored Mia's glaring look. He didn't need it to know that it was time he put his father in his place.

"Lay off Mia, Pop. I don't intend to tell you again. I didn't bring her here for you to make her uncomfortable. And I'm not going to ask her to remain here if you continue to treat her this way. She's trying, why can't you?"

"I thought I was. Sorry, Mia. I didn't know you couldn't take a joke."

Mia glared at both Damien and Charles and left for the bathroom. She was shaking so hard that she could feel it reverberating through her. She heard Kathy behind her calling out to her but didn't answer her until she was inside the lounge of the ladies' room.

"Welcome to your future, Mia," Kathy said.

"What are you talking about?"

"I'm talking about Damien. I tried telling you before. He's just like his father. He's my son and I love him, but I'm warning you that this is what you have to look forward to.

"I don't blame Damien for the things Charles said. Why are you?" Mia turned from the sink to face Damien's mother. "I thought you said you liked me."

"I do, Mia."

"Then why are you constantly trying to make me doubt Damien? We're getting married in just a few more days." Mia wanted to cry. She'd done her best to like Damien's mother and in some ways she did, but the woman made her uncomfortable. For some strange reason she reminded Mia of her own mother and that she didn't like at all.

"Listen," Mia said, trying again. "You don't have to worry. Damien would never treat me with disrespect. You heard what he said to Charles. He loves me, he won't hurt me."

"Trust me, he will. You're new, this relationship is new. Yes, Damien is in love with you. In time the newness will fade and he'll hurt you. Ask Ashleigh. She thought the same thing. Look how the two of you met. That doesn't bother you? It should. Mia, you met the man when he was at his ex's home trying to beg his way back in. If she had said yes, do you think you would be here right now with him? He has no idea how to be faithful."

Mia gazed at Kathy in disbelief. *What's wrong with everyone*, she wondered. *Even if they're not, can't parents stand the thought of their kids being happy?* A picture of Charles lashing out at Kathy flashed before Mia, making her decision for her. She would not do the same; the woman needed someone to be kind. Mia could do this. It was her profession.

"Why are you saying this?"

"I'm not trying to hurt you, Mia. I'm trying to save you."

"I don't need saving, not from Damien."

"I wish someone had done this for me. You're going into this thinking that everything is going to be all roses, that the two of you are going to love each other always and that Damien is never going to look at another woman. I thought the same thing about his father."

"Damien is not his father."

"That's what you think. The two of them are alike. He loves his father, he looks up to him and his father intends on making him remember his old ways, their old ways. I'll admit Damien has changed since he met you but for how long? I don't believe he can keep this up. Maybe you can be happy, but just don't count on Damien being faithful."

"You're his mother. Why would you tell me this?"

"Because you're a woman. I can see how much you love Damien. I see the stars in your eyes. I'm just trying to tell you what's in your future." Kathy paused.

"Mia, as horrible as it's been for you tonight, I think it was good that it happened. Charles will always be a part of Damien's life. If you marry him he'll also be a part of yours. At least you can see now what you're in for before you make a mistake."

Mia ran her teeth back and forth over her top lip in a sawing motion. It was becoming clear that talking rationally to the woman wasn't working. This was the last thing Mia needed today. She didn't want to remain in a bathroom with Damien's mother trying to convince her that things would be different between Damien and herself. She wanted to say, "Shut the hell up!" But if she were going to be good at her job she couldn't tell her patients to shut up, could she?

"Are you saying that my marrying Damien is a mistake?"

"I'm saying that it's a mistake if you think my son is going to be faithful to you. I believe he finds that your being a virgin is some kind of prize and he's determined to be the one to win."

Mia cringed and an uneasy feeling settled in her stomach. Her own mother had said the same thing. Even Mia had thought that the night Damien proposed. She didn't know how much more of this she could stomach. Kathy was not her patient and even if she were, her patient wouldn't be discussing Mia's private life.

She stared for a long moment at Kathy. "Listen, I think it's best if we don't discuss my sex life."

"That's the point of this conversation. You don't have one. You're a virgin and all men are intrigued by virgins."

"Damien never pushed me, even before he found out that I was a virgin. I think you're wrong." Mia's voice was firm, her resolve to be kind slipping a bit. But then the woman was butting into her private affairs, in places she didn't belong.

Kathy smiled at her. "I hope you're right, but don't ever say you haven't been warned."

Both their heads turned as they looked toward the door, wondering who was knocking.

"Mia, you okay in there?" Damien's voice called out. Both women shared a glance.

Mia blinked several times, feeling the tension building inside her like a pressure cooker that was about to blow. But she wouldn't right now; she didn't have the time. Mia looked toward the door, then smiled at Kathy. "He loves me."

"I know. I never said that he didn't."

"Mia," Damien called again, "are you okay in there?"

"I'm okay," she answered and glanced back at Kathy as she walked out of the bathroom.

Damien lifted her chin with the tip of his finger. "I'm sorry about my father. We can go if you want. I thought he would love you. I know he was nasty the last time you met but I thought it was because he'd been drinking. I've only seen him act like this with my mom."

Mia had a brief flash of insight. Of course! Charles was jealous of the women that Damien loved. It made perfect sense. She felt proud of herself for diagnosing the man's behavior so quickly. Maybe she was cut out for the line of work she'd chosen.

"Listen, I should have been prepared for this." She smiled at Damien. "I'm going to make my living giving advice to people on how to get along with…well, people they may have problems with. So I might as well give it another try with your father."

"You sure you want to? I meant it when I said you don't have to. I'll take you home if you want to go. "

"It's important to you that your father and I get along, so it's important to me."

Mia walked back to the table and smiled at Damien to show him that she was definitely going to try.

"Did I hurt your feelings, Mia?" Charles asked with disgust in his voice.

"Not at all," she answered. "I have allergies and something in the food must have triggered it." She smiled indulgently at him and dug into her salad.

"Glad to hear that," Charles answered.

Mia continued to smile, not answering because of the food she was chewing, but she knew Charles was hoping his actions would drive a wedge between her and Damien. She'd have to keep her guard up and remember that.

"So where are the two of you going to live?"

Charles looked at her, glared for a few seconds. Then his glare turned to a definite leer and his eyes fastened on her bosom. It was official. The man was deliberately trying to make her angry. Maybe he was trying to show that he was the one Damien would choose should it come to a showdown.

Mia was saved from saying anything when Damien spoke. "We're going to stay in Mia's apartment." He glanced toward Mia. "She has a very nice place."

"But it's hers." his father said.

"So what? Once we're married it will be ours."

"No, it won't. If she wants to kick you out she'll tell you, 'Get your ass out of my house.'" He turned to glare at Kathy. "Won't she?"

"I won't," Mia said. "I have no plans on ever saying those words."

"Plans," snarled Charles. "Every woman has plans until they marry you, then those plans change. Damien, listen to me. Don't live in a place that belongs to some woman. Get your own."

"I thought you always thought that was okay?" Damien said to his father. "I remember you told me that I shouldn't ever have to pay rent if I could find someone else willing to do it."

"That was before you lost your mind and decided to get tied down with one woman. Now I'm telling you, don't move into Mia's apartment. Give me one good reason why you should."

"I own the apartment," Mia intervened.

"You own it?"

Mia bit her lip slightly, knowing she'd said the wrong thing. "Actually my brother Keefe owns it, but I don't have to pay any rent."

"And you think your brother is going to keep that arrangement when Damien moves into it? Do you think your husband is going to want your brother living in the same crib?"

"Keefe doesn't live with me. He doesn't even live in the same building. He has several apartment buildings."

"And your brother doesn't have a key to your apartment?"

"Of course he has a key." Mia winced. This was harder than she'd thought. "But I also have a key to his apartment."

"Who cares? There is no chance that Damien is going to walk in on your brother. But he can walk in on you. Are you going to get your key back from him?"

Mia sucked on her tongue and glanced once again at Damien, who was watching her with a curious expression on his face. She'd never thought of the fact that her brother had a key to her apartment. "I can ask for it back," Mia said softly, ignoring Charles and speaking instead to Damien.

"You don't have to do that, Mia. I don't mind that your brother has a key. In fact, I think it's a good idea in case of emergencies and stuff like that."

For a long moment Mia stared at Damien. Then she smiled. "If you're sure you don't mind," she answered.

"Damien!" Charles nearly screamed. "Man, what kind of bull is this? I knew this girl had you whipped. Now she's got you kissing her brother's ass too. She's punking you."

"But it's me she's punking. Evidently I like it." Damien stared hard at his father before seeing the pleading look in his mother's eyes. Then he glanced at the woman he loved, at Mia and knew he'd let things go on much longer than he should have.

For thirty years he'd been a pawn between his parents, each of them using him for their own purposes. His mother constantly found fault with him in order to have his father step in and parent. Only it had never been to parent him but to see her, if only for a few brutal words. Then she'd soothe his father with food and sex. Damien had watched the game for many years. His father had told him in plain English how weak his mother was and although he'd known his father was right, he had still felt sorry for his mother for pining over his father, a man who was mean, ill tempered, and charming only when it suited him.

He'd tried telling his mother that more than once. But she'd either not wanted to listen or she'd cried. What was Damien supposed to say to that? He'd gone along with both of their manipulations all of these years because it hadn't mattered. He'd always known what they were doing. The only thing he hadn't known was why. He didn't fully believe he was their main reason for fighting.

He glanced again at Mia. For one night he'd hoped that Mia could work the same magic on his parents that she'd worked on him, that his mother would become strong, that his father would become a little less mean to his mother, that maybe he could have a normal family with sane parents, just maybe.

Well, it was obvious that wasn't going to happen. It appeared that the best he could hope for was to start his own sane family. He should have never allowed his father to bully and disrespect Mia. If lines were to be drawn in this family saga, from now on the battle would be more in Mia's favor. The two of them were now a team, because he was joining in. He was joining Mia.

He leaned over and kissed Mia, then stuck his fork in her salad. For the look of love she'd just given him, he didn't give a damn at the moment what his father thought of him.

He grinned at his father. "If this is being punked, then I'm for it. Maybe if you tried it you'd stop yelling at everyone. Fine, Mom's not the one to make you feel this way, so go find someone who will. Mia makes me happy."

Charles grunted. "Happy?"

"Yes, happy." Damien turned from his father, ending the conversation. "I'm sorry, baby girl," he whispered to Mia. "I should have stopped him sooner." He tilted her head slightly, kissed her throat, felt her tremble and was grateful he'd not lost her love. Then he pulled Mia into a deeper kiss, right there at the table.

CHAPTER EIGHT

The ride back to Mia's apartment was quiet. Damien would have liked nothing more than to cuddle up with Mia, kissing her until she threw him out. But not tonight. Tonight he had to set things straight with his parents, sever ties if need be.

He sighed out loud. He knew in his heart he didn't want it to come to that. But tonight was the last night he would stand by and listen to his father abuse Mia. It wasn't going to happen again.

"What's wrong?" Mia asked.

"Nothing."

"You're sighing. You have something on your mind and you don't want to tell me."

Damien smiled and dared a peek at Mia. "Are you reading my mind, baby girl?"

"Would you mind if I did?"

"If you're reading it right now I don't mind." His mood was lifting. "Tell me what I'm thinking."

Mia laughed. "What you're always thinking. That's not so hard to read." She laughed again before issuing a sigh of her own.

"Okay, now you're doing it," Damien said. "Suppose you tell me what's got you doing it?"

"I was just thinking that I wish I had listened to you, just hopped on a plane with you and eloped."

"We still can."

"Keefe would kill me."

"Family," Damien said. "That's the problem we both have. Too many people in our lives we're trying to please and they're causing a problem."

There was a tightening in Mia's belly that quickly spread upward. "Do you think we're rushing things?" she asked softly.

"Rushing things?" Damien answered. "Do you know how long it's been? I'm about to burst from all this pent up energy. No way, baby, are we rushing things."

"Don't joke. Not about that, not tonight."

"What's wrong? You sound so serious. You know I'm kidding."

For a moment she didn't answer, but just looked at him, licking her lips as she searched for the words.

"When your mother and I were in the bathroom she warned me about you. She said basically that I was a novelty, that no woman had ever turned you down." Her voice trembled and she stopped. "I know that you love me, Damien. I know that. But...I...I just wish you would stop saying that...you know...like what you just said. It does sound like you're marrying me for one thing."

Damien didn't answer. He shook his head instead. What did he have to do to prove to Mia that she was more important than sex? Even though he kept an erection whenever he was near her, and he wasn't going to lie about that, sex didn't have a damn thing to do with why he wanted to marry Mia. He needed her and more than anything he needed her to continue believing in him.

He rubbed his palm against her thigh and sighed again. This time she didn't ask what was wrong. She merely laid her head on his shoulder and entwined her fingers with his. In a few minutes they reached her apartment and he walked her upstairs, pulling her into his arms for a kiss, making no move to enter the apartment.

"Aren't you coming in?" she asked.

"Not tonight, baby. Tonight I have to deal with my parents. I can promise you, Mia, that you'll never have to live through another night like tonight."

"You can't control your father."

"No, but I can control myself and if he ever acts like that toward you again, we'll get up and walk out."

"Don't feel too bad. You haven't met my mother yet. After you do, you might be the one having second thoughts." She laughed, but he didn't.

"Say you didn't mean that, that you're not having second thoughts?"

"It bothers you that I said it," Mia teased. "No, I'm not having second thoughts. But how would you like it if I kept saying that?"

"I wouldn't."

"Then stop saying you're marrying me so that you can sleep with me."

"I've never said that." Damien looked at her. "At least not like that."

"It doesn't matter. That's how it sounds."

"Mia, I told you the first day I met you that I wanted to sleep with you. You've never agreed, so I don't see why you're getting so worked up."

"Because then it was different. Now we're getting married."

"And now that we're getting married my mind is supposed to be off sex?" Damien groaned. "Tell me that isn't true."

"Stop making me laugh. You know what I mean."

He took her in his arms and kissed her thoroughly. "Mia Black, you're working my nerves but I love you. Now good night. I would love to continue this conversation but I have to go home and scold my parents."

"Good luck."

"You know what we need?"

"I can just guess what you think we need."

"Well, you're wrong. We need to go on a date, just the two of us. What about tomorrow? I just need to run by the zoo for a couple of minutes and I'm free."

"I thought you were off tomorrow."

"I am but we have a bear cub due any day and I've been trying to catch the birth."

"That's why you've been spending so much time at the zoo?" Mia grinned. "Now I'm in competition with the animals."

"You're in competition with no one. But the animals are a pretty close second." He laughed. "Do you think you can drop everything and spend the day with me?"

"I can always drop everything to spend time with you."

"In that case I'll pick you up at ten. We can go to Navy Pier and ride the Ferris wheel." He kissed Mia again, then ran down the stairs. As usual he glanced at the window to see her waving goodbye at him.

Mia's other senses kicked in once she wasn't in such close proximity to Damien. She heard her answering machine beeping and went to answer it.

"Mia, got your invitation to the wedding. Thanks for inviting me. I was surprised that you wanted me to give you away but of course I'll do it. Give me a call, okay?"

Mia listened to the message, stunned. This was really happening. Jerry was going to give her away. She couldn't believe it. The next voice stopped what could have been an emotional meltdown.

"Mia, I thought you'd gotten married already and forgot to call me. You said a month, and it's way past that. I talked with your cousin, Tanisha. She told me you won't be getting married for two more weeks. Give me a call and I'll see if I can make it."

Mia pulled her bottom lip into her mouth and sucked down on it, then shook her head and lay across her bed. She hadn't called her mother since the last disastrous time.

She replayed the message. It was clear that her mother had heard her but hadn't even bothered to find out when the wedding was. Mia didn't know why her mother now wanted to come. As for herself, she wondered why she'd never bothered to call her mother back.

She shuddered, acknowledging the reason. She didn't want her mother to come, not after all the things she'd said. She put both her hands atop her head, sliding her thumbs downward to massage the base of her skull. *Let it go, Mia*, she commanded. *Let it go*. But this time the pressure remained. Too many things were happening too quickly.

For the first time in her life Mia wished her mother would do as she'd always done—miss another important moment in her life. Damien had been right. Their families were proving to be a problem.

Damien walked into his home knowing that it would be unpleasant, but it had to be done. He had no intention of letting his father get away with what he'd done tonight.

"Didn't expect to see you back here tonight," his father sneered. "Oh yeah, I forgot she won't give you none, so you come back here like a whipped puppy."

"Stop it, just stop it and leave Mia the hell alone," Damien shouted. "I didn't expect to see you here. You don't live here, just like you told Mia. So why are you here?"

"Unlike you, I won't be sleeping alone tonight." Charles glanced over at Kathy, a sneer on his face. "You couldn't pay me to date a woman like Mia—too much work."

"Who the hell asked you to date her? She'd never have you." Damien was angry. It was the first time he'd ever shouted at his father but he didn't regret it. His father's face stretched with fury and for a moment Damien thought his father was going to hit him. Chuck stood only inches away from Damien's face and shouted back at him.

"Boy, who the hell do you think you're yelling at? Don't disrespect me like that."

"That's nothing compared with the way you disrespected Mia tonight. I'm not going to just stand still and let you talk to her like that. You're not messing things up with Mia, either one of you." Damien glared at his father before turning to include his mother.

"Why would you tell Mia that I was only marrying her to get into her pants?"

"I like her, Damien. I didn't want to see her get hurt."

"With the number that Pop was pulling on her," Damien stopped and shook his head, "I could have lost her. Don't you see that? Listen, Mom." He turned to his mother, shutting his father out. "I want to believe that you think you're helping and I know that you think I'm going to treat her the same way…," he paused, "that you've been treated. But I promise you I'm not. I might be my father's son," he walked toward his mother, "but I'm yours also and I would never treat a woman the way you've been treated."

"But you have." Kathy teared up. "Don't you know how many women you've hurt, women that loved you? What about Ashleigh? You were going to marry her. Do you think you can just say you're sorry and that makes it all okay? Yes, I told Mia to be careful. You tell me that I'm wrong. Tell me she's not the first woman to say no to you."

"Mom, I love Mia."

"I know that but I still think you're wanting something you've never had. I can't help it if I believe that you look at Mia as a challenge. I think she deserve better than to give her entire soul to you and wake up one morning to find you don't want her anymore, that she's given you all that she can and you're bored."

"That's not going to happen."

"I wish I could believe you."

"I'm not responsible for the things that Pop did to you. Don't you want me to be happy?"

Damien's voice was soft and his eyes held his mother's. "I just want you to like Mia."

"I do like her, Damien." She rose to embrace her son, "I like her very much. I liked her even before I met her. She's good for you. I'll admit that you're trying to change. I'll just wait and see. Don't hurt her, though. She doesn't deserve that. If you don't think you can be true to her, don't marry her."

Damien kissed his mother. She didn't understand what she'd done and his explaining wouldn't help. She really was trying to keep Mia from repeating her own fate. *Two weeks*, he thought, *two weeks and this will be over.*

"This is a cozy little scene," Charles sneered. "But I don't like her. Mia's a stuck up little snob acting like she's too good to listen and laugh at my jokes.

"You were being crude," Damien answered, his voice sounding as tired as he was feeling. "Not only that, you spent the entire evening first grilling her, then glaring or leering at her. What did you think she was going to do? I told you Mia wasn't like that." Damien's temper was rising and his voice rose as well. "I don't like you talking to her like that."

"You can't tell me what to say or who the hell to say it to. Who do you think you are? You might be a man but you'd better think hard about it before you ever step in my face again."

Damien shook his head. "Look, Pop, I wasn't trying to disrespect you, but you're going to have to show some respect to Mia. She's going to be my wife and I'm not going to allow you to talk to her like that."

"Are you threatening me? Just make it plain what you're saying."

"I'm saying that if you can't behave civilly around Mia, then I think it's best that you aren't around her."

"So now what? You're telling me how to act for a piece of tail that you're not even getting?"

Damien pushed away from the table, balled his fists and turned to his mother. "Tell me why you've wanted this for thirty years? You're a good-looking woman. You don't have to put up with this, with him coming over to sleep with you when he can't find anyone else.

"And to answer your question, yes, Mia is the first woman who said no to me. I think you could learn a lot from her. She respects herself and she isn't going to let me walk all over her."

He saw the intake of breath and his mother lowering her eyes. He'd hurt her. Damn. He hadn't intended to do that. His frustration with his father had allowed him to strike out at his mother. She didn't need that. He glanced toward his father. One of them being a bastard to her was enough.

"Can we start over? Mom, I'm sorry I snapped at you. Pop, listen to me for a minute. I know it's partly my fault. I started it when I told you months ago that Mia thought she was better than me. I was just pissed. She broke things off with me to wait until she told her fiancé. I didn't like not being with her. I was angry. Hell, I was scared that she might realize that I wasn't good enough for her, that her fiancé was the one for her."

Damien laughed, then shook his head. "Do you want to know something? She thinks I'm special. That's right," he repeated proudly. "While the two of you might think I'm worthless, that I'm going to cheat on Mia, she doesn't. I've never asked anything of either of you. I thought that the one time I did, you'd know how important it was to me, that maybe you'd come through. And in case you're interested, you didn't scare her away, Pop. With all that you did, you didn't scare her away." He stared at his father and walked out of the door.

He was lucky that Mia hadn't run away screaming after the number his father had pulled. Between his parents and her brother glaring at him, it was a wonder that either of them felt like having a wedding.

He remembered Mia telling him how she wished she'd taken his suggestion and eloped. Well, now he was wishing she had also. At the time Mia had looked at him as though he had two heads, kissed him and told him to deal with it. But now he was tired of dealing with it. He wanted the wedding to be over before anything else went wrong. He wanted to make Mia his wife before she came to her senses and changed her mind.

Damien drove around aimlessly for hours. Finally he headed down Lake Shore Drive. It was much too dark to see anything but he drove anyway. The Ferris wheel beckoned and he turned on Grand Avenue, parked and looked skywards. He and Mia deserved a day together. They were seeing less and less of each other since they'd become engaged and that had to be rectified. Tomorrow he would make sure they did just that.

Another few minutes of looking at the Ferris wheel and Damien left, hoping that by the time he returned home his parents would be done with their fight, and that his father would be gone.

Damien groaned inwardly as he pulled up to his home and spied his father's truck. He shook his head, not wanting to deal with more drama, not tonight. The drive had done him good and he wasn't about to allow his parents to spoil the way he was feeling.

Without thought Damien eased his key into the lock, holding the door as he opened it, making sure he wouldn't be heard. Too late he realized that though his parents didn't hear him, he could hear them. He waited for a second before deciding to ease past the den. He couldn't believe they were still going at it.

"I'm sick of playing the bad parent."

Damien stopped at his father's voice and almost laughed out loud at his father's words. *What the hell kind of parent does he think he's been?*

"You are the bad parent," his mother came back. "You should have married me."

"Married you? Are you crazy? You're lucky that I didn't just leave you and never come back."

"My God, are you going to throw that up in my face for the rest of our lives?"

"Yes."

Damien heard his father growl but the growl contained something else. There was pain there. Damien sat at the foot of the stairs listening to his parents. Something was wrong. This was different from any of the fights he'd ever walked in on.

"Big deal. I had an affair. So what? I wasn't the only one to have one," his mother said.

Damien's stomach fell. His mother? He wouldn't have believed it if he hadn't heard it from her own mouth. What was wrong with this picture?

"I never slept around on you while we were together and as far as your little affair, you conveniently forget that you cheated on me twice." His father's voice was ragged with emotion. Damien thought about making noise to alert them that he was home but he found himself unable to move as his mother's voice screamed out in anger.

"It didn't mean anything. I've tried telling you that. I was confused and angry."

"And that makes a difference? Why, Kathy? That's all that I want to know. I loved you. I was good to you. Why?"

"Isn't it obvious? I was unhappy. Chuck, it isn't going to do any good to keep going over this. The first time I was just confused, I thought…"

"I know what you thought. You thought you could do it and I would never find out."

"I still wanted to marry you."

"You were sleeping around two days before we were going to get married. I found you in bed with a man, remember? Did you really think I was gong to marry you then?"

"I was pregnant. You should have married me."

Damien begin to shake. His mother had slept around. She'd been pregnant and sleeping around. How could his father even be sure he was his son?

"My son was the only good thing that came out of our relationship."

"You know, Chuck, sometimes I wish Damien wasn't yours."

"But he is mine. I made sure of that."

"Don't you think your putting me through that was revenge enough? You've used the threat of telling Damien for his entire life."

"And you've used me being the bad guy so he would hate me for his not having a family."

"You are the bad guy. He's seen it his entire life—you've taught him your ways."

"To protect him, Kathy. Yes, he knows my faults but I'm not the only parent he has that has faults." Charles grunted. "I don't know, maybe neither of us had what it took to be together. We tried, but it didn't work."

"We still love each other. We could try again. Damien will be gone soon and you could move back in."

"I told you the last time you threw me out I would never live with you. 'Fool me once, shame on you. Fool me twice, shame on me.'"

"Then why do you keep coming back?"

"Because you keep calling me." Damien heard the bitterness in his father's voice from the stairs where he sat with his head in his hands. This was the missing piece, the reason why his mother put up with his father, the bitterness his father displayed toward his mother and women in general. He was making her pay for betraying him.

"Kathy, I guess a little part of me will always love you but I can never trust you again."

"So you've decided to make it your mission to destroy your son's happiness."

"I don't want him to allow some little girl to make a fool of him like I did. I don't want him to love her so much that he forgets to protect himself. You think men don't hurt, Kathy? They do."

"I'm sorry."

"Yeah, I know you are. But we both know that you play this doormat role in front of Damien. It's not who you are. It's never been who you were and I'm not buying into it again."

"I've put my life on hold waiting for you to forgive me, to take me back. It was so long ago. I couldn't help what I did. I was young."

"You didn't try to help it. It wasn't enough that I loved you," Charles spat out bitterly, his anger renewed. "You thought you were going to use my son against me. Well, you see that didn't happen. I have the last laugh on you as far as Damien's concerned. He's more like the way I should have been from the beginning, and I'm not going to let him allow love to screw him up.

"You just think you have control over him. I'm his mother. When all is said and done, he will chose me over you."

Damien couldn't believe what he was hearing, all these years, all the fights, them pitting him against the other. It wasn't because they hated each other as he'd always thought. In some sick universe, they actually loved each other.

Damien walked into the den, glancing from one parent to the other. "Are you two for real?" he asked quietly. "All my life you've been using me to hurt each other because you couldn't find a way to make your relationship work."

He looked toward his mother. "I can't believe you always brought up Pop's faults, but never once mentioned it was you who cheated on him." He turned his gaze on his father. "Why didn't you ever say anything?"

"That's your mother, boy. You don't disrespect your mother."

"But you do it. You've disrespected her my entire life." He saw the look in his father's eyes change and saw him glance at his mother.

"It's none of your business what goes on between us."

"It is when it affects me. Look, if it hurt you so much when you caught her cheating, why didn't you just leave and go on with your life, forget about her?"

"Because he wanted to make me suffer," Kathy yelled, "and you were the best way to do that."

"You're the one that used Damien."

Damien's head swiveled from one parent to the other. "I'm through," he announced. "That's it. Kill each other, love each other. I don't give a damn."

Kathy looked at Charles. "I'm not going to keep begging you to forgive me. I made a mistake. Okay," she amended, "I made a bunch of mistakes, but through the years you've more than repaid me. Damien's right, it's time we end this feud. I'm moving on. The dance ends tonight."

Halleluiah, Damien thought and headed up to bed.

CHAPTER NINE

Mia snuggled next to Damien, enjoying the feel of his arms around her. They were looking out over Lake Michigan, the spray from the water misting them. She had always enjoyed watching the boats, and now with the fog rolling in, they looked even more beautiful and a bit mysterious.

Damien was unusually quiet, and Mia wondered what was up. "Anything wrong?" she asked.

"No, nothing."

"You sure?"

"I'm sure."

"Did something happen at the zoo?"

Damien stared at Mia for a moment. "Why do you want to be a psychologist?"

"I want to help people figure out their problems. I want to give them tools to keep themselves sane. I think if more people had tools they wouldn't feel so hopeless and do things that can't be changed."

"Mia, you can work a lifetime with the garbage that's in a person's mind and never be able to help them."

"You're not going to keep telling me nothing is wrong. It's in your voice. You're upset about something. Tell me what it is. Maybe I can help."

"Baby girl, I don't need a therapist, I need a wife." He grinned. "This is not the way I wanted us to spend the day. My parents got into a messy fight last night. I caught act one and two." He saw her lips pull down and sadness fill her eyes.

"No baby, no sadness over this, not today and not ever. They're adults. They'll have to work out their problems for themselves. Some people like drama, Mia; they like being miserable and no one can help them out of it. I don't plan on allowing them to sap my energy or to ruin our day."

"You'd make a good counselor yourself," Mia teased.

"I'd rather shovel manure all day and all night at the zoo than deal with all the crap most people come with. Come on, I promised you a ride on the Ferris wheel. After that maybe we'll walk down to the edge of the pier and listen to a little jazz." He held Mia's hand tightly in his own. Their lives would be a hell of a lot different than his parents' or hers. He would do everything in his power to make sure of that.

At the top of the wheel Damien pulled Mia into his arms and kissed her, wishing that they could stay locked forever inside their safe little box. But they couldn't and he knew that. As the ride came to an end, Mia begin pulling him towards one of the boats for hire, but then stopped and grinned.

"I'm hungry."

Damien laughed, wondering where she was putting it all. They had both been eating constantly the entire day. "I can't believe it but what would you like?" he asked, grinning back at her.

"I want a pretzel." She kissed him. "I'll wait here and watch the boats."

When Damien returned with the pretzel Mia wasn't where he'd left her. He'd almost panicked, unable to spot her in the increasing fog, when he caught sight of her at the end of the pier staring out at the lighthouse.

Damien stood for a long moment watching Mia. The sight of her took his breath away. Dressed in a silky blue dress that stopped just short of her ankles, she was extending her arms as though inviting the Lake Michigan mist into her soul. He could hear her tinkling laughter as if she were being tickled by unseen hands.

He could stand watching her forever, but she turned and held out her hand for the pretzel, her smile lighting a fire in him and igniting a memory.

"I didn't know you were aware I was there."

"I always know when you're around. Why were you standing there watching me?"

"I was thinking how beautiful you are. I wish I had a picture of the way you looked. Words from a song came to mind as I watched you."

"What song?" Mia laughed, "You're making that up."

"'You make my whole world misty blue,'" Damien sang in her ear, loving her more with each passing second.

"What?"

"What do you mean, what?" Damien nipped her ear playfully. "The song, you remind me of the song."

"I have no idea what song you're talking about."

"Gladys Knight. You're kidding, right?" Damien pushed back to look into her eyes. "Mia, if you don't know 'Misty Blue,' I'm afraid I'm going to have to take back your black card."

He waited a moment until she got it and laughed. Then he pulled her close for a hug. "Come on, let's go hear some music." Together they walked away from the end of the pier, the sounds of Motown pulling them toward the open pub a few steps away.

Finding a couple of empty seats was next to impossible. When Damien left saying he was going to check for something closer, Mia gave him a look of skepticism. *Good luck*, she thought. A few seconds later he was back and grinning.

"Okay, Mia, the band is playing this one just for you."

"'Misty Blue?'"

"'Misty Blue.' Now dance with me," Damien said softly. "Listen to the words, Mia. This is us. This is how you make me feel."

Mia was fighting the jitters that had claimed her in the last few days. Everywhere she went, everyone she talked to thought they should warn her about Damien. She'd stopped going to the club altogether because she realized the women hit on Damien partly because they wanted to, partly to rile her up. Even when the women didn't choose to confront her face to face, they made nasty insulting remarks they knew she could hear. She was tired of hearing them, tired of the doubt that kept trying to rear its ugly head.

Seeing less of Damien had two side effects, one good, one bad. On the one hand, she had accomplished a lot. With less than a week left until she was married, she was glad they'd taken a day for themselves. She pulled up that memory whenever she felt overwhelmed.

On the other hand, Mia had not seen her brother as much as she would have liked. If she didn't know better she would think he was avoiding her. But why would he? she thought. Still, Mia realized that she missed him. The quick calls and short visits weren't nearly enough but that would be remedied soon. Keefe and Ashleigh were taking her out for her birthday.

Not seeing the people that meant the most to her, especially Damien, was the downside to her being so busy. She had not seen nearly as much of Damien as she'd wanted and she missed the reassurance of having his arms around her. In his arms she never doubted.

She looked at the clock. Damien would be there in a few minutes. When the knock came at her door, she was ready. She opened the door with a huge grin, ready to fall into his arms and kiss him.

"About time," her mother said as the door opened. Mia stared in shock. "Mom, what are you doing here?"

"I talked to Tanisha a couple of days ago. She happened to mention that it was your birthday. Silly me, I'd forgotten. Anyway, you never called me back. Your cousin reminded me you were getting married in a few days, so I figured you'd either forgotten to call me or the message got lost on my machine. I was going to meet a friend in Windsor, so I thought, 'Hey why not stop in and see my baby girl, stay with her a few days and see her get married all in one shot?' Are you surprised?"

"Yeah, I guess I am. Lucky for me that my birthday and wedding came at a time when you were on your way to Canada. At least that way you didn't have to go to any trouble."

Mia saw her mother's mouth form a look of surprise. Mia didn't blame her. She had surprised herself when she heard the words come out of her mouth. She refused to meet her mother's gaze. Having said it, she didn't want to change it. In rapid succession the words from her last conversation with her mother came back and try as hard as she could, there was no shoving the memory away.

Mia heard voices on the stairwell and stood for a nanosecond gawking at Keefe and Ashleigh. She managed to say, "Look who's here," as she moved aside to allow everyone to enter.

"Are you okay?" Keefe whispered to her as he entered.

Oh how badly she wanted to tell him that nothing was wrong, but his mended fence with their mother was fragile at best. Nevertheless, she gazed directly into her brother's eyes and whispered, "No, I'm not okay. I don't want her here." Then she calmly closed her door, aware there was a crack in her facade, microscopic but there.

The look on Keefe's face told the story. He was surprised. Mia had never behaved as she was doing now. She was always the one who welcomed their mother with open arms. This time Mia couldn't even fake it. So she didn't try.

Another knock sounded on the door and Ashleigh, who was standing there, looked toward Mia for permission, then pulled it open. Mia could tell from the look on Damien's face he'd been prepared to kiss her and had pulled back on realizing that it was Ashleigh.

"Hey," he said when he entered the room. Then he stopped and stared.

"Hello. You two must be Ashleigh and Damien. It seems the cat has my childrens' tongues. Otherwise I'm sure they would not be so deliberately rude as to not introduce their mother."

Mia blinked, stuttered and looked toward her brother. This was stupid and yes, rude. Though she was trying hard to make the proper introductions, she couldn't get her mouth to work and was grateful when Damien stuck out his hand. Icy fingers of dread touched the core of her soul as she watched her mother's reaction to Damien. Her mother gave him a long appraising look and she held on to his hand, not letting it go.

"My, my, my, you are handsome, aren't you? Mia didn't lie. And your voice. It makes me melt."

Mia's face burned with embarrassment and she glanced once again over at Keefe, not saying a word.

Bless Ashleigh, Mia thought, as Ashleigh stuck her hand out for her mother to shake, forcing her to release Damien's. But Mia couldn't help noticing that even though she'd released his hand, her eyes followed him like a hungry cat. Either Damien didn't notice or it didn't bother him, for he came toward Mia and kissed her as though nothing odd had happened.

Her mother shoved a box at her. "Here, Mia, I brought a birthday gift for you."

"Thanks," Mia said softly, taking the box and opening it. "Peanut brittle," she announced, unable to stop herself from once again searching out her brother. His gaze met hers and Mia swallowed the lump of sudden pain.

"Peanut brittle?" Damien asked as he looked at the box in Mia's hand. "Aren't you allergic?" he questioned as he took the box. "Do you mind if I have some?" he ripped into the box before Mia could answer.

"He's right. Mia's allergic to peanuts, Mom," Keefe said. "Ashleigh, Damien, meet Lillian Black, the woman who brings her daughter a gift that could kill her."

And that was everyone's introduction to their mother.

Mia groaned inwardly, wishing for a moment that she'd handled things differently. She should force herself to smile, to pretend. But she couldn't. She was rooted to the spot, her skin tingling with awareness. Her mother was there to cause problems. She knew that as surely as she knew she'd allow it to happen. She remembered Damien's words from the week before: Some people create the drama. Mia wouldn't deny she'd started the ball rolling with her remarks to her mother.

"Kill her? How would I know that?" their mother said airily. "You can't expect me to remember everything, now can you?"

It was as though Mia were watching a play. She felt the increasing tension. She shouldn't have told her brother that she didn't want her mother there, but it was true. She didn't. She watched Damien whom she'd never seen eat candy, munching on the peanut brittle. She saw him smiling at her mother and a sense of betrayal tugged at her frayed nerves as she remembered bits of the last conversation she'd had with her mother. *The first woman that comes along. Oh God, she didn't want to have those thoughts.* She touched Damien's arm, needing to look into his eyes, to see—

"This hits the spot," Damien said. "I wanted something sweet." He looked toward Mia. "Something edible, some candy. This was perfect."

Mia smiled. Damien's words were just what she needed, his jokes and innuendos, his look when his eyes settled on her. She saw her mother staring and she stared back, determined that her mother wouldn't get to her. She had nothing to fear. Her mother's vile remarks meant nothing. Damien still wanted her.

There was an intense building up of electrical energy. The room practically sizzled with awareness. In slow motion Mia observed the players and tensed, waiting for the fall-out. She saw the anger in her brother's eyes and knew he would have his say.

"Damien, I can't believe you would think peanut brittle is a perfect gift for Mia. Yeah, if she was trying to kill Mia it was perfect."

Keefe sputtered and all eyes turned in his direction. He was protecting Mia, the same as he'd done her entire life. Mia couldn't deny that she'd known any negative comments she made about her mother would cause Keefe to rush to her defense, to save her. He always had.

"Keefe, why the hostility? I thought last time I was here we buried the hatchet." Lillian turned toward Keefe and smiled. "I thought you had forgiven me?"

"I never said that. I said I would try and I have." He shook his head. "How could any mother not know or care what her daughter is allergic to? Oh forget it, you would never understand."

"Good. It's best forgotten. It's not as though she ate the candy. Come on, big deal. She's a grown woman. If she ate something that she knew she was allergic to, that would be her fault, not mine. Now enough talk on that. The two of you are making me feel unwelcome. Mia, you haven't given me a hug. Is something wrong?"

Mia blinked three times in rapid succession, not wanting to turn what was a little thing into something big. She had always hugged her mother but this visit felt different. Something had changed. Mia glanced once at Keefe but still couldn't move.

"I have a cold," she lied. "I don't want you to catch it."

"You didn't seem to mind having Damien catch it. I noticed when he kissed you you didn't move away."

"I gave it to her," Damien answered.

Damien stepped alongside Mia and rested his arm around her waist. Mia could have given him another kiss just for that. It was up to her to diffuse the situation. She wouldn't force Damien into the role of peacemaker for her family. From the look of things he had enough problems of his own on that front. She searched her mind for something that would pull her mother out of the room. Maybe not seeing her, Keefe would declare a cease fire.

"Do you want to see my gown since you're here?" Mia said at last, finding a topic and changing the subject. She headed for the bedroom without waiting for an answer. Instead of the tension lessening, however, Mia felt it increase. This was an important moment in her life. She should be thrilled to have her mother surprise her on her birthday, to be there for her wedding. But she wasn't thrilled; she was angry with her mother for being there. And she was angry with herself for caring. She was trembling and underneath she felt an unwarranted anger and couldn't quite place it. Her face felt hot and flushed as she opened the closet door.

"Here it is," she said, lifting the heavy bag from the closet.

"Is this the gown that Ashleigh made?"

"Yes," Mia answered. "Do you want me to try it on?"

"No, that won't be necessary."

Her mother smiled oddly, her expression sending chills skittering down Mia's torso.

"Is there something wrong, Mia? You're acting kind of funny, more like your brother. What's up? You're not happy to see me?"

For a moment Mia toyed with answering that question truthfully, for she wasn't happy to see her mother. "I'm just surprised, that's all. If you thought I was getting married weeks ago, why didn't you show up then? Why now?"

She watched while her mother's smile changed into a scowl and her voice lost the sweetness.

"You're getting more and more like your brother every day. Nothing I do for the two of you has ever been enough. Look at my thoughtfulness in bringing you a gift. Are you grateful? Nooo, and what does your brother do? He attacks me. Sometimes I wonder why I try so hard with the two of you. I'm here now, be happy with that."

Then she turned on her heel and marched out of the room, leaving Mia to stare after here.

"Be happy," Mia muttered to herself. For what? *Exactly what am I supposed to be happy about? That you didn't care enough to find out exactly when I was getting married or that it was convenient for you to stop by now because you probably need a place to stay?*

Mia caught sight of her own face in the mirror and recognized the bitterness in her eyes, for it was in her heart. She shook her head, trying to let go of the feelings, but they persisted and she couldn't deal with them at the moment. She had Damien, Keefe and Ashleigh waiting for her to take her out to celebrate her birthday. *Well, happy birthday to me.*

Mia stepped back into the room in time to witness her mother pressing her body into Damien, backing him into a corner. If Lillian weren't her mother, she'd be tempted to snatch her bald. As for Damien, she wanted to smack the silly grin off his face. Why didn't he move away? It was as though her mother had sensed her presence and had orchestrated her little performance for Mia's benefit. That thought was confirmed when her mother turned to her and smirked.

"Mia, I can't believe you're going to wear the gown that Ashleigh was going to wear to marry the man that Ashleigh was going to marry."

She burst into laughter at the same moment embarrassment flamed Mia's cheeks. This was payback for what had happened in the bedroom. She should have known not to cross her mother.

"Mia looks stunning in that gown. It was made for her," Damien interjected, moving away from her mother at last and returning to Mia's side.

"It was made for Ashleigh," her mother cut him off, "to marry you."

"The gown belongs to Mia," Ashleigh volunteered. "Damien's right. She looks gorgeous in it."

Though she was looking down, Mia could see her mother turn and focus on Ashleigh.

"So what? Mia is a gorgeous girl. She would look beautiful in rags. She's my daughter. But the gown wasn't made for her. It was made for you." She turned toward Mia. "And if I were you, Mia, there is no way I would wear it. It's bad luck, pure and simple."

"That's nonsense," Keefe snarled. "It's only a gown. No luck is tied in with it. Mia's wearing it. It was bought and paid for and she loves it. She's going to wear it."

"You're still worried about money, aren't you, Keefe? You bought the gown I suppose?"

When no one answered she continued. "Mia, who do you think Damien's going to see coming down the aisle to meet him, you or Ashleigh? Or will he be able to tell the difference?" She smiled sweetly again. "I'm only thinking of you, sweetie. I don't mean to offend anyone."

They all watched as she turned on her heel and strutted over to Damien, her hips undulating to some unheard music. She was acting like a seductress and it was obvious she didn't care that they were all watching her vulgar display of sexuality. Mia knew that what her mother was doing was meant either as a reminder of her warning or as a direct challenge.

Daring a glance at Damien, Mia saw that he was staring at her mother, and her heart fell. Of course he would find her mother attractive. She was beautiful. And the one thing her mother had always been good at was turning the heads of men. But Damien was her man. Mia wished she could take back what she'd said and done to her mother since her arrival so she would stop. She wished now she had hugged her. Maybe then she wouldn't have to witness her mother making a play for Damien. Now she had to stand there and pretend with everyone else in the room that it was a joke.

Mia turned slightly to look at her brother. His scowl spoke for him. With a grunt of disgust, Keefe left the room. With what she knew was a sick smile on her face, Mia glanced at Ashleigh, who gave her a pitying look. Mia blinked, pretending to herself as well as Ashleigh that nothing was wrong. But as she watched her mother grinning up into Damien's face, her own skin burned with shame.

"I'll bet you're still a dog, aren't you, Damien?" her mother drawled as she glued herself to him.

"I used to be before Mia," Damien answered, "but not anymore." He pushed her away gently but firmly, then pulled Mia into his arms. "There's only one woman for me," he said, hoping Lillian would get the message.

"I still think there's a bit of a dog in you. It would just take the right woman to bring it out. And frankly, I don't think Mia's that woman."

"Would that woman be you, Mom?"

All eyes turned toward Keefe. None of them had heard him reentering the room.

"Keefe, I was only teasing with him."

"I know teasing and I know you. You were flirting with the man Mia's going to marry." He glared at her, then turned to Mia. "Mia, he's your fiancé. What do you think?"

What do I think? Mia cringed inwardly. *I think I want to die.* To think that only a few seconds before she'd wanted an intervention, but not this. She stumbled to speak. It wasn't that she didn't agree with Keefe because she did. And it wasn't as though she weren't used to him rushing in to save the day, to save her. She'd always encouraged it. But with everyone looking at her, she felt like an incompetent child.

"I think we'd better get going," she answered her brother. "This is my birthday and I'm ready to celebrate."

"We're taking Mia and Damien out for Mia's birthday, Mom. We'll see you when we get back," Keefe said, heading for the door.

"You're crazy if you think I'm staying here while the four of you go out on the town," Lillian countered.

"We have reservations. It's too late to change it all now." Keefe answered.

"That's bull," she retorted. "I'm not staying here. I'm going with you. If you made reservations at some fancy, smancy place, that's not my fault. Either call and change the reservation to five, or pick some place else, because I'm going."

They all watched as she stormed to the door and stood as sentinel. If anyone had lit a match at that moment no doubt the room would have gone up in flames.

Damien looked at Mia, then Keefe. He'd felt the undeniable tension from the moment he came into the apartment. Had Mia not told him about the relationship her brother had with their mother, he would have been confused but it made sense.

And regardless how pompous he thought Keefe was, he was right about one thing: Lillian had definitely not been playing. He'd seen the hunger in her eyes and knew that her come-on was serious. He'd been taken aback and had waited as long as he dared for Mia to handle her mother as he'd handled his father. When he'd seen that wasn't going to happen, he'd been forced to push the woman away. If he hadn't, Damien wondered how far she would have gone. It was obvious that she didn't care that Mia had witnessed her actions. But it wasn't up to him to chastise Mia's mother. That was Mia's job.

The room was completely silent for more than a minute after Keefe told Lillian she wasn't going to dinner with them. Damien noticed that Ashleigh, too, was aware of the tension and was attempting to make conversation with Lillian. Mia and Keefe, however, were standing no more than a foot apart and staring at each other. And Damien could swear they were communicating. He watched as Keefe jerked his head angrily to the side and Mia's head tilted up as though pleading with him. When Keefe clenched his fists and closed his eyes, Damien knew he'd been right. Brother and sister had been communicating without words.

"Mia, I was just thinking you're not going to have much time alone with Damien before you get married. Your going out when you have only a few days to complete things was a bad idea. I'm sorry, that's my fault for not planning this better. Maybe instead of going out tonight, you should stay home. It's going to get crazy in the next couple of days."

"But you've gone to so much trouble," Mia answered. "It would be selfish of me to change all the plans now."

Damien was amused at the interplay between the siblings. It was obvious what was going on. Mia no longer wanted to go out to celebrate her birthday if her mother was tagging along. That had been the reason for Keefe's clenched fists. He had to take dear old mom off Mia's hands. Damien smiled at Mia and waited for his cue.

"Damien, would you mind if we stayed in? I am sort of tired and there are some things I need to do."

"Mia, it's your birthday. You're not even married yet. Do you want this hot man to think you're some little stick in the mud, stay-at-home drudge?" their mother chimed in.

Though Mia was avoiding looking at him, Damien had his cue. "Mia is definitely not a drudge, nor is she a stick in the mud." He saw Mia's eyes lift toward him and continued. "I would love for us to be alone, baby girl. We can order a pizza."

"Pizza? What kind of birthday is that?"

"The kind that won't kill her," Keefe growled. "At least it's not peanut brittle. Besides, it is Mia's birthday. She can do what she wants."

"Then I'll stay here and have pizza with Mia and Damien."

"God, don't you get it? They want to be alone. You'll go to dinner with us. Come on, Mom." He took his mother's elbow and steered her toward the door, ignoring her protest.

Keefe glared at Mia as he walked out, confirming for Damien what had just happened.

"So your brother saved you again, huh?"

"What are you talking about?"

"I was watching. I saw what just happened. You asked him to get your mother out of the apartment. I gather she was getting on your nerves. It's the first time I've seen you jealous. I like it, though you had no reason to be."

"I wasn't jealous."

"Like hell you weren't. You wanted to kill her, don't lie."

"I wanted to kill you. Why were you encouraging her?"

"I didn't encourage her. Don't you dare put that on me. She had me backed into a corner."

"And you were too afraid to move? Ha."

"Mia, don't start. I tried to give you a chance to put your mother in check. You didn't. I did. If I didn't do it fast enough to suit you, maybe you should have said something." Damien grinned.

"Were you tempted?" Mia asked, hating herself for having to ask, hating that she had been jealous, hating that as a professional she didn't have better control. A chill went through her body and she attempted to walk past him. But he reached out for her and tugged on her arm until she relented to his touch. "Were you tempted?" Mia repeated.

"I'm tempted, baby girl, by you and only you."

His lips came down and she let go of her hurt, her passion rising to the surface with the speed of lighting streaking through the sky. She was trembling. She wanted to seal their marriage, have it slut proof, prove to her mother that she wouldn't be able to turn Damien's head.

"What's wrong, baby girl?"

"I don't know. I just…I wish she hadn't come."

"I thought you had invited her."

"I did, weeks ago. But after she said some really nasty things, I never called her back. Now I'm wondering why she bothered coming. I can't get over the feeling that she came here to start trouble."

Mia couldn't voice what she really thought. How could she tell the man she loved that she believed her mother, the world's biggest slut, had come there deliberately to take him from Mia. Damien would think she was crazy. He wouldn't believe her. Who would?

"You okay, baby? You're shivering."

"I'm okay. Tell me something. How did you figure out what Keefe and I were doing?" Mia said, forcing a grin.

"I may not be your brother but I do know when something is bothering you. Hell, I knew from the moment I came into the apartment."

"I would never have known by your actions. You seemed to be infatuated by her, eating that darn peanut brittle." Mia frowned and shook her head. "It would have been better if she'd not brought anything."

"Why didn't you just say something to her, tell her to knock it off?"

"I wish I could. I have a hard time whenever I talk to my mother. It's like I'm a kid again. I'm working on it but," she shrugged, "she's my mother, you know. What am I going to do? It's not like she's constantly in my life, so why make waves?"

"I remember you wanted me to make waves with my pops."

"That's not true. He irritated me, but I didn't ask you to intervene."

"Maybe not with words, baby girl, but the look in your eyes said if I didn't handle my business I wouldn't have any to handle."

Damien chuckled and pulled Mia toward the couch. "Neither of us are kids anymore. Sometimes we have to do the hard jobs and just hope for the best."

"You're right, I know. It's just I've never had this particular problem with my mother. It feels kinda strange. It's generally her and Keefe that are fighting and I'm always the—"

"Let me guess, you're the peacemaker?"

"Yeah."

"You gonna be okay letting her crash here? Maybe it would be better if she stayed in a hotel." He smiled. "Do you think your brother would let her stay at his place? From what I hear he spends most of his nights in Ashleigh's bed. He shouldn't mind."

It wasn't the first time Damien had made mention of Keefe and Ashleigh's sleeping arrangement and Mia knew without a doubt that he'd meant nothing by the comment. Still, her stomach tied in knots. Every word her mother said was now ringing loud and clear in her ears. She wasn't giving Damien what he needed. He'd go elsewhere. *God, how was she going to survive the next few days living with her mother and her vicious accusations?*

"Mia."

"I'm sorry," she said. "I was just thinking. No, there's no way Keefe will allow her to stay with him or to use his apartment, even if he were living with Ashleigh, which he's not," she said sharply. "He wouldn't have anyway, but I'm sure after tonight there won't be the slightest chance. And all the begging in the world is not going to change that."

"I hope your brother doesn't kill your mother while they're out. He looked as if he wanted to strangle both of you."

"He did." Mia laughed, remembering the incredible scowl on Keefe's face. "He'll make me pay for that, don't worry."

"Well, he can't touch you. I'm going to be your new hero. I'll save you, just ask me," Damien purred and leaned in to nibble at her neck.

A cold breeze blew across Mia's face and she trembled. There was no way a breeze could have occurred. She held tight to Damien, feeling as if she'd just been given a warning. Her need for knights riding in to save the day, to save her, had to end. If there was some saving to be done, she needed to do it herself.

Once again Mia vacillated between thinking her career choice was a complete sham and thinking that she would do a good job. First, she knew she needed to get her own house in order. Only how? She had no ideas. The books covered it, but theory and practice were two different things.

She allowed Damien to pull her into his arms. Kissing him some more was what she needed right now.

"You really liked me in that gown, didn't you?" she whispered as he kissed her.

"You were beautiful in that gown. I've been dreaming of ripping it off you for months."

"You do know I'm not going to wear that wedding gown, don't you?"

"I kind of got that feeling after that comment your mother made. Mia, you don't have to worry. If you still want to wear it, your mother's wrong about it. And she's wrong about me. Still, if you want something else, go ahead. I'm not marrying the gown, I'm marrying you. I told you I would buy you a new gown weeks ago." Damien began kissing her forehead with every intention of working his way down to her lips.

"Good," Mia murmured, "because no way am I going to be wondering if you are looking at me and thinking of Ashleigh. Not on our wedding day."

"You don't have that worry," Damien moaned as his hand went beneath her sweater. "I have no problem telling the two of you apart. Every thought that I have is of you. I promise you, Mia, that will not change. My heart, my soul, the breath of my very life, are yours to command."

CHAPTER TEN

The sound of glass shattering spoiled the only moment of quiet that Mia had known in the last four days. Her gaze fell on her trembling fingers. Because she felt unsteady, She didn't kneel to pick up the shattered glass.

Of course Mia knew the reason. Her mother. She was constantly talking to Mia, laughing at her inexperience, complaining that she'd not been given anything to do as the mother of the bride, demanding a new dress, telling her how she'd been right, that Keefe didn't want to give her away. She suggested Keefe's absence was because he was glad to finally be ridding himself of Mia.

While everything else might have had a touch of validity, Mia knew that one statement was a bald-faced lie. Keefe wasn't coming around because of their mother. The real mother they'd known had returned with a vengeance. She didn't even bother to try to pretend as she usually did. She seemed driven and Mia feared her mission was to destroy Mia's life. Her mother's words were getting to her and Mia was holding on by only a thin thread. Glancing again at her trembling fingers and at the broken glass that had slid from her grip as easily as if it had been a buttered noodle, she thought of her old therapist and friend, Dr. Grey, and wondered how she'd handle this situation.

The thing that bothered Mia the most wasn't her mother's words but her actions. She'd wasted no time in trying to make a play for Damien, rubbing her body against his every chance she got. And then she'd had the nerve to smile. But if she could just get through the next couple of days, it would be over. She would be married, and her mother would leave and go to Windsor.

At least at the rehearsals Jerry would be enough of a distraction to keep her mother's interest. She knew her mother would waste no time making a play for Jerry. She couldn't stand the thought that he was happily married, that he'd gone on about his life without her. She'd told Mia many times that all she had to do was crook her little finger and she'd have him back. So God forgive her, Mia was hoping her mother would concentrate on Jerry tonight and leave Damien alone, keep her hands off him.

"Ashleigh, hi," Mia said, making her way toward her.

"What about me?" a booming voice said. Mia suddenly changed directions and ran toward the man who'd called out.

"Jerry, it's so good to see you." Mia smiled as she hurried toward the man who was going to walk her down the aisle, the man who'd given them so much help. If it wasn't going to be her brother doing it, then yes, she'd want no one other than Jerry.

He crushed her in a bear hug, then pulled away beaming at her. "I can't believe it. Little Mia's getting married. With the way your brother protected you, I'm surprised that you ever got a chance to meet anyone. What happened to that James fellow? I knew you weren't going to marry him."

"How did you know that?" Mia asked. Now she was the one surprised.

"You weren't in love with him."

"How about him? Was he in love with me?"

Jerry looked down.

"Don't worry," Mia assured him. "It won't hurt."

"I didn't see it, Mia. He liked you well enough, but there was something missing between the two of you, some spark that wasn't there." He leaned back to take a good look at her. "Like the spark that's in your eyes right now." Then he turned to face the front and saw Damien coming in with his parents.

"That's him?" he asked as he watched Mia's face split into a grin.

"That's him," she answered.

Damien's gaze sought hers and she smiled more broadly as he made his way toward her.

"That boy's in love, Mia."

"I hope so." Mia glanced at Ashleigh, unable to help it. Jerry looked sharply at her and she rushed to explain. "He was engaged to Ashleigh about a year ago."

"Don't worry, Mia, it's not Ashleigh he's looking at, just you. He's in love with you."

Mia wrapped her arms around Jerry and hugged him to her, thinking how strange it was that a man not of her blood was able to be more supportive than the woman who'd given her life.

Damien came to stand beside her and slid his arms around her waist. His warmth filled her with longing and she turned her face up for his kiss.

"Umm, just what I've been waiting for all day," he whispered in her ear before turning to Jerry. "I'm Damien. You must be Jerry."

After that the introductions moved along rapidly. Kathy and Charles had come to the front of the room and were being introduced to Jerry when loud voices caused them all to turn toward the back of the banquet room where Keefe was entering with their mother. The two appeared to be fighting about something. Nothing new there.

It was as though some invisible force seized control of Jerry and Charles because they turned simultaneously to gawk at her mother. Mia refused to look at Damien, praying that he was immune to her mother's spell. Then she felt it. As insignificant as it was, she felt it. His hands loosened slightly around her waist, and to Mia, it felt as if his hands lingered on her body merely out of habit.

She sucked the feeling inside, willing the pain to go away, knowing that some of what she was feeling was in her mind. She'd reached her limit; the crack was widening. And as it did, it brought with it the memories of their mother's neglect. She closed her eyes for a second and reopened them. It wasn't working. Her method of handling her pain was failing her. She could no longer push aside the frustrations that had gnawed at her for almost her entire life. Her eyes caught Ashleigh's and they both attempted to smile.

"Damn," she heard Charles murmur.

Damien turned to his father. "That's Lillian, Mia's mother."

"Introduce me."

"Pop, just go over there and introduce yourself." Damien glanced at his mother, then Mia. "You don't need me for that."

"Boy, bring your ass on." Charles grabbed Damien's arm and pulled him along.

"Before Mia had a chance to wonder if she should be the one giving the introduction to Charles, she heard Jerry's booming voice shouting, "Lillian," before he practically ran down the aisle to where her mother stood. She watched as Jerry hugged her mother and wondered why he didn't hate her for dumping him. Damien was looking uncomfortable as he introduced her mother to Charles.

Rolling his eyes in disgust and barely shaking hands with Jerry, Keefe made a beeline for Mia and Ashleigh.

"So that's your mother?"

Mia had almost forgotten Kathy was standing there. "Yeah, that's her, Lillian Black. And this is my big brother Keefe," she said to Kathy as Keefe reached them. Mia smiled as Keefe made polite talk with Kathy, making up for the rudeness of the other men.

For a moment or two Mia watched as her brother chatted amicably with Kathy. No one else would have known that he was angry. No one else would have been able to sense the degree of tension in his body. It wasn't until Kathy turned her attention to Ashleigh that Keefe finally got a chance to tell Mia what had him so riled.

"Like bees buzzing around a pot of honey." He jerked his head toward the men surrounding their mother. "Can you believe her?" he whispered to Mia. "She thinks I should give her an apartment for free, forever. When I said hell no, she told me that I should at least pay for her place in Arizona. I just wrote her a huge check less than three months ago. Mia, she was trying to blackmail me. Every time I see her she has a new angle."

"I was hoping the last time she was here that her change for the better would be permanent."

"Mia, you're so damn naïve. Grow the hell up, will you?" he snapped and walked away.

The sting of tears burned the back of Mia's eyes and she felt more alone that she had in a long time. Her brother had never taken out his anger for their mother on her. She caught sight of Damien. Even though she knew his father had insisted that Damien introduce him to Lillian, it didn't matter. She didn't want Damien anywhere near her mother. A shard of betrayal pierced her. He should be standing by her, not beside her mother.

As though he'd read her thoughts Damien moved a few inches from his father and turned to look at the her. He was staring at her, and she glared back at him. Maybe she was being petty, a baby, but she was the one getting married, she was the bride. It was her time. If anyone was due adulation, shouldn't it be her? Mia shuddered and took a deep breath. It was just nerves, she told herself, nothing to worry about.

Still, she felt like an outsider. Kathy was talking to Ashleigh, Keefe was sulking on a chair and everyone else…everyone else was crowded around her mother. A wave of nausea rolled quickly upward and she fought it, just as she'd fought the pain. She wouldn't let her emotions control her. She had the tools.

Keefe sat watching Mia. He'd seen her reaction to the way he'd snapped at her. Well, hell, he'd been biting his tongue since this nonsense began. He was doing what she'd asked. What more did she want?

After a minute Keefe turned away. No matter how hurt he was, he couldn't bear watching her pain. She seemed so lost and her face, though smiling, broke his heart. When he looked at his sister he didn't see the newly twenty-four-year-old professional standing across from him, but the frightened little girl that he'd promised to protect.

Groaning, Keefe closed his eyes. He'd kept his promise. Mia had been the one to shut him out of her life.

The sound of their mother's laugher grated on him. She'd never been a mother. Hell, she'd never even felt like family. Mia was the only family that he claimed, but now that she was getting what she wanted, marrying Damien, she was behaving as if she no longer needed anyone else in her life. So now his entire family was gone.

When he opened his eyes and followed Mia's line of vision to their mother surrounded by Damien and his father and Jerry, he couldn't help feeling sorry for Mia.

A warning began inching its way up Keefe's back. He knew his sister well. He studied the group in the back of the room and saw Damien staring at Mia and Mia glaring back. Something was definitely wrong. Mia looked as though she were ready to explode. His eyes finally lit on the culprit. Lillian Black.

Mia looked away quickly when she realized her brother was watching her watch their mother and her admirers. She was fighting to hold her tongue, not lash out and call Damien to her side. He should be standing beside her because he wanted to be, not because she'd called him.

"Hello everyone."

Mia saw the minister Damien had secured coming toward her. He barely glanced at her mother or the men but instead headed for Mia.

Thank God, Mia thought. If the minister had halted in his steps she would have been tempted to call the whole thing off.

"Mia, how good to see you again," he greeted her warmly, hugging her. "You need to call on me more than when you're getting married."

Before she had a chance to get embarrassed, he laughed. "Don't worry, I love playing that little gag on people. Okay, everyone gather round."

Mia heaved a sigh of relief as the minister let her go and called everyone. She hadn't been the one who'd had to break up the admiration society.

After receiving instructions, she went out of the room with Jerry. But when she walked back into the room she faltered, This wasn't right. Then she saw her brother walking toward her, his face filled with hurt and he stopped.

Keefe had pushed away the vacant chair near him. He didn't want his mother anywhere close and she knew it. But her voice carried as she'd meant it to as she announced to the men around her that she was thinking of moving to Chicago. If she thought that by threatening to move near them he would pay her upkeep in Arizona, Keefe thought, she was sadly mistaken. He was done attempting to keep her in Mia's life. He would no longer pay for that slight peace of mind for his sister.

Then he caught sight of Mia coming through the door and all his anger drained away and he was left with only hurt. He saw the smile on Jerry's face and a look he couldn't read on Mia's. This wasn't the way it was supposed to be. Mia was the only family he had and right then he decided he wasn't letting go of his family that easily.

Before he knew it, Keefe was on his feet and walking toward his sister. He felt everyone staring at him but he didn't give a damn. Sure, his timing needed some work, but he had to find out what he'd done to make his sister stop wanting him in her life.

"We need to talk."

Keefe strode purposefully up the aisle toward Jerry and Mia. He took Mia's arm and pulled her after him, ignoring her protests. He tried door after door until he found an empty room. Then he shoved her in, followed and locked the door.

"What's going on?" Mia asked.

"You tell me," Keefe answered her. "What the hell is happening to us? Did Damien tell you that he didn't want me in the wedding?"

"No."

"Then why? Why are you letting Jerry walk you down the aisle? Why don't you want me?"

"It's you who didn't want to do it."

"What the hell are you talking about? I always wanted to, you know that. I told you a hundred times."

"That was when I was going to marry James."

"You think because it's Damien I don't want to? Why? What in hell would make you think that?"

"You."

"That's a lie! What did I do?"

"I asked you if you minded if Jerry walked me down the aisle and you said no."

"I said no because you wanted him. What was I supposed to do?"

"You were supposed to tell me that you wanted to do it."

Keefe clenched his jaw in frustration, blowing out the huge breath of air he'd just taken in. He had to calm himself, find out what the hell Mia was talking about. She'd been behaving strangely for weeks and he was determined to get to the bottom of it.

"Mia, whatever gave you the idea to ask in the first place? We've talked about this a million times. It was all set, always. There was no need to ever have a discussion on who would walk you. That was my job to do. I wanted to do it," he said, looking at the pinched look on his sister's face, knowing it was there because he'd said walking her down the aisle was a job. But that wasn't what he'd meant and he didn't have time at the moment to play word games. He needed to find out what had happened. The words he'd straighten out later.

"Okay, Mia, let's try this again. We made plans and the only thing I could see that changed them was you no longer wanted me."

Keefe looked at his sister shaking her head no. "Then if it wasn't you, who didn't want me to do it? Tell me why the hell I'm not doing it? What gave you the idea I didn't want to?"

"Mom."

"Mom?" Keefe repeated dumbly. "Mom," he frowned. "What did she have to do with all of this?"

"I called her when Damien asked me to marry him and she told me that I've taken advantage of you my entire life, that I should stop. She said that you would be uncomfortable walking me down the aisle to marry Damien because you're sleeping with Ashleigh."

For one long moment Keefe just stood and stared at his sister. "Mia, how could you believe her?"

"She told me to tell you I had someone else. She said that you would be relieved and wouldn't put up a fight, so I did and you didn't."

He watched as tears slid down her cheeks.

"Mia, why would you ever listen to her? More than likely she's jealous that you're marrying a man that absolutely adores you. She can't stand that."

"But she helped me last time."

"That was either a fluke or a miracle. She doesn't really give a damn about anyone but herself, Mia. I've told you that a million times. You've got to stop thinking you can change her, that it's your fault that she left us. It isn't. We're not the reason she's the way she is." He hugged her tight.

"Keefe, I knew it was stupid, but I wanted to believe she could change. How can I make a good psychologist if I don't believe people can change?"

"Some people can change, some can't. You're not going to be able to help every single one of your patients, Mia, so don't try to take on that burden. Now stop crying and tell me who's going to give you away?"

"I always wanted you to," Mia sniffed.

"Then let's go and fire Jerry."

Mia pulled on his hand. "Can I ask you a question?"

He saw the brooding look on her face and knew something more was bothering her. "Yeah, what is it?"

"Have you ever been with a virgin?"

All the blood drained from Keefe's face and he shifted uncomfortably from side to side. He'd talked to Mia as little as possible about sex, telling her only the things he thought she should know, nothing personal. Now she was asking him straight out.

"Why are you asking me?"

"Please, Kee, just answer it, okay?"

"No, I haven't."

"Do you think…I mean Damien is really experienced. Do you think he's going to compare me?"

This was the last conversation that he wanted to be having. "What are you worried about?"

"I'm worried that Damien is going to be disappointed, that I won't really know what to do."

"I think you're going to be just fine." Keefe turned to walk out the door, indicating the conversation was over.

"Mom said he would leave me and find someone who could satisfy him."

This made him stop and turn back to face his sister. "Don't listen to her. How the hell would she know, Mia? She's been married eight times and she's lived with more than a half dozen men and slept with God knows how many more. If she's such an all fired expert, why is she alone?"

"But—"

"No buts, Mia. She's alone. That guy she was with left her a couple of months ago, right after she came to visit. When you talked to her she was probably just pissed and took it all out on you."

"Why would she do that?"

"Because that's the way she is."

"But she was so nice to me the last time."

"Mia, honey you can't depend on her."

"But what if she's right? What if I don't know enough? I mean Damien might…he might go back to playing around."

"He loves you, Mia, he can hardly keep his hands off you. I'm surprised that he has waited this long." He finally looked directly at his sister. "Why didn't you ever…"

"Have sex, you mean?"

"Yeah. I mean, didn't James ever try?"

"A couple of times. I told him that I was staying a virgin until I married and he seemed fine with it. We had fun together. We were good friends. We enjoyed each other's company. Anyway, it was never much of a temptation. He never made me feel the way Damien does. With Damien that's all I think about." She blushed and turned away. "I think about being with him all the time and I don't want to stop him. Sometimes if it wasn't for him…" She smiled. "He's helping me keep my vow."

Keefe smiled in spite of himself at the thought of Damien talking Mia out of having sex. That must have gone against everything that was in Damien.

"Mia, the two of you are not going to have any problems. I can promise you that. You can barely keep your hands off each other. Relax, okay."

"But, Keefe, what if…Mom said… Well, what if I'm not any good? What if he thinks of other women he's been with and compares me? Do you ever think about…" She hesitated. "Do you ever think of Damien with Ashleigh when you're making love to her?"

Keefe groaned. God, this wasn't a conversation he'd ever expected to have with his baby sister. "Mia, come on. I think we've spent enough time in here. I'm sure everyone's looking for us."

"I don't have anyone else to ask," Mia said. "Mom said there was no way I could make him happy." She bit her lips. "She's been flirting with Damien and I don't think she's kidding."

Her voice lowered and she barely squeaked out her words. "I hate to think that my own mother would…" She trembled. "I hate knowing what she's capable of."

The one thing Mia was right about was she did need someone to talk to. And for sure that someone shouldn't be their mother. She'd done enough damage. Keefe was left with no choice but to answer Mia's question.

"First, Damien's not able to see anyone but you, so it doesn't matter if she does try. It won't work. And do I believe this of her? Yes, Mia, I do. I'm glad she was able to help you before, but I've always told you she was a bit of a slut. That hasn't changed. In fact I was being nice. She's not a bit of a slut. She's a total slut." He watched as Mia's eyes turned watery and sad.

"What about the other thing? Do you? I mean, have you ever thought about it, that Ashleigh was with Damien? Does it bother you?"

"Yeah, a couple of times it happened, but I worked through it. I love Ashleigh and she loves me. No, I don't want pictures of her with any man in my head when I'm with her, so I push them away. And if it happens to you, Mia, you do the same."

"What if I can't?"

"Why are you so worried about this? You weren't before."

"Mom told me that I should find a guy and get some experience before I get married. She—"

That was the last word Keefe heard before he unlocked the door and tore out of the room. He'd been stupid to give his mother another chance. She didn't deserve it and she didn't deserve to be at Mia's wedding. Mother of the bride. What a joke. They could pick up any woman off the street and she would have done as much for Mia, maybe more. He was going to kick her out, send her packing.

"Kee, Kee, please don't say anything."

Keefe kept marching, the sound of Mia's running footsteps not stopping him. How could the woman tell Mia all of those crazy things, as if she hadn't already screwed her up enough? Now this. She was always trouble. She hadn't changed.

"Kee, don't. Please don't make a scene, please."

Mia was beside him, holding on to his arm, pleading, and at last he slowed his steps and grabbed his sister's arms. "You haven't, have you?"

"No, I haven't."

"You're not thinking about it?"

She shook her head. "No, I just don't want...I love Damien, Keefe. I don't want him to stop loving me."

"Talk with him, Mia."

"I can't, I can't tell him this stuff."

"You're getting married in two days. Tell him and let him put your mind at ease."

"I can't."

Keefe looked into her eyes. "If you don't, Mia, I'll talk to him." The look that came into his sister's eyes chilled him to his very soul. She was really afraid. She'd never voiced concern over her inexperience before. Damn their mother. God, how he hated the woman. He shook his head, knowing he couldn't blame Mia. He'd hoped their mother had changed also.

"Mia, listen to me." He tucked his finger under her chin and lifted her head. "This is important, Mia," he said softly. "Love doesn't stop that easily. You have to believe that. There is nothing in this world that you could ever do that would make me stop loving you. Nothing, Mia. And if Damien loves you the way that he says that he does, he won't stop loving you because you're inexperienced. You can learn." He rubbed at the tears on her cheeks.

"You have to let yourself believe this because we both know what's at the root of this. You did nothing to make Mom go away. It's not us, you're not to blame. I know she told us it was us. She lied. It wasn't us. It was never us."

"I know that, Kee."

"You say it, but you don't believe it. Don't you think I know why you always forgave her, why you always wanted to give her money when she drifted back and forth into our lives? You thought if you were perfect, if you made her happy she would love you, that she wouldn't leave you again."

For an answer tears streamed down Mia's cheeks and she shook her head.

"It is true, sweetie. I know it is. Don't blame yourself. I felt that way for a long time myself. I mean, why wouldn't we? Whose mother doesn't want them, for God's sake? You'd have to think you'd done something wrong. But you didn't. And she's not Damien. Damien is not going to leave you and he's definitely not going to stop loving you. He's proven that already. He hung in there and waited when you sent him away. He loves you, Mia. Now tell him so you can stop worrying."

"Do you think he likes Mom?"

"Not in the way that you're talking about. Of course I know Mom's been making a play for him, she can't help herself. But he's not buying into that. He's being nice to her but that's it."

"Are you sure?"

Keefe wanted to throttle their mother but right now he needed to comfort his baby sister. "Mia, don't let Mom take away your trust in Damien. She isn't worth it. Don't let her ruin your wedding or your life. Talk to Damien, tell him." Keefe saw Damien over Mia's shoulder.

"He's coming, Mia."

Mia turned around and spotted Damien walking toward them. In a panic she turned back to her brother. "Don't tell him, okay?"

"Then you promise me that you will."

"I promise."

"Mia, I mean it."

"So do I," Mia answered. "I promise."

"Good. Now I'm going to have a talk with good old mom."

"No, Keefe." Mia put her hand on his arm. "Please don't ruin things. She'll be gone in a few days."

"As long as she doesn't make you cry again." Keefe wiped at the last tear, then smiled at her as Damien came to stand alongside them.

"Everything all right?" Damien asked, looking first at Keefe then at Mia.

"Yeah, it's all straightened out now. Keefe is going to give me away."

Damien smiled. "I knew that. I never thought your brother would let it get his far."

Keefe cocked his head. "You don't mind?"

"Why should I mind? You're Mia's brother. She loves you. Period." Damien smiled wide, "And you did help get us back together."

Mia glanced at Keefe. "I guess I'd better go and tell Jerry."

"Don't worry about it, I told him already."

Both Mia and Keefe looked at Damien.

"How did you know?"

"Because Keefe loves you. If I had been in his position I would have done the same thing. I told you all along that he wanted to."

"You did," Mia grinned. "I guess I should have listened to you." She kissed Damien, feeling consumed by her love for him as she always did. "I love you," she murmured, "more than you know."

As Keefe walked ahead of them, Mia said, "I think we need to talk." She spoke in a voice loud enough for her brother to hear.

It took only a few minutes for Mia to tell Damien of her worries. When she was done she tried to look away but he prevented her.

"Baby girl, you're worrying about nothing. I know all that you need to know. Don't worry, I have enough experience for the both of us."

He kissed her and as usual she melted in his arms. Deep inside though, a little voice whispered, *That's just the problem, Damien. You have more than enough experience.*

CHAPTER ELEVEN

It was her wedding day. Mia had been awake for hours, trying to quiet the butterflies in her stomach. Keefe had been partially right. Talking with Damien had made her feel somewhat better. At least for the rest of the night Damien had behaved as a proper bridegroom. And for that one night her mother had not bothered trying to get his full attention. She had Jerry and Charles fawning over her.

Mia felt sorry for Kathy. She knew exactly how she felt. She'd glimpsed the sadness in her eyes and prayed that she would not wear the same look. All at once Mia shivered, feeling cold, though she knew the outside temperature was over eighty degrees. How could her mother's mere presence in her home drop the temperature? She hoped it wasn't an omen.

"Mia, get up," her mother called out to her. "I want you to take your shower and do whatever it is you have to do so that I don't have to be bothered while I'm trying to get dressed."

Mia winced. *Whose day is this?* Instead of voicing her thought, however, she called to her mother, "I have two bathrooms. We won't get in each other's way."

"I'm using the big one and I don't want your stuff all over, so get up now and get ready."

Just today, Mia said to herself. *Tomorrow I'll be on my honeymoon and I can forget her, forget that she was even here.*

She went into her own bathroom, ignoring her mother's voice telling her not to take forever, hoping that the sound of the water would block her out. It did. Mia took her time underneath the spray, grateful for that little respite. When she began toweling off she heard her mother call and refused to answer until she heard her scream that Damien was on the line.

Wrapping the towel around her, she was out of the door in ten seconds flat and snatched the phone from her mother's hand. She hated having her mother even talk to him on her wedding day. The frown that appeared on Lillian's face as Mia put the phone to her ear told Mia that she'd done the wrong thing. Again.

"Hey," she said into the mouthpiece after going into her room and closing the door.

"Hey, baby girl, are you marrying me today?"

Mia smiled, thanking God for Damien. "Yes. Are you marrying me?"

"Only death could keep me from it. I've got a surprise for you, Mia."

Damien's deep voice sent shivers of desire coursing through her. Their long wait would be over in a few short hours. She wouldn't have to beg him to stop or push his hand away when he went a bit too far. "What's the surprise?" she asked.

"If I told you it wouldn't be a surprise."

"Then tell me you love me."

"I love you, baby."

"I love you too."

"So, are you getting excited? I know I am. I can hardly wait to undress you, to kiss my way down your body, to lick your thighs, to put my tongue—"

"Mia, are you done?"

Mia blinked. She'd not heard the door open. She looked into her mother's face, feeling a new surge of anger. It felt as if her mother had walked in on her and Damien making love. "No, I'm not done," Mia managed to say between clenched teeth. "Please close my door."

"Mia, you okay?" she heard Damien calling to her.

"That was my mother."

"I guessed that much. What did she want?"

"She wants me to hurry up and get ready so I won't bother her."

"Damn, Mia, it's your apartment. Tell her to knock it off."

"You have no idea how close I just came. If I can get through the next few hours it will be alright."

"You know, baby girl, eventually you will have to have that battle."

"I know, but not today, not on my wedding day. Don't forget my surprise," she laughed. "I'm going to need it by the time this day is over." With that she hung up the phone, but the good feeling Damien had brought was being rapidly eaten away by the banging around her mother was doing outside her door. Mia knew the noise was deliberate, to drive her bonkers, and she was doing everything in her power not to give in to it. Unfortunately she hadn't listened to Keefe when he'd suggested putting their mother up in a hotel room, so she'd just have to suffer through the rest of the day. After that, it would be smooth sailing.

She thought of Keefe saying their mother was trying to blackmail him to get her to stay in Arizona. She didn't have to blackmail Keefe. Mia would gladly help with their mother's expenses if that meant she wouldn't live anywhere near the state of Illinois. Keefe was right: The fact that she'd actually helped a few months ago was something that more than likely would never again be repeated.

Mia grinned at Keefe. He'd hardly blinked when he saw her new gown. "I couldn't wear it, Keefe, not after everything Mom said. This feels right. It's my own."

"You're still beautiful, Mia, and believe me, Damien is not going to notice anything but you when you walk down the aisle."

"Thank you, big brother, for putting up with me, for all the things I've put you through in the last year." Mia stopped as tears filled her eyes. "Kee, I'm serious. Let me say this. I appreciate so much what you've done for me and what you've given up. Thank you for raising me and for giving me such a good life. I love you."

The last words were said through her tears because try as she might, she couldn't prevent the tears from streaming down her face. Her brother hugged her hard, his own voice husky with unshed tears.

"Stop crying or you're going to be walking to marry Damien with tear tracks down your cheeks. That just won't do." He brought her head up and wiped at her tears. "Is everything okay now? I mean, you talked things over with Damien. Did he help to put aside your worries?"

"Yes," Mia answered. "He did. I was just being silly. He loves me and I know that. I think Mom caught me off guard. She's always had that effect on me."

"I know. She makes you feel guilty. Me, she just makes mad as hell. What a gift for one woman to possess."

Just then the music began playing and Mia looked at her brother. "That's our cue," she said, looking into the banquet hall that had been transformed into a beautiful flower garden. The doors were held open by two of Stavros's employees who were playing ushers. "It's showtime," Mia said to her brother and began walking, holding on to his arm as much to steady herself as because it was the ritual.

Damien watched Mia coming toward him on her brother's arm. He couldn't believe it. How the hell had he managed to convince someone as wonderful as Mia that he was worthy of her love? He had no idea how he'd gotten that lucky but he sure as hell intended to make her happy. He'd prove his parents wrong. He was definitely not like his father. He wanted one woman and one woman only. And that was Mia.

Though the last few days had been crazy, Mia's mother had at last stopped cornering him and had focused on his father and Jerry instead. He felt bad for his mom but was hoping that maybe she'd finally let go of the hope that she and his father would become a permanent thing.

When he saw Mia smile, his heart nearly burst with longing. How had her crazy mother managed to convince Mia that he would not be happy with her? He was already happier than he'd ever been in his life and when he made love to Mia, all of his dreams would be complete. He'd remember to take it slow. Damien thought of the surprise he had waiting for her, a gag gift really, just something to show her how silly she was being worrying that they would have problems in the bedroom. That, he could guarantee her, would never be one of their problems.

"I now pronounce you man and wife. You may kiss the bride."

Damien was grinning at her from ear to ear. Mia looked deep into his eyes and lost herself. Then his lips lowered and he whispered. "I love you, baby girl." His mouth closed over hers and she tasted the sweetness of his tongue. Want and lust tumbled around inside her. But it wasn't either of those emotions that made Mia feel that she would burst from happiness. It was the love she felt for Damien. She couldn't believe it. After everything that had happened, they'd found themselves here at this moment.

When he released her from the kiss, she almost swooned and his arms supported her. He smiled down at her.

"How does it feel to be Mrs. Terrell?"

"It feels like heaven," she whispered.

"Ladies and gentleman, may I present for the first time Mr. and Mrs. Damien Terrell."

The sound of applause caught Mia off guard. She'd almost forgotten others were there. She turned with Damien toward their guests and accepted their good wishes.

When the men filed up to kiss the bride, Mia held Damien's arm, thinking his father would try something. But he didn't. He merely kissed Mia's cheek and turned to look for her mother. If it weren't for the look of desolation on Kathy's face, Mia would have been happy. Although she'd wanted to steer Charles's unwanted attention away from her, she hadn't wanted it at the expense of Damien's mother. It looked as if her mother and Damien's father shared the same DNA. They were both selfish people who didn't care who they hurt. Mia was determined that would not be her and Damien's legacy. They would make a new start.

Within moments, the makeshift altar had been removed and Mia had been hurried along with Keefe and Charles, who'd been Damien's best man, to take pictures. By the time Ashleigh, who'd acted as her maid of honor, had joined them, and all the pictures were taken, the flower garden chapel had been revamped into a huge ball room. Orchids, lilies, roses and flowers that Mia didn't know the name of sat atop the tables and adorned the room. She smiled at her brother, knowing he was the one who'd taken care of the flowers. She'd ordered only daisies.

Mia danced with her new husband, feeling the constant new shivers that he created in her. She felt his arousal through the fabric of his tux and laughed. "How do you plan to hide that?" she asked as the music stopped and everyone hit their glasses with their silverware.

"I have no intention of hiding it. I couldn't if I tried." He laughed as the tinkling sound grew ever louder. "I want you, that's no secret. Now you're mine," he teased. "No more running from me."

Then he kissed her.

And she melted.

If she were a man the entire room would have been aware of her own burning desire.

The father-daughter dance was announced and she danced first with her brother, then with Jerry. For the next half hour Mia danced with every man in the room except her husband. Him she followed with her eyes as he twirled one guest after another past her, always swooping in to kiss her when he came near.

When he danced with her mother, she couldn't help noticing that her mother was pressing her body in much closer than she had to. She saw Damien repeatedly pulling back. In fact, he looked as though he were about to leave her mother on the dance floor. Good, she thought. Mia was not aware that she was frowning until her mother called out loud enough for all to hear, "Lighten up, Mia. It's only a dance."

Jerry, her dance partner, smiled at her. "Don't worry, Mia. She's trying really hard to get you angry. Don't let her." He gave Mia's shoulder a squeeze but it wasn't until a couple of seconds later when

Damien cut in that Mia felt better. "I want to dance with my wife," he said. "Do you mind switching?" Jerry smiled. "No, I don't mind at all."

"Thank you," Mia whispered, laying her head on her husband's chest.

"For what?" Damien asked. "I meant it. I want to dance with my wife. All of this," he looked around the room, "is nice but you're the only woman I want in my arms."

For the longest time Mia stayed right where she was, not stirring when someone came up to ask her for a dance. She could feel the movement of Damien's head as he shook his head no. He'd asked the band to play only slow numbers for awhile and that was alright with her. It wasn't until Keefe came up to them that it even occurred to her that they were being rude.

"You two need to mingle."

Mia blinked. "We have been."

"Not for the past forty-five minutes. Stavros said he's going to start serving dinner in ten minutes. Now you two let go and allow someone else a chance," he said as another guest came up. This time Damien relinquished his hold, but Mia knew it was reluctantly.

The next few hours passed in a blur, eating, dancing, kissing Damien and sipping champagne. Mia was deliriously happy, enough so that she was able to ignore most of her mother's barbs.

It seemed Jerry had appointed himself one of Mia's knights. Every time her mother got within shooting range, he'd come and whisk her away to dance. And always he'd smile at Mia, his smile telling her that he wasn't going to let her mother ruin her special day.

Even Charles helped, although his reasons were his own. He was hitting on her mother hard. Mia finally saw what Damien had meant about his father's charisma. He'd charmed more than half of the women there, her mother included.

"Mia, how much longer do we have to stay here?"

Damien leaned over to kiss her and she tasted the champagne on his tongue. The crisp sweet taste was an extra bonus.

"Not long," she answered. "I think an hour or so. We haven't cut the cake yet. After that we can leave."

"I'm glad we only have to go upstairs," Damien whispered. "Otherwise I'd have to make love to you right in front of everyone, or in the car." He grinned wickedly as his hand wandered across Mia's chest, dipping inside the bodice of her gown.

She tapped his hands. "Stop that. People can see you."

"We're married; I don't care if they can see me."

"I do. Now stop."

"God, Mia. I want you." He grabbed her hand and brought it down. "Feel me," he ordered.

She felt his hardened flesh and tried to ignore the burning that had pushed its way to her face. "As soon as we cut the cake." She felt as if she were falling backwards. Damien had her under a spell, one she hoped to never be out from under.

"You'd better make it quick." He grinned at her, looked around the room and zeroed in on her mother. "There are other women in this room that find me simply irresistible and can't seem to keep their hands off me." He kissed her quickly. "Let's hurry and cut that damn cake. I'm tired of waiting. I want to make love to you. Now." Then he walked away across the room to her mother.

The spell was broken. *Oh Damien*, Mia moaned inwardly. *I know you're teasing, but...* She reached for her glass, surprised to find her hand trembling. Mia downed the contents of her champagne, the bubbles tickling her nose. She wasn't much of a drinker. Truth be known, she didn't drink, had never felt the need until now. Now she needed something to help her get through her wedding day. *How ironic*, she thought and held her glass up for a passing waiter to refill.

"Don't you think you'd better slow down?"

"Keefe." Mia looked at her brother. "I haven't had that much."

"Yeah, but you're not used to it. It could really hit you later."

She ignored her brother's warning, bringing the glass to her lips and sipping, trying her best not to look at her husband dancing with her mother. He was grinning, waving at Mia, and pointing his finger in the direction of the cake.

"You okay, Mia? Why are you staring at Damien like that?"

"No reason."

"You sure?"

Mia smiled at her brother. "He's ready to go upstairs. He's trying to get me to hurry."

"By making you jealous?"

"I'm not jealous."

He chucked her under her chin. "Tell that to someone who doesn't know you. Mia, honey, she gets to you so easily because you care. Damien's your husband now. Tell her to keep her hands off."

"I can't."

"You can."

Mia smiled. "I want to."

"Then do it."

For a moment she thought of doing just what her brother had suggested. "Maybe I'll thank her for coming, tell her how much I enjoyed her visit." She laughed and raised her glass to her lips only to have her brother take it away.

"Are you ever going to stop worrying about me, Kee, or stop trying to protect me?"

"Not as long as there's breath in my body." He smiled and kissed her forehead. "Go dance with your husband."

She pulled her brother in for a hug. "Have I told you lately how much I love you, big brother?" She smiled as he finished off her champagne. "Why don't you take your own advice and go and find Ashleigh?" Mia stood grinning. "Can you believe it? We made it. We're both happy."

Damien felt the woman's hand brush against his crotch and ignored it. Surely it had been an accident. Then he felt her fingers groping him, kneading him right there on the dance floor. He couldn't believe it. In a flash he searched for Mia. Good, she wasn't looking at him at the moment; she was talking with her brother. He maneuvered his own hand and roughly brought Mia's mother's hand away from his crotch.

"Lady, you're sick," he mumbled, determined to keep his voice low, not to ruin the day for Mia.

"And you have a hard-on."

"Big damn deal. I've had a hard-on the entire day but it's not for you. I've been flirting with my wife the entire time I've been dancing with you. Are you crazy?"

"Do you really think she's going to be able to give you what you need?" She laughed. "God, you're both pitiful."

"I think you've got that wrong. You're the one that's pitiful. Listen, if you ever put your hands on me again I'll tell your daughter." He walked away in disgust, no longer caring about not causing a scene.

Damien debated whether to tell Mia. He saw her smiling as she talked with her brother and made up his mind. He needed something a lot stronger than the champagne they were serving, he thought as he made his way to the bar, glad that there was a bar. He nearly collided with Ashleigh as he made a hasty beeline in the opposite direction of the banquet room.

"Whoa, Damien, where are you going?"

For a moment he stared at Ashleigh, then shook his head, deciding to tell her. After all, he believed she'd eventually marry Keefe and she'd be subjected to the same craziness. She might as well know what was coming.

He pulled her away. Finding a secluded corner he began talking. When he was done, the shock on Ashleigh's face told him what this would do to his new bride.

"Do you think I should tell Mia any of this?"

"My God, no," Ashleigh answered quickly, "not on her wedding day. I don't know if you ever should."

"Can you believe it? The woman's sick."

"Maybe she's just drunk."

"She's not drunk, Ashleigh. You were there the first day that she came. She's been coming on to me ever since. I've been staying out of her way. Some of this is my fault. I was kidding with Mia, trying to make her leave the reception, so I danced with her mother to speed things up. I never expected the woman to go that damn far. I didn't for a minute believe she would, not until she pulled that number. And she has the nerve to think that I would actually want her." He trembled in disgust. "God!"

"Poor Mia and my poor Keefe."

"You gonna tell him?"

"I'm not sure but he can deal with it better than Mia. I'll wait and see. I know it won't be today."

Damien sighed, shaking his head. "You have no idea how much I love her, Ashleigh. She means everything to me. The thought of someone hurting her..." He shook his head again. "It makes me so angry. I just want to protect her."

"You're beginning to sound like her brother."

"But I'm not her brother. I'm her husband. Taking care of Mia will be my job from now on."

"You both talk about Mia as though she's a child. It's not your job to take care of Mia. It's Mia's job to take care of Mia. Your job is just to love her, Damien."

"That part's easy," he smiled. "I don't know how I lived without her."

Mia saw Damien leave her mother on the dance floor. She'd undoubtedly said something to him because he looked very angry. Mia glanced at her brother, then down at her empty champagne glass.

"You don't need it," he assured her.

"You're right. And you're right that it's time I told Mom to keep her hands off of my husband." She couldn't hold back her smile. "I have a husband. I'm Damien's wife." She laughed, hugged her brother and headed off toward the dance floor, thinking maybe she'd give her mother a dose of her own medicine. She'd dance with Jerry.

"She's not going to be able to satisfy him. Look at him. She's still a virgin for God's sake."

"Are you lusting after Mia's husband now?" Jerry asked.

"He'd be better off with me. The girl is dull as dirt. Matter of fact, both she and Keefe are the dullest people I've ever known. I've always wondered if I weren't given the wrong babies. Really, I don't think they're mine, they can't be. Poor Damien, he'll probably fall asleep in the middle of the deed."

"You're so crude. Damien is wild about Mia."

"If he's so wild about her, why did he have an erection when he was dancing with me?"

"Hell, he's had an erection the whole damn day. I joked with him about it earlier when we were talking. His dancing with you didn't do it. He has it because he can't keep his eyes off Mia. It's not you he wants, it's his wife," Jerry answered.

"You think so? Wait until he has her tonight. I'll bet you by morning he'll be wishing he'd taken me up on my offer."

Mia stood behind her mother, her smile frozen into place. She was paralyzed by the words she'd just heard. Unintentionally she moaned aloud and Jerry's head snapped up and his eyes connected with Mia's.

"Mia, honey, your mom was just kidding," Jerry said and Mia knew he was warning her mother that she was there. As her mother turned and faced her, Mia knew the words she had heard had not been said in jest.

Once more she had to acknowledge that Keefe had been right. As much as she'd wanted it, her mother hadn't changed for the better. If anything, she'd gotten worse.

"How could you?" Mia asked. "I hate you, Mom. I'm not trying anymore."

"Like you ever tried, Mia. You were only afraid of losing your brother. Nothing you ever did was because you wanted me around. As for your husband, he's not here with me now, yet I don't see him by your side. Maybe it's not me you have to worry about."

"Mia, don't listen to her. She's been drinking, she doesn't mean it."

Jerry pulled on Lillian's arm, trying to get her to leave. For a second longer Mia stood there and stared.

"When the reception is over, I want you gone. I don't want you going back to my apartment. I'll have Keefe give you your things. Since you've never wanted to be a mother, you no longer have to worry about it. You mean nothing to me now."

With tears stinging her eyes Mia finally walked away. She spied her brother walking toward her and shifted her direction. She couldn't talk to Keefe right now. He would be too angry. He'd toss their mother out without a second thought, and she knew her mother wouldn't go quietly. Her wedding day would be ruined. Well, actually it already was. But Mia didn't want the day ruined for Damien.

Mia continued walking, ignoring Keefe calling her. She needed to feel her husband's arms around her. If she talked to her brother, there was no doubt she would fall apart.

"Damien," Mia whispered, spotting him at last standing in a secluded corner talking quietly with Ashleigh. She stared for a moment before changing her mind and heading for the bathroom. She couldn't allow her sudden intense feelings of jealousy to surface. Her mother was a liar, plain and simple. Damien loved her. She was the woman he wanted, not Ashleigh and not her mother.

Mia walked away from her husband, wishing once again that they'd eloped. She did nothing to stop the tears that flowed down her cheeks, no longer caring if anyone spotted a bride crying.

Keefe ignored his own hurt. Something was wrong with Mia. He'd seen the tears in her eyes as she'd glanced briefly at him and walked away, not bothering to turn when he called out to her. He saw her hesitate when she found Damien and Ashleigh talking. He didn't know what had happened but he'd be willing to bet their mother was the source of Mia's pain. That's all she'd ever really given either of them.

Keefe stood there watching Mia watch Damien. He almost followed her when she turned away, but instead walked up to Damien and Ashleigh, a bit annoyed that they were so engrossed in their conversation that neither had noticed Mia or him.

"What's going on?" Keefe said a little gruffer than he'd intended, interrupting them.

Surprised, Ashleigh turned to him with what he thought was a rather strange expression on her face. Damien wore almost the identical expression and it made Keefe wonder if it was guilt. Because they were damn sure getting ready to tell him a lie. He could tell by the knots forming rapidly in his abdomen.

"Keefe, we're just talking," Ashleigh answered at last.

"I can see that," he answered her. "It must be something pretty important." He glanced at Damien. "Mia was just looking for you. She's upset about something."

"I didn't see her," Damien answered

"Just my point. A bride in a wedding gown is pretty hard to miss."

"Where is she?" Damien asked, ignoring Keefe's sarcasm.

"She went into the bathroom."

A look passed between Damien and Ashleigh that puzzled Keefe. Maybe for once it wasn't their mother who'd put the tears in Mia's eyes. He glared at both Ashleigh and Damien before turning to walk away.

"Keefe, what's wrong?"

For an instant he thought not to answer Ashleigh but took a deep breath instead.

"What were you two talking about?" he asked.

"Why?"

His head tilted to the side and he stared at her. "It just seemed important."

"It was."

"That's it?"

"No, it was also personal." Ashleigh laughed. "I know you can't be jealous. First off, I'm madly in love with you. Secondly, Damien's madly in love with your sister. He can't see anyone else when she's around."

"That's not true. She was looking for him and he didn't see her."

"Would you stop that?" Ashleigh teased, leaning forward to kiss him. "Your sister has changed Damien, believe me. He's going to make her happy."

"He'd better," Keefe growled before turning his full attention to kissing Ashleigh thoroughly.

Damn. Damien was hoping that Mia had not witnessed her mother's vulgar display. But Keefe said she was upset. Now it seemed as though she'd seen it all. He had to explain to her, let her know it was not his fault, that he'd not done a thing to make her mother behave the way that she had.

Without checking to see if other women were in there, he pushed the door open and went inside. He saw Mia sitting there looking forlorn with obvious streaks on her face, a tell-tale sign that she'd been crying. His heart lurched and he shook his head. Damien couldn't believe that on their wedding day she was hurting. He'd already broken his promise to make her happy. Damn.

"What are you doing in here all alone?" Damien said, going up to Mia and kneeling on the floor beside her. "Keefe said you were upset."

"This is the ladies' room," Mia said quietly.

Damien's heart swelled with love for her. She sounded so sad and he wanted to make that sound go away.

"I know it's the ladies' room," he grinned. "I just wanted to make sure that you're alright. You're not angry with me, are you?"

"No. I'm not angry with you. Whatever gave you that idea?" Mia gazed at her new husband. He was smiling at her and lust quickly filled his eyes. She'd been holding onto the thought of that look since she'd left her mother. He took her in his arms and a tremor of desire shot through her.

"Damien, what if I don't satisfy you?"

"Shh, baby girl, stop. I thought we had this all settled. I don't know where the hell this keeps coming from, but I know it's not coming from me." He kissed her eyelids, her nose, and her lips. "That would be impossible."

"Let's just say I don't. What then?"

"Mia, stop worrying. I love you. I'll always love you." He kissed her deeply, his passion for her making him hard instantly. "How much longer do we have to stay?"

"We don't. We can go cut the cake and leave." As she answered, the door opened and three women entered at once.

"We're leaving." Mia smiled, reached for Damien's hand and pulled him up and out with her. She should have known Keefe would be standing outside the door waiting for them.

"You were in the ladies' room?" he said to Damien.

"I went looking for my wife." Damien grinned. "I do like the sound of that," he added, kissing Mia.

"So do I," Mia agreed as she kissed him back. Then spotting her mother, she quickly ended the kiss and looked away. When her brother's glance connected with hers, she dropped her eyes, knowing as he looked in their mother's direction that he was aware something was wrong. She'd tell him later to give Lillian her belongings.

"Come on everyone," Mia said, including Keefe and Ashleigh as she entwined her arm in her husband's. "We're going to go and cut the cake." And she marched away without looking again in her mother's direction.

CHAPTER TWELVE

Mia was trembling. The cake had been cut, the pictures taken and the catcalls begun as she and Damien made their way from the banquet hall to the elevator door that would take them to the bridal suite. This was it, the beginning of her new life, their new life, as man and wife.

It was as though she were on display. Mia felt the eyes of everyone piercing her back with the knowledge of what she was about to do. She hated that. It was a private matter.

When the elevator doors opened, Damien swung her up into his arms, taking her breath away, and fell backwards against the wall of the elevator.

"Damien, you're drunk," she whispered, not able to keep the disappointment from her voice.

"I'm not drunk, baby girl, and even if I were, it wouldn't make a difference."

He was so wrong, Mia thought. She had never thought that her husband would be drunk their first time together. Damien wobbled a little and Mia closed her eyes. "Put me down before both of us fall."

"No, I'm not letting go of you."

He kissed her and the taste of scotch on his tongue was not as pleasant as the taste of champagne, but she ignored it.

"I love you, Mia," Damien said, putting her down as the door to the elevator opened. "Thanks for making this the happiest day of my life."

Now the scotch no longer mattered, just Mia and her new husband. She clung to him. "I love you too," she said, once again giving in to the feeling of desire that had claimed her body for almost an entire year. It didn't matter that her husband was slightly drunk. It would still be the best night of her life.

When Damien slid the card down the side of the lock and lifted her once again into his arms, she didn't protest. She knew it wouldn't do a bit of good. He was bound and determined that he would carry her over the threshold.

Once inside the room, Damien carried her to the bed and laid her down and lay next to her. Mia looked around and spotted their luggage on luggage racks.

"Turn around," he said, his voice raspy. "Let me get you out of this dress."

In a matter of seconds Damien was tossing her wedding gown on the floor and his hands were all over her body. This wasn't part of her dream. She smacked at his hands. "Damien, I want to put on the negligee I bought."

"Why?"

"Because."

"Because what?"

"Because it's part of the way I thought it would be. I want the romance." She smiled shyly.

Damien leaned up on one elbow and looked at her. "Let me get this straight. You want to get up from this bed and put on more clothes?"

"Yes," Mia answered, embarrassed.

"Why?"

"So you'll remember how I looked."

"I'll remember better seeing you naked."

"Damien."

"What? I'm just being honest. We've waited too damn long as it is."

"Then a few minutes won't make that much difference," Mia answered, laughing as she tried to untangle herself from her husband's hands that were all over her body. She was shivering with anticipation. Still, she wanted to put on the gown and watch his face as he saw her in it.

"I still don't see the point," Damien said, sitting up now. "Because the moment you come out of the bathroom I'm going to take off whatever garment you've put on, and you're going to be naked anyway. So why not just start there? Cut out the middle man?"

Mia hopped off the bed and went to her bag and opened it, taking out the negligee she'd bought for her wedding night. She held it in front of her body. "I promise I'll be quick and you'll like the results." She went into the bathroom.

Damien fell back on the bed. "Mia, if you think being in white lace is going to make you more appealing than you lying here naked next to me, you're insane."

Suddenly Damien remembered the gift he'd bought for his bride and went to retrieve it from his own bag. He laid it on the corner table. "Mia," he yelled. "What the hell is taking you so long in there? God, I'll never understand women. Only a woman would think about putting on clothes just so a man can rip them off her. Come on out here, Mia, I'm horny as hell."

"Keep your shirt on," she yelled back, making him laugh. The only item of clothing he still had on was his briefs. He would have taken those off but thought it would be sexier if Mia took them off.

Alright, he thought. Maybe Mia had a point. Maybe she wanted the sexiness of her gown. He opened the champagne and poured himself a glass, shaking his head. He was beginning to feel the combined effect of the day and the alcohol. "Mia," he called again. "Come on out." He lay down as a feeling he'd never experienced in his entire life overcame him. He recognized it for what it was: contentment, bliss, joy. Any of the nouns could apply. Mia had made him whole, made him complete by marrying him and he would spend the rest of his life making sure she never regretted her decision. His heart swelled with love.

"Mia," Damien attempted to call out again but felt his tongue heavy and fuzzy. *What the hell?* He thought, as his eyes closed. He'd never passed out a day in his life. Damn, what a time to start now. "I love you, baby girl," he whispered as he gave up the fight and succumbed.

Mia took another glance at herself in the bathroom mirror.

She was ready. She trembled with the thought of what was about to happen. She walked out the door of the bathroom and stood there in what she was hoping was a provocative pose. "Damien, I'm ready," she whispered, surprised that he'd not turned around when she entered the room.

"Damien," Mia called more loudly. Finally hearing the sounds of his soft snoring, she put her hands on her hips and struck a pose. *Oh no he didn't.* Surely he was just kidding. She hopped on the bed and rolled him over. The sound of his snoring increased. And with the sound came her mother's laughing words declaring that Damien would fall asleep in the midst of the deed.

"Oh Damien," Mia pleaded, leaning down, kissing his lips, his eyes and his cheeks. "Please wake up. This is our wedding night."

It was no use. Damien was dead to the world. This was just a coincidence, she assured herself. It had nothing to do with Damien's desire for her and everything to do with how much he'd had to drink. That was all. Still, she felt sorry for herself. She was a bride and she'd waited her entire life for this night. It could never be repeated.

Mia lay down next to Damien, her head on his bare chest. With nothing else to hold her interest, she began looking around the room, her eyes lighting on the gaily-wrapped package on the corner table.

At least Damien hadn't forgotten about her wedding gift. She'd forgive him now. She hopped from the bed and rushed to rip the paper from the package. Mia stared in shock and dropped the box. A porno tape. *Fifty Ways to Please Your Lover.* She looked back at Damien snoring on the bed and the tears slid beneath her lashes. This wasn't the gift she'd had in mind. Her thoughts had ran more the way of jewelry, or at the least, a sexy gown.

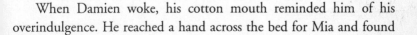

When Damien woke, his cotton mouth reminded him of his overindulgence. He reached a hand across the bed for Mia and found only empty space. He squeezed his eyes shut to blank out the jack-hammers going off in his head. A moment later, he realized that the sound was actually running water.

"Damn, how long does Mia need to put on a gown?" he muttered. He attempted to sit but fell back to stop the spinning. That was odd, he thought, but decided to give it a few more seconds to pass. Then he would drag his wife out of the bathroom. It was their wedding night.

Silence, blessed silence. The water had stopped its infernal racket. Mia should be out in a minute. Maybe he wouldn't have to drag her out, just wait for her to join him on the bed. The bathroom door opened and his wife stepped out.

Dressed.

Not in the sexy white negligee that he'd seen her carry into the bathroom with her, but in jeans and a blouse. Damien frowned and continued his inventory. She even had on shoes. What the hell was she planning?

"Baby girl, what happened to the sexy gown?"

"That was last night," his wife answered him.

He froze. Something was wrong. She wasn't looking at him and she definitely wasn't teasing him. Hell, she wasn't happy.

"Mia, what happened in that damn bathroom?"

She glared at him.

"Mia, what's going on?"

"Look at the clock. You'd better get dressed; we're meeting our families for breakfast. Then we have a plane to catch."

"What the hell are you talking about?" Damien's eyes shifted to the clock and he groaned. No wonder his new bride was pissed, he'd passed out and totally blown their wedding night.

"Come here, baby girl, I'm sorry. Come on, let me get you out of those clothes."

"We don't have time."

"We have time for a quickie." He looked at her face. Damn. Mistake number two.

Kicking away the covers, he jumped out of the bed and reached for Mia. "Baby girl, forgive me." He pulled her close, ignoring her resistance and holding on for dear life. "Don't be mad at me. Do you have any idea how mad I am at myself? I've been waiting all this time to make love to you and the first chance I get I blow it."

Oomph.

"What the...Mia," Damien moaned, offended. "Why did you elbow me?" He moved away from her, knowing he'd somehow made mistake number three, even though he didn't know what it was.

"I was trying to apologize, baby." He groaned, still smarting from her blow to his ribs.

"You're not doing it very well."

Okay, so she was really pissed. He'd never seen her so, he thought, *cold as ice.* "Mia, what the hell happened to you when I passed out? Did I do something to you? If I did, tell me. I don't remember."

Damien was worried, wondering if the reason Mia was staring at him as if she no longer knew him, no longer loved him, was because of something he couldn't remember. He was trying desperately to pull himself together, to remember. He'd wanted her so badly, but that was nothing different. He'd always wanted her and he'd never attacked her in the past. Still, there was something in her eyes. But no matter how hard he tried, he was drawing a blank. Surely his first time with his wife had not taken place without him being able to remember it.

"Mia, if I was a little rough or impatient last night, I'm sorry. I didn't know what I was doing."

"What are you talking about, Damien?" Mia asked.

It was the way she said his name that chilled him, as though he were some insect to be stepped on. He decided to ignore her temper and answer her question. "I'm talking about our making love. I'm sorry if it wasn't good for you."

"We didn't make love. You were asleep."

Mia turned from him and began putting her wedding gown on a hanger. "You'd better get dressed," she said.

He tried again. "I'm sorry about our wedding night."

"Not as sorry as I am," she answered.

Damien snapped Mia's bag shut. "Do you have everything?" he asked.

"Yes."

She was still giving him one word answers. He had hoped by the time he got out of the shower she would have thawed a little. He smiled, their first fight as a married couple. He lifted the bags and made his way toward the door. A strange crinkling sound made him pause. Damien looked down and spotted the torn wrapping paper.

She got my gift. That would melt her, he thought and carried the luggage downstairs to leave at the desk until it was time for their flight.

Mia carried the bag with her wedding gown as she walked behind Damien. Keefe had agreed to take that home for her. She hated that they'd made plans to meet their families for breakfast. She'd hated it from the first time that it was mentioned. She knew what everyone was going to want to know. She didn't want them staring at her, imagining what she'd done or hadn't done.

She shuddered. If she were talking to Damien, she would ask him to cancel, to call everyone and tell them they were eating in…but then she'd have to do what she hadn't done last night and she wasn't quite ready for that particular intimacy. To think that they'd both been so looking forward to it.

"Mia, are you not going to talk to me at all?" Damien asked as he turned from the check out desk and reached for the bag that his wife carried.

She sighed. "I don't have anything to say."

To that he laughed, moving closer to her, holding her tight and singing, "'Just the thought of youuuuu…'" He felt a tremble ripple through her body and chuckled. She'd thaw. Then he brought his lips around to hers, kissed her lips softly, then the hollow of her neck. Again she trembled and he smiled.

"I knew you couldn't stay mad at me," he whispered.

"Hey, you two, get a room. Oh, that's right, you just had a room," Charles said coming up to them, talking in a voice loud enough for the entire lobby to hear.

Damien let go of Mia, sensing a change in her mood. Inside he cursed his father's bad timing. In a matter of moments their entire family was assembled and he wished they'd never made plans to have breakfast with all of them. What a dumb ass idea.

"So, Mia, how are you this morning?" his father sneered. Damien felt Mia stiffen and closed his hand around hers, giving her fingers a squeeze. "I'm good," Mia answered at last and Damien headed the group into the restaurant, smiling down at Mia, grateful that she was still holding his hand.

For over an hour they all behaved. True, Mia was quieter than usual, not looking at her mother, and he couldn't blame her. He hadn't looked in the woman's direction either. He was surprised to see her there but hadn't made a fuss.

For now at least even his father was behaving. Well, almost. The majority of his father's attention was concentrated on Lillian. So when it happened, Damien had been lured into complacency and had let down his guard.

"So, Damien, tell us. Was your bride worth the wait?"

He was getting ready to answer his father's damn question, to tell him that Mia was definitely worth the wait, when he caught the smirk on his father's face, saw the hidden meaning. Before he could stop him, his father started laughing and Mia's mother joined in.

Before Damien got a chance to say one word, Mia was up from the table and walking away. Though he wanted to tell both her mother and his father to go to hell, to keep their noses out of their private affairs, he leaped up and followed Mia. She was more important. Behind him he heard Keefe's voice raised in anger. Damn. This had been a bad idea.

"Mia, wait up. Don't let him get to you." He caught Mia's hand as she raced to the desk and saw her eyes glimmering with unshed tears. He cringed. "Mia, he's…" God, what could he say? "Mia, he was way out of line. I'll take care of it."

She was ignoring him, asking the desk to call for the bags and a taxi. Damien peered out the door and saw a taxi waiting. The door opened as if fate had known this would happen.

Mia stormed out the door and he followed, putting the bags in the cab and climbing in beside Mia. "Aren't you going to say goodbye?" he asked Mia, pointing to her brother who'd run out the door.

"No," she said. I just want to go. Please."

No amount of consoling, singing or pleading worked. "I don't believe this," Damien mumbled low. "Why are you blaming me for what my father said?"

Mia glared at him, her anger intensifying with each second. "Who would you like me to blame?" she asked, her voice shaking. "God, what did you do, take out an ad, Damien?" She'd held her emotions in for hours and she really didn't want to cry, not here in a taxi, but she couldn't stop the tears that came. She pushed Damien away, not wanting his arms around her. She ignored his, "*This is one hell of a start to a honeymoon*" and cried even harder. She agreed completely.

CHAPTER THIRTEEN

Sin City, the capital of fun. Mia winced as she woodenly followed Damien from the elevator and down the hall to the room. Because he had decided to bring the bags up himself, Mia said a catty thing to him. "Can't wait to see what you got, I bet." His jaw clenched and he ignored her. She was feeling evil, evil and scared as hell. Everything was falling apart. It wasn't supposed to be like this.

Damien set the bags on the floor, then turned to her. "Are we going to keep fighting," he asked. "Because I don't think I want to."

"I don't want to either," Mia whispered. "I thought...I hate this."

"What do you hate exactly?" Damien asked slowly. "That we're fighting, or that we're married?"

"I hate that I'm being judged, that everyone I know is probably right now taking bets on us. God, Damien, how could you tell your father something so personal? He's making jokes about me right now. I can feel it."

"Don't let him...don't let anyone interfere with us, Mia, we have a good thing here. Come on, let's stop fighting."

He held his arms out and she went willingly into them. She was crying and she needed him to comfort her, tell her that she was wrong, that they were all wrong, that he really did love her, that sex was only a tiny part of it. But he was undressing her, pulling her blouse off her shoulder and she felt his hardened flesh pressing against her. Just the thought of what was on his mind made her angry. Comfort was what she needed now. Not sex.

"Let me do that for you," she snarled and yanked her clothes off, not stopping until she stood before him naked. "Come on, Damien, it's what you've been waiting for. You might as well see if I'm worth the wait." Without a thought she ran to the bed, threw the covers back and lay down spread-eagled.

"Is this what you want? You've got it. You married me, I'm your wife. Let's see if the wait was worth it."

"What the hell are you doing?" Damien asked, the anger seeping through. "You're taking this way out of proportion. Listen, I didn't ask for a virgin sacrifice."

"Then what is it that you want?"

"I want the woman that I married a few hours ago. I want the one who begged me to help her keep her vow because she found it difficult to say no to me. I want the woman who gets hot when she looks at me, Mia, that's what I want. And please, for God's sake, tell me where she went because she sure as hell isn't here."

Mia stared at Damien. He was right. She wasn't the same woman. She stared until she burst into tears again. Then she pulled the covers over her nude body and burrowed her head in the soft down pillows.

"Mia, I'm going downstairs for awhile. I need to cool off and so do you," Damien said, as he closed the door behind him. He stood for a minute listening to the sounds of Mia's sobs through the door. He put his palm against the door and whispered, "Stop crying, baby girl. I'm sorry, it's going to be okay." But he wasn't so sure. He shook his head and walked back toward the elevator thinking, *What a difference a day makes.*

For over two hours Damien sat in a bar at Caesar's Palace. He smiled dully at the scantily clad waitresses coming and going. This wasn't how he'd envisioned his honeymoon, his bride crying in their hotel room while he sat in a bar nursing a drink and feeling sorry for himself. He also hadn't envisioned his bride remaining a virgin.

With that thought he got a renewed surge of energy and his erection pulsed in his pants. But his erection was the thing that had made Mia go off in the first place. How the hell was he supposed to control it? He wanted her. Hell, he'd always wanted her. Their honeymoon was definitely no exception.

Damien threw a few bills on the bar and walked out, heading for the house phone he knew was just outside the door.

"Mia," he said as she answered. "I'm sorry, baby. Can I come back up?" His voice was raw with his need. He didn't want to frighten or anger her but he needed to feel himself inside her body. He needed to cement their relationship. Once they made love, he knew all would be forgiven. That was his talent, his gift. If only he could get the chance to show his bride just how good he could be.

"I'm sorry too," Mia answered. "I'm acting like a child. I know that. I think...I think maybe all the wedding preparations. My mother, your father. I think everything just made me hormonal. Come on up."

"Are you still undressed," he asked.

"I'm still undressed," she replied, a bit of the frost returning.

"Do you think you could put on that lacy thing I didn't get to see last night?" Damien could practically see Mia smiling through the phone.

"I can do that," she answered.

"I love you, my sweet wife."

"You can't possibly love me as much as I love you," Mia answered.

She hadn't ruined things. Mia raced for her bag, dug around and found the gown, ignoring the wedding gift her husband had gotten for her. Mia washed her face with a cool cloth and quickly brushed and gargled. Yeah, she was more than ready to make love to her brand new husband.

When Damien returned, Mia was waiting by the bed. Her heart fluttering, she lifted her eyes to his face and smiled. "Damien, I love you and no matter how I've been acting this morning, I'm glad we're married." Then she was in his arms and he was kissing her and she was kissing him, laughing as he kissed her nose, her ears, and nibbled at her lips. His heat consumed her and became her own.

"Mia, we've waited so long," Damien moaned.

She sucked in her breath, holding in her own moan. "I know," she answered, giving in to the hunger, touching him with delight. As she felt the heat from her husband's body, desire flared in her and exploded. Together they undressed him and Mia stood for a moment in shy embarrassment, watching him as his flesh jutted forward. She'd never seen a naked man this close, only in the movies, only in her mind. She shivered as her desire burned her to the depths Of her very soul.

"Damien," she moaned as she felt herself being lifted into his arms. Her hands trailed down his side, feeling the hard rippling muscles. She had never before touched her husband's flesh without the barrier of clothes between them. Her fingers twitched. This was a dream she wanted badly to fulfill.

Under the covers, her thoughts centered greedily on her own pleasures. Damien was touching her in her most intimate of places, probing all the areas she'd before smacked his hands away from, and she could feel the juices, her own juices, racing through her body, pouring out of her. She was moaning at his touch. Such ecstasy, such wonder. He suckled her breasts, licked her ears, her belly and all the time his fingers probed. And she was touching him in return, feeling his hardness in her hand, exploring his body with the pads of her fingers. She was burning with the heat, the lust, the wonder of it all.

Then he rose up, instructing her to open her legs. She complied and then he was there, at her entrance and she tensed without thinking as he pushed against her.

"Don't tense up, Mia."

She ordered her body to relax. Damien pushed a little harder and a sudden pain and intense burning ripped through her. This too she could handle. It would go away. She knew that.

"Mia, you don't have to worry about a thing, not with me, and, baby, you're going to be a fast learner. I can tell."

Her needs took on a life of their own. She was doing whatever Damien asked without question. Liquid fire crawled through her.

"My God, Mia, you're so tight."

She chuckled. That was a good thing, she knew at least that much. Despite the feeling of her flesh being on fire, of being ripped apart, Mia wanted more. She trembled with the knowledge, and clung to Damien.

"Come on, baby girl, wrap your legs around my back, Damien urged.

Sweat covered their bodies, so much that Mia's hand fought for purchase on Damien's flesh, only to slide away. They were both grunting, deep, guttural, almost animalistic sounds.

"Raise your hips to meet my thrusts, Mia."

She did as he asked, wincing in both pleasure and pain as Damien plunged even deeper inside her.

"Mia, you're a natural. You were born for this. It's in your blood."

A natural? In her blood? It couldn't be. She didn't want it to be her mother's blood that was awakening these feelings in her. All at once a tremble of awareness started in her belly and spread throughout her body. She shivered, thinking of all the things she was doing, all the things she was enjoying. She liked the things Damien was doing to her. Were virgins supposed to enjoy themselves the first time? She'd always heard they didn't. Did their bodies respond as hers was doing? Mia didn't want to be a natural. It could mean only one thing…

She opened her eyes and looked at her new husband, his face contorted in lust, and a shiver traveled down her spine, chilling her soul. She knew that look. It was the same look she'd seen on the face of a man Mia had found lying atop her mother. She knew in that instant that if she looked into a mirror her own face would be distorted by the lust. Just like her mother's had been. She shut her eyes tighter as the memory forced itself into her thoughts-the memory of how at five, hearing her mother's screams, she'd run into the bedroom to find a strange man on top of her. She'd thought he was hurting her mother, had tried to help her but her mother had screamed at her to get out and she'd run into another room and hid in a corner, covering her ears and crying until Keefe came in from riding his bike and found her there.

Oh God, what was she doing? Her hands were clawing at Damien and she was moaning and grunting like some animal in heat…like a slut…like her mother. Terror skittered down her spine, and Mia struggled desperately to shove the image of her mother out of her head. She didn't belong there, not now when her husband was making love to her. She tried hard to remember that this was Damien, the man she loved, whose touch she craved like flowers crave rain. This was Damien, her husband now. The man she'd wanted to make love to her for months, the one who'd made her melt, made her feel things she'd been unaware existed. She'd wanted him with every fiber of her being, risked her relationship with her brother by lying to him.

Suddenly it was as though a bucket of ice water had been dumped over her entire body, freezing her, freezing every emotion except shame. Mia loved Damien, she truly did. But she was helpless to resist the horrible images and thoughts flooding her brain. Every doubt, every worry she'd ever had about herself coalesced into this one moment with Damien. She was her mother's daughter! Mia closed her eyes against the horror of that thought but what awaited her was even worse. She saw her mother laughing, her finger pointing and the tears worked their way from beneath her closed lids.

A wave of revulsion swept through Mia. Her husband's touch that only moments before had filled her with a sweet intense heat, making her crave more, now filled her with a different heat. She was burning up alright-burning up with shame.

Mia screamed out, the pain of the images more that she could bear. "Stop! She screamed. "Stop, Damien!"

Damien had everything he wanted, Mia as his wife, him buried deep inside her. Damien groaned in pleasure, feeling his release getting the better of him. He was taking it damn slow, making sure he didn't frighten Mia, didn't hurt her with his intense need, his greed. But he'd promised her he'd teach her, that she'd enjoy it and he was teaching her. He hoped like hell she understood the gruffness of his voice when he called out encouragement to her, little hints of things that would increase their pleasure.

He dove into her again and again. God, how he loved her. Then he heard her calling his name just as he'd always imagined, just as he'd told her she would and the sound of her voice pushed him farther over the edge. She was almost as incoherent as his thoughts.

"Stop, Damien."

He wasn't sure if that was what she said but he knew she couldn't want him to stop. She hadn't come. He knew that. Maybe he was still hurting her. "Don't worry, baby girl," he consoled her. "It won't hurt much longer, just a few more seconds." Just then his entire body trembled and he could no longer control it. His release shook him all over and he growled, clutching Mia to him. Then he collapsed on her chest.

"Stop, Damien," she screamed again and he shook his head to clear it. As he attempted to rise up, he felt himself being shoved upwards with such force that he slid to the floor with a thud.

What the hell! "Mia," Damien called to her as she snatched a rumpled sheet to cover her body.

"Leave me alone," she sobbed and ran into the bathroom.

Damien stood up, panic filling him. He looked toward the bed, then the bathroom door, not knowing what to do, what had happened. I *must have hurt her*, he thought. But he'd been so gentle. He'd made sure of that. If not, they would have been done the moment he slid into her wetness.

"Mia, why are you crying, baby girl? Did I hurt you, Mia? I'm feeling like hell out here. You know I didn't mean to hurt you, baby. Sometimes it's painful for virgins the first time. I promise you it'll get better. Come on out, Mia."

The sound of rain came from the bathroom and Damien frowned. "Are you taking a shower? Let me come in. We can shower together." He was having a difficult time getting his voice normal. He knew what Mia was doing. She wasn't just taking a shower. She was washing his scent off her.

An intense pain filled his chest and he groaned again but this time there was nothing pleasurable about it. Without warning his mother's laughing words returned to him. *"It will serve you right if the one woman you want to please, you can't."* He looked again at the bed. *"Stop, Damien."* He now heard the words loud and clear. *"Stop, Damien."* They were reverberating in his head. She'd wanted him to stop. What the hell did it make him that he hadn't? Shivering, he looked down at his nakedness and felt foolish. As unbelievable as it seemed, he was still hard. That knowledge disgusted him. He'd scared the hell out of his wife, and even now she was washing the smell of him away. She was disgusted by him. And he had an arousal.

⚘

Mia stood beneath the hot water crying, her heart breaking. She'd loved Damien touching her, the feel of his hands on her body, inside her, and even with the pain she'd welcomed him inside her. "Oh, God," she moaned, "God, please don't let me be like her."

Despite the running water she could hear Damien calling to her. What could she tell him? How could she explain her behavior. How could she tell him that she'd tried to control the images and hadn't been able to. He'd think she was crazy. She just needed time to work her way though this…to apply her process. *But how did a woman get over finding that she was a slut-just like her mother?*

All she wanted was to make Damien happy. She cried harder. She loved him so much. How was she ever going to face him. "Oh, God," she moaned. "Damien, I'm so sorry."

⚘

Mia came out of the bathroom at last, wrapped in one of the hotel's huge fluffy white towels. She wished she'd thought to take clothes with her into the bathroom. She didn't want to cross the room in only a towel but she had no choice. She aimed for her open bag, averting her eyes from the bed.

"Mia, what happened?"

She blinked, startled. She hadn't seen Damien sitting at the table near the bags. Her eyes flicked over him and she was grateful that he was at least partially dressed in sweats.

"I won't know what's wrong unless you tell me." Damien's voice was hoarse, the words ripping from his throat with the rawness he was feeling. "Help me out here."

Mia remained silent, searching her bag for clothes.

"Answer me, Mia."

"What is it you want me to say?"

"I want you to tell me what happened. Did I hurt you, baby?" He started to rise from the chair but was stopped by the look of terror in her eyes. "You're afraid of me?"

She opened her mouth to speak, only the words wouldn't come. She wanted to tell her husband that it wasn't him, she was afraid of, but her own emotions.

Damien tried again, this time not allowing the look of fear in Mia's eyes to stop him. He walked toward her, reached his hand out to pull her close. If he could just hold her, he thought, everything would be fine.

"No, no, no. Please don't touch me, Damien."

Mia was trembling so hard that the clothes fell from her arms. "Please, just go back to the chair. I need to get dressed, Damien. Just let me get dressed." As he bent to pick up the dropped clothing she moved away, nearly snatching them from him as he held them out to her. "Leave me alone, Damien, just leave me alone."

"How can I just leave you alone, Mia? Something is wrong, I need to know what it is. You're afraid of me and I have no idea why. Now you're angry and I don't know what I did wrong or what you think I did. Please, baby girl, tell me at least why you're angry."

She turned and stared at him. He was right, she was angry, but not at him. She wanted to tell him that she was angry at herself, at her mother, that despite all of her years of waiting for the right man, for marriage, blood had won out. Damien deserved so much more than to marry someone who'd been cursed to have Lillian as a mother.

As she stared at him, she thought about all the things that had gone wrong since they'd taken their vows. She should have known what she was. How could she have so easily fallen in love with Damien? After all, she'd been engaged at the time.

Even now she wanted him, wanted his hands on her, wanted him to repeat the things he'd done before she'd leapt from the bed like a lunatic. Mia looked away briefly, before bringing her gaze to rest on Damien. That was what she feared and what she could not tell him. That was the reason she was angry.

Then a quiver began in her toes and continued until it was a full shudder ripping through her at the knowledge of what she was. The pain of knowing was killing her. Mia closed her eyes, attempting to shove it away, to forget. That had been her habit for more years than she cared to remember. That was how she dealt with her pain. She submerged it, afraid of what would happen if she allowed the pain to explode.

"Mia, talk to me," Damien pleaded. "If you're angry about something I did, tell me, we can deal with it."

Anger she could deal with, unwanted memories, she couldn't. Her first time making love had been marred by ugliness. If she were to share the images she'd seen in her head with Damien he would think she was crazy. "Not now," she said, "give me some time." She backed away from Damien, turning only when she felt the bathroom door at her back.

In the bathroom she thought of her patients, of some of the things they confided to her, things that didn't sound nearly as ridiculous as what she had to tell her husband. And she knew first hand that she thought they were nuts. Mia's eyes closed as she leaned against the door. Some psychologist she was. She thought her patients were crazy. And then she screamed, loud and long. But it was only in her mind.

Damien sat where he was, watching Mia as she reentered the bathroom, her arms loaded down with her clothes. He was still sitting there when she came back out fully dressed, avoiding him. He couldn't let this go on. He had to know what the hell had happened. Maybe this happened with all virgins. He didn't know. But there was only one virgin he was concerned with and that was his wife. "God," he moaned. "Help me."

He walked toward her. "Whatever it is, baby girl, we can talk about it. I must have hurt you. You have to know it wasn't deliberate. It's all part of lovemaking. It will get better, Mia, the pain will go away and you'll…you'll enjoy it." He swallowed, but stopped short of making her a promise. He'd made her several promises in the last few months and it was apparent that none of his promises were coming true.

He reached out for her, believing that if he could only put his arms around her it would be okay. He'd take away her pain in his arms.

"Don't touch me."

"Don't touch you?" Damien's mouth dropped. This was a bit more than his new bride being fearful. More than a virgin's skittishness. He looked into Mia's eyes and saw fear mixed with loathing.

"Mia, what did I do?" he whispered hoarsely, wracking his brain for the answer. They'd been married less than twenty-four hours. He was sure that look hadn't been there when she'd said 'I do.' Hell, he was positive it hadn't been there when he'd begun making love to her. No, just a short time ago her eyes had been filled with love that had rapidly changed to lust as he kissed her. She'd wanted him, loved him. He was certain of it.

"Mia, what's wrong? Did I hurt you?"

"No, you didn't hurt me," she said softly, and walked away.

If he hadn't hurt her, then it could only be one thing: His new bride hated his hands on her, hated his lovemaking. Damien cringed inwardly, praying for that not to be so. He was a good lover, he knew that. He'd prided himself on giving pleasure to the women he'd been with. His chest was hurting with the effort it was now taking him to breathe.

"Tell me what to do," he pleaded. "Just tell me what's wrong, Mia."

What was wrong was Mia couldn't stand the hurt she was hearing in Damien's voice. "Damien," her throat closed with the lump lodged there. She couldn't talk and she didn't want to continue crying.

"Mia, please—"

"I need to have time to work through this, Damien," she whispered, wishing he would stop talking and allow her to begin her process but he wouldn't.

"I know there was some pain, baby. I'm sorry."

She wanted to tell him that the pain she'd known about, had expected it. What she hadn't expected was to have her worst nightmare come true.

"Mia, I love you. Just let me hold you."

If only it were that easy. There was nothing Mia wanted more than to turn to her husband, tell him that she loved him too. But if she did, he would touch her, hold her, and as much as she loved him, as much as she loved his touch, the thought of being like her mother disgusted her to the point of not being able to have him touch her at all. She feared her passion for him. In his arms she would succumb. She knew that.

From the moment Mia met Damien, she'd felt the fervor. Now she knew it was a danger to her. She wished she could tell him all of that, that she was hurting far worse than he could ever imagine. But that wasn't how she did things.

All her life she'd been brave. She'd kept her pain buried deep inside, sharing it only with her brother, but mostly keeping it to herself. Her brother had told her time after time that she had to be brave, had to be strong, had to not let anyone know they'd hurt her. She'd done that time after time. She'd played her part, never giving in to being scared, never crying when their mother would leave her alone and she couldn't find Keefe. And she'd kept the pain inside whenever her mother would drop in wanting money instead of them, loving a different man and never them. Mia had become an expert at keeping her feelings hidden. She'd done that time after time.

Yes, Mia was very good at being strong. This pain, too, she would handle alone. She'd learn to deal with it as she had every other pain in her life. But she knew this would require more time. For now she couldn't allow Damien to touch her. Her hysteria was just below the surface, having it return wasn't a chance she was ready to take. She needed him gone. She needed to mend on her own.

For two days the two of them shared a room and little else. Mia refused to talk and Damien was so bewildered by her attitude that he didn't know what to do, how to change things. He'd decided to wait it out, make small talk, eat with her, sleep in the bed with her, knowing that the moment she thought he was asleep she got up and slept on the overstuffed couch. They were both nearing the breaking point and he knew they couldn't take much more without one or both of them saying things that they would regret.

"Mia, I'm going to run downstairs for a little bit, maybe play a few slots. Do you mind?"

"No," she answered, surprising him. It was one of the few answers she'd given. She must be happy at the thought of him leaving her alone. And that saddened him.

"Okay, then I won't be long."

The pain had not subsided but Mia had shoved it into the nether regions of her mind. She hadn't run screaming from the room and she'd even gotten into the bed with her husband, knowing that if he touched her she could not maintain the calm façade. But if she told him how she felt, it would drive a wedge between them.

Like my actions aren't already doing that, she thought.

She was positive that Damien thought she was crazy. And the longer they went not talking, the harder it was.

She'd cringed at the look of confusion on Damien's face. She saw the hurt in his eyes and was affected deeply. Sometimes she found herself wanting to ease his pain; other times she wanted to ask him to get a separate room. She did neither. She was brave; she held it all inside.

When the door closed on the room Mia picked up the phone and dialed her brother's cell. Mia shivered as she waited for him to answer.

Keefe must have known what would happen. She remembered Keefe's reaction when he'd caught her kissing a boy, how he'd yelled at her, something he rarely did. Her brother had told her he would not allow her to become a slut like their mother. That was the first time Mia had doubted her character. She'd liked the kiss. Since that day Mia had shut herself away from those feelings, until Damien. And though both she and Keefe had tried to keep her from turning into Lillian, it had happened anyway.

"Keefe, you lied," she began.

"Mia, I don't understand. Lied about what?"

"You told me it would be fine, that Damien's and my love would be enough to make it work. But it's not. You were right to worry that I'd turn out like Mom. I am like her…just like her," she sobbed, then hung up the phone.

The call had happened so quickly that Keefe was not prepared. A call from Mia was the last thing he'd expected. She was on her honeymoon. What could have gone wrong? He replayed Mia's wedding day in his mind. Mia walking away from their mother crying, her coming upon Ashleigh and Damien and changing direction, her asking him to give their mother her things, and the morning after. Keefe remembered the crude remark Damien's father had made.

Any of those things could have ruined Mia's honeymoon. He punched in Ashleigh's number. He was going to narrow down his choices.

"Ashleigh, I need to know what you and Damien were talking about at the wedding."

"I thought we'd settled that," Ashleigh answered. "That was days ago. It's over. Let it rest."

"Ashleigh, this is important!" Keefe snapped. "I need to know and I need to know now. It has nothing to do with my jealousy. Now tell me."

When she was done, he groaned. Even he found it hard to envision that his mother had run her hand over Damien's crotch, cupping him. God, what a mess! Do you think Damien told Mia?" he asked.

"Not unless he's stupid. I advised him not to. Can you imagine what that would have done to Mia? It would have ruined her honeymoon."

Exactly what Keefe was thinking. "Thanks, Ashleigh," he said. "I'll talk to you later."

Keefe got the number from the operator and called the hotel, not knowing what he would use as an excuse if Damien answered. Lucky for him it was Mia.

"Mia, you scared the hell out of me. Do you want me to fly out and get you?"

"Get me?" Mia asked in a hushed voice. "What are you talking about?"

"Mia, you were crying. Something's wrong."

"Just a momentary lapse," she answered. "But I'm being strong. I'll handle it, Keefe. Don't get involved," she continued. "You can't help me on this one." Then she hung up the phone.

And that worried the hell out of Keefe.

CHAPTER FOURTEEN

Mia and Damien sat on opposite sides of the living room of Mia's apartment. Correction, *their* apartment, their new home. Damien looked first at his hands, then at his bride.

"We have to talk about this, Mia. We can't just keep going on like this, pretending nothing is wrong."

"I know." she answered.

"Then are you ready to talk?"

"Not now," she answered. "I need more time."

"Anything else?" he asked, curious as to her hesitation.

"I could use some space." There, she'd said it. They stared at each other.

"So my father was right. This is your crib and you want me out."

"No, Damien, that's not what I said. This is *our* home. I only want some space."

"What does that mean exactly?"

"I think for a little while, if you don't mind, I'd like to sleep alone. You can take my bedroom…I mean, you can take the larger room," she corrected herself. "I'll take the other one."

"I didn't get married to sleep alone."

"But you told me you didn't marry me for the sex."

"I'm glad I meant it because from what you're saying, it looks like I won't be getting any."

He was pissed. He had done nothing to warrant the abrupt change in her. "What's going on, Mia? Does this have anything at all to with all the questions you were asking me before we got married? Is this why you were quizzing me? Whatever your mother told you, she was wrong. She lied. I'm happy, well, not at this moment, but you were fine, Mia, you didn't disappoint me."

Mia closed her eyes, wondering why he was bothering to lie, wondering how many more lies he'd told her. How could her screaming out for him to stop not disappoint him? What sane woman ran from her husband during their honeymoon and how could he not regret falling in love with her?

"Are you sorry you married me, Mia?"

"No," she answered truthfully. She was only sorry that she feared her reactions in his arms.

"I don't understand how our sleeping in different rooms is going to help. You're running away. If there's a problem, then we need to fix it. But I'm not a mind reader, baby girl. I'm just a man."

Mia sighed. She should have known Damien was not going to go along with her suggestion so easily. He was a man and a man that was not used to having a woman say no. She knew that for a fact, he'd admitted it. Mia stared for a moment at her husband, wondering if some of his anger wasn't coming from that.

"This is part of my process. I do it for a living. I know that pretty soon I'll be able to talk to you about it, just not now."

"Part of your process? I'm not your damn job. I'm your husband. And do you want to know how I deal with a problem? Directly, Mia Terrell. You're my wife now and I'll deal directly with you as my wife, not as a shrink." He ignored the brief flash of pain that pinched Mia's lips.

Instead he walked up to her and threw the bag she had in her hands to the floor. He held her for a second, their eyes locked. "Welcome to my process, Mia."

Then he kissed her.

And she kissed him back.

The hunger he had yet to feed rose up in him like a lion. It roared through his blood, inflaming his senses with need. He'd married Mia because he loved her, needed her to make him whole, and right this moment he needed her more than ever. He needed to know that she still thought he was special. He plunged his tongue into Mia's mouth over and over, ravishing her, feeling her tremble, and he increased the assault until he felt as though he were drowning in need. Then he lifted his wife into his arms and carried her toward the bedroom.

"Mia," he moaned as he carried her to the bed, his lips buried in the softness of her neck. He held her tighter to stop the squirming, afraid that he might drop her. "Stop kicking your legs, Mia," he moaned again. Then it hit him. She was trying to get away.

With great effort Damien pulled back and took a good look at Mia. The fear in her eyes chilled him. She was still afraid of him. He set her down and watched in shock as she backed away. The woman he loved was afraid of him. What the hell had he done to deserve that?

"Mia, for God's sake, tell me what did I do to make you look at me like that. Why are you afraid of me?"

"It's not you," she said, backing toward the door. "It's me. I'll take care of it."

Before he had a chance to object, she was gone. He heard the door to the room close, then the tumblers click into place. He closed his eyes in agony. Mia was locking the door against him, fearing him, afraid that he'd what? Rape her? He shuddered, remembering her words. "Stop Damien." Is that what she thought he'd done? Is that what it really boiled down to? He fell on the bed. Why hadn't he heard her?

Mia was shaking. She sat on the bed to calm down, running situations and applications through her mind. She knew what was happening and she had the tools to work thought it. She'd be her own patient. She'd treat herself and when she was healed, she'd go to her husband.

She ran her fingers across her lips, where the pressure from Damien's kisses still lingered. She'd liked his method, his process and it had almost worked. She'd felt the same desire for him she always had. It wasn't until he'd begun carrying her into the bedroom that the memories had returned and she'd panicked. Mia wasn't ready to face that again. The thought of lying beneath him while pictures of her mother making love played in her head was more than she could bear.

She lay across the bed and brought a pillow to her chest. She'd work her way through it. She'd learn to control the images, stop them from coming. She could do it. She'd always done it. Her brother had taught her how. Now more than ever she needed to be strong. Her five-day-old marriage was at stake. She only hoped Damien loved her enough to give her the time she needed to work through it.

For two weeks Damien and Mia lived together in a polite existence. Damien had not tried to kiss Mia again. His head swarmed with confusion. He'd rewritten their wedding night and honeymoon so many times that now he was convinced that he must have raped his wife.

Every instinct that he had told him that wasn't true, but the fearful look she gave him if they so much as accidentally brushed hands told him she believed differently.

Damien was glad for his increased work load and Mia's increased classes. Before the wedding they had bemoaned the fact that they would not have much time for each other. Now it killed him to know that Mia welcomed it. Nevertheless, he pasted a fake smile on his face when he went to work and pretended that he and Mia were happy.

"Damien, can you come out for a few minutes? You have a visitor."

Damien glanced toward the door his co-worker had just come through. For a moment he dared to hope that it was Mia, but quickly gave that up. The only people who'd ever come to see him at the zoo were Keefe and Ashleigh.

Sure enough, it was his new brother-in-law. Damien walked toward him warily, stuck out his hand and waited.

"You really seem to like working here," Keefe began.

"I do. I love the animals, I like taking care of them."

"Did you ever think about making a career out of it?"

Damien laughed, "As a matter of fact I have. Being a vet wouldn't be such a bad thing."

"No joke," Keefe whistled. "You're thinking about becoming a vet?"

"The thought's in the back of my mind but there are other things I have to take care of first." Damien couldn't help smiling. "You know you didn't come here to talk to me about a career move. What do you want?"

"How was the honeymoon?" Keefe asked.

Damien noticed that he looked away. "What are you asking me exactly?" He wasn't going to let Keefe off the hook. He saw that he was uncomfortable. Hell, he should be. What happened on his honeymoon was none of the man's damn business.

"I was just…I wondered…did everything go okay?"

Damien shook his head. Unbelievable, unmitigated gall, that's what it boiled down to. "Look, man, before you go any further with this I'm going to tell you straight out I'm not talking to you about my sex life. It's none of your damn business."

Damien watched as Keefe swallowed and seemed to be go through some kind of internal struggle. He waited.

"Mia's not used to the things that you might have wanted to do. You knew she was a virgin, Damien," he said accusingly.

There, it was out. Damien laughed. He read between the lines and knew he was being called a pervert. He wondered briefly if his wife thought he was a rapist and a pervert.

"Exactly what sort of things do you think I'm used to?"

"Don't make me say this." Keefe looked away. "We both know what I'm talking about."

"I'm stupid, you're going to have to tell me." Keefe glared at him and he glared right back.

"She might think some of the things you might have tried to do were dirty."

That did it. "Why you arrogant son of a bitch, who the hell do you think you are? Mia is my wife, get it! You don't control her anymore and you sure as hell don't control me. Like I said, I'm not discussing either my sex life or the lack of one with you."

"The lack of one?" Keefe asked quietly.

The two men stared hard at each other and before he knew it Damien had told Keefe everything, beginning with their wedding night, him passing out, and ending with the fact they were now living together like brother and sister.

"What did I do? What made her freak out like that?" He swallowed, feeling strangely better, not believing that he'd unloaded on the one person he'd never have thought he would, Mia's brother.

"I don't know," Keefe said quietly.

"I was patient and gentle. I swear I was." He pleaded with Keefe, wanting to see someone believe him, wanting to believe himself that he was not a monster.

"I believe you," Keefe answered. "I don't think it's about you or what you think you may have done."

"That's what Mia said. She told me it's her problem but she won't tell me what the problem is."

"Did she say anything else?"

"Yeah, she told me this is her process. That she would work it out. She's shutting me out and it's killing me," he admitted. He glanced ruefully at Keefe. "It seems you're still her knight. What did she do? Call you to save her from me?" He closed his eyes, willing the hurt to go away, but it wouldn't.

"Mia didn't call me. She's avoiding me. I even met her between her classes and she wouldn't talk."

"Tell me something, Keefe. This process of Mia's, do you know anything about it, how long it takes, anything?"

Keefe looked away. "It's something I taught her when she was a little girl. I always told her she had to be brave, to be strong. When she'd tell me that she couldn't, I would tell her that it took time, that it was a process that she had to go through, her process until she could be strong. I taught her to bury her pain inside until she didn't feel it anymore."

Damien stared at Keefe. "Why, man?"

"To get her through the pain. Mia has had a hell of a lot more than her share of pain. I did what I had to do to get her through it. I had to make her strong in order for her to survive."

Damien was getting scared. There was something Keefe was not telling him and he had to ask. "And when she's done with the process, when she's strong, then what happens?"

"She doesn't feel the pain."

"There's more, Keefe. What is it?"

"I taught her to be strong and not care, that if she didn't care, she wouldn't be hurt."

"And that's what she's trying to do with me, process me out of her system?" Damien asked in horror.

"I think she just wants to find a way to be with you. I don't know what happened but she's trying to deal with it."

"By processing all of her feelings for me away until there's what? Nothing left? I don't want Mia to not care about me."

"I'm sure she's just trying to find a way to be a good wife to you, Damien."

"You mean Mia's trying to find a way to make herself able to be with me, stomach my touch? I don't want that. I want the passion she's had for me this entire time. I don't want her submitting to me. And that sounds like what you're talking about."

"I didn't say that. I think whatever happened when…when the two of you…I think she's just trying to find a way around it."

"The hell with that," Damien shouted, enraged, ignoring the fact that he was drawing attention to them. "Her process ends tonight."

"Damien."

"Don't. You stay out of it, Keefe. I'm not a lab rat or a psychology experiment. I'm her damn husband and she's going to have to learn to deal with that. She can process that information."

"Mia doesn't do well with fighting. She'll just tune you out."

"That sounds a hell of a lot better than processing me out. Hell, fighting with Mia right now sounds exactly like what we both need.

She needs to know that we can fight and I'm still going to be there."
He shook Keefe's hand. "Thanks, man. And don't look so worried. I
think you actually helped."

"So what are you going to do now, save her?" Keefe asked.

"No, she's going to save the both of us. I love Mia and I know that
she loves me. I have no intention on being someone that she just learns
to tolerate."

Damien could hardly wait. He'd seen Mia for all of five minutes
when he'd gone home to shower and change before going to the club.
Tonight would be the night they would initiate his process. He was
tired of sleeping alone.

"Ashleigh, thanks for letting me come over." Damien hugged her
and kissed her forehead. "I'm glad I didn't manage to throw away our
friendship."

He smiled at her, at the irony that he was coming to her, the
woman he'd screwed over royally, for help with the woman he loved.
But he had to ask some questions of a woman he'd been involved with,
and Ashleigh was the one he'd chosen.

"Listen, I just wanted to ask you, did I ever hurt you?" He watched
as she squinted her eyes and frowned at him. "I mean, physically, when
we, well, when we were together. Did I hurt you?"

"No," Ashleigh answered and Damien knew she was more than a
little curious. He looked down. "Did I...I mean...was I okay?"

Ashleigh laughed. "I don't believe you're asking me that. I think sex
is sex until you find somebody that you love. Then it becomes making
love. You and I had sex. Keefe and I make love." She looked at him
sharply, "Like I'm sure you make love with Mia. As for the sex, it was
good. Why?"

Damien squirmed. He wasn't going to tell Ashleigh everything.
He'd already gotten the information that he came for.

"No reason. Thanks, Ash."

"That's it?"

"Yeah, I guess I should go home now."

"Wait a minute, Damien. I don't know if I should say anything about this or not, but there is a chance that Mia might know what happened with her mother at the wedding."

"How?" Damien faltered. "I didn't tell anyone but you. Did you say something to Mia?"

"Not her, I told Keefe."

He stared at her. "Why?"

"He called me when you were in Vegas and he demanded to know. He said it was important. I got the feeling that Mia had called him, that something was wrong; maybe the two of you had a fight or something. He never told me but I just thought you should know."

"Yeah, thanks," he said as he walked to the door. He hugged her close for a second, then let her go.

"Good luck, Damien. I hope everything works out with you and Mia. Now I know that even when you love someone you can still have problems. Keefe and I," she smiled. "Even you and Mia. If anyone should have had smooth sailing, I would have put my money on the two of you."

"Don't give up on us just yet. I have no plans on throwing in the towel. Thanks, Ash." He waved and headed home.

Damien stuck his key into the lock, praying that what he was about to do would work. He knew one thing for certain. What they had done thus far definitely hadn't worked. "Mia," he called out. "Are you awake?"

"Your dinner is on the stove," she answered.

Damien looked toward the kitchen. If he'd needed a cook he could have gone to any restaurant. He marched into her bedroom and stood there staring down at the surprised look on her face.

"Why the surprise? This isn't the eighteenth century. Surely you expected to see me in here at some point."

"What's wrong?" Mia asked. "Are you okay?"

"No, baby girl, I'm not okay."

Damien scooped Mia up into his arms, ignoring her protests, her look of sheer panic. He carried her to his bed. "We're married, Mia. I didn't get married so that I could sleep alone." He unceremoniously dumped her on the bed, then sat beside her. "You're my wife. From now on you sleep in my bed."

"But—"

"No buts, Mia. Is that clear? You sleep beside me, in this bed, from now on."

She didn't answer and he wanted her to. Damien wanted to fight but the tears forming in Mia's eyes pushed the fight right out of him and he turned away from her. "I can't do this," he said quietly.

"Can't do what?" she asked.

"This," he pointed toward the bed. "This caveman routine. I can't do it. I can't understand what happened, why you stopped loving me, but I can't force you to love me and I sure as hell can't force you to make love to me."

He turned to her again, "Not with that look of fear in your eyes. Mia, just tell me what I did or what you think I did that made you stop loving me?"

"I haven't stopped loving you," Mia answered.

He watched as the tears slid slowly down her cheeks and he traced one with the tip of his finger. "Then why the tears? You keep telling me nothing is wrong but you cry if I just look at you."

"Tell me where you were tonight before you came home," Mia whispered.

He shook his head slowly, trying to understand what his wife was asking. "You know where I was. I was working at the club."

"I mean after you left the club, where were you?"

He glanced at the clock and cringed. He'd taken a little longer than he'd thought talking to Ashleigh.

"Mia, I haven't done anything wrong. I swear it."

"Then tell me where you were."

She waited and when he didn't answer, she looked at him and said softly, "Alright, then I'll tell you. I smelled the perfume when you picked me up. It's Ashleigh's. I recognize the scent."

"Do you think I'm screwing around on you? Is that what this is about?"

Now Mia was ready to talk. She swiped at the tears on her face. "You're changing the subject. Tell me you weren't just with Ashleigh, that she wasn't in your arms. She had to be close to you to leave her scent."

Damien groaned. How the hell could he tell his bride what he'd gone to Ashleigh for? "I went to see her as a friend. She gave me a hug, that's it."

"Was my brother there?"

He knew where this was leading. He took a deep breath and sighed. "No, Keefe wasn't there. I called Ashleigh earlier and asked her if there was a way that she could be alone, that I needed someone to talk to."

He saw Mia wince and he got angry. This was all her fault. Why the hell did he have to explain anything?

"She agreed, as a friend, Mia. She listened to me and yes, she hugged me. And she didn't have the look in her eyes that you do now, that she was afraid that I was going to rape her."

Damien didn't know what had happened but knew his own fears, that he wasn't good enough for Mia, that she wouldn't make love to him because he'd failed to satisfy her, were very close to the surface. His heart lurched within his chest and his worst fear, that Mia didn't love him any longer, surfaced. That he couldn't accept. He was determined to make her remember, to make her love him again. He reached for her and crushed her to him, thrusting his tongue into her mouth. Then he fell on her and pushed her flimsy nightgown above her hips and shoved his fingers roughly inside her.

"Damien." She was whimpering and somehow her arms were wound around his neck. "I do love you. I've never stopped. How can you think that?"

It was her words that brought control back to him and he released her. "You still love me?" he repeated, doubt making his voice husky.

"Of course I do."

"Then tell me what the hell is going on. For nearly a year we haven't been able to keep our hands off each other. Now you cringe whenever I get near. Just talk to me, Mia, tell me what I did wrong. You said I didn't hurt you. Then why won't you let me make love to you? Why does my touch make you cry?"

"It's not you," Mia answered. "It's nothing you've done. "It's me. I'm trying to deal with it. I just need a little more time."

"That's just it. You need a little more time to tolerate my touching you? You're shutting me out, Mia. We should be working through this together. I don't want to be a job for you, or a patient that you're learning how to handle. Trust me to help, trust our love." He reached for her again but this time when she moved away so did he.

Damien stood and frowned, "I love you, Mia, and I want to work things out but you're going to have to help me. I meant what I said. You're not sleeping in a different bed. You're my wife."

"Are you saying you're going to just do it, no mater how I feel?"

With more control than he knew he possessed, Damien turned to face Mia who was still on the bed and looking at him strangely. He'd never felt such anger or such love.

"That would make me less than a dog. I have no plans on raping you." He thought he saw a flash of relief in her eyes. "I know you're inexperienced and I have no idea what's going on in your head, especially since you won't talk to me, but I do know that what we did was perfectly normal. There may have been pain, but I didn't rape you, Mia. I know I didn't. One other thing. I also have no plans on staying celibate." He saw her wince again and knew he'd hurt her.

Good, he thought as he marched out of the room into the bathroom. He held his fingers to his nostrils and breathed in his wife's scent. A deep longing filled him as he washed it away.

Mia needed help. She knew that. Treating herself wasn't working. She hadn't called her therapist as a patient for years but she needed someone to talk to her, to help her enforce the things she already knew. She needed someone to help her exorcise her nightmares. She needed someone to help her save her marriage.

Damien thought she'd stopped loving him. That she thought he'd raped her. Why shouldn't he? She knew that was the way she'd been behaving. She had really tried getting her fears under control. She'd tried to be strong, to go it alone but the stakes were now too high for her process. She'd do whatever it took to make her marriage work.

CHAPTER FIFTEEN

It took several weeks and the changes were subtle but Mia felt them. She was glad that Damien had demanded she sleep in the bed beside him. Her therapist had confirmed that he'd made the right move. She'd also suggested that Mia confide in him or bring him to a session. Like that was going to happen. That was the last thing her marriage needed, for her husband to think she needed someone to help his wife be the wife she wanted to be.

It was true. She did, but she wasn't ready to tell him that. She was making progress. Whenever Damien fell sleep she lay on his chest, touching him, kissing and caressing him. She fell asleep each night curled around him and only moved away when he woke in the morning.

Damien lay as still as he could, barely breathing. For the past several nights Mia had begun touching him as he slept, kissing him, whispering words of love to him. At first he'd thought to confront her but she'd always moved away when he made the slightest movement. And at least she was touching him, so he didn't say anything. When the alarm went off, he pretended to wake, knowing that as he did Mia was going to move away.

He sat up and looked down at her. Damien was tired of what they were doing, how they were behaving. He felt they were suffocating in the apartment. He knew they needed to get out, to at least return some form of normalcy to their lives. He stared at her a moment longer until she stopped the pretense and opened her eyes.

"Mia, we're going to stop behaving as hermits. We're going to my mother's for dinner tonight. She called and I accepted." He waited for her to object.

"Is it just your mother?"

"Yes."

"What time?"

"As soon as I come home and shower."

Mia licked her lips and he waited for her to try and get out of it but she didn't. At least that was some progress.

When they arrived at his mother's home, Mia shocked Damien by putting her hand in his as they walked toward the door.

"Is this for show?" he couldn't help asking.

"I don't want to have everyone asking questions. We've only been married a few weeks. I don't want your mother to think we're fighting," Mia answered.

"Damn, Mia, couldn't you have just said you wanted to hold my hand?" He dropped her hand. "Until you want to touch me because you want to, don't do it. I don't give a damn what my mother says or think. I'm not putting on an act for her or for anyone," he said, walking ahead of her. "And you might as well get used to us going out, because we're going to start living. Do you understand?"

"Damien, I'm not your child."

"No, but you're my wife."

"You can't order me around."

Damien glared at Mia. "We can finish the fight here or we can take it up when we get home." Just then his mother opened the door and Mia sailed past him.

"Your choice," Mia answered. "I don't care."

She was angry and the knowledge nearly made Damien smile. Her anger was better than her apathy. At least she was behaving as if she were still alive.

"You two fighting?" Kathy asked when dessert was served and Mia had not spoken more than ten words.

"Yes," Mia answered, "your son seems under the mistaken opinion that marrying me meant he became my father. He thinks he issues orders and I am just to obey them."

"How could I have that impression?" Damien came back. "Keefe already holds that title."

"I'm getting sick to death of hearing you throw my brother's name up every time something doesn't go your way." She stood up. "I'm ready to go."

Kathy started laughing and Mia turned toward her. Her anger was rapidly spreading to include Kathy. "I'm happy to know that we're amusing you." Mia reined in her temper, trying not to allow all of her anger at Damien and herself to spill out on Kathy.

"I'm just thinking that I told you how it was going to be and you didn't believe me. I warned you that Damien is just like his father."

Mia frowned. "What are you talking about?"

"Your fighting. I can figure out what it is. Damien is running the streets and doesn't want you questioning him about it. I knew it."

Mia continued frowning. She glanced toward Damien and saw the sadness in her husband's face.

"You've got it wrong, Kathy. Damien is not running around." She glanced again at her husband and pain pierced her heart for what his mother had done to him and for what she herself was doing to him. He didn't deserve it nor did he deserve the bad rap. Well, that was one thing she could and would take care of. Mia had already told Dr. Grey that she was ready to try and make love with Damien again. Despite their fighting, or maybe because of it, tonight would be a good time to take charge of her life.

"Kathy, it's not Damien who's causing the problem. It's me. He's been the best, most patient husband that I could have asked for. He hasn't done any of the things that you said. You just gave me the wake-up call that I needed." She turned her attention to her husband. "Damien, can we go now?"

When they were inside the car, Mia turned to Damien. "I'm sorry for making you live this way." His face was hard and his jaw was clenched. He wasn't answering her.

"Damien, I love you. I want to work things out." She kissed his cheek and ignored his pushing her away.

"Mia, I'm not a yo-yo. You can't keep pushing me away, then pulling me back when you want."

"I'm not going to push you away anymore. You can count on that."

Damien held both her hands in his, his breath ragged. He couldn't look at her, he didn't dare hope. "Unless you mean what I'm taking this to mean, then stop right now. I can't take anymore of this. So you either mean it, or move over to your side of the car. You don't have to feel sorry for me that my mother is happy thinking I screwed up. I'm used to it, Mia. I've put up with it my entire life."

She pulled her hands from his grasp and held his face between them, her eyes probing the depths of his. Her lips claimed his as she closed her eyes and held on to him, hoping that he'd forgive her, that she was still in his heart. He clutched her to him and their tongues battled for dominance. She felt his heat, intense and urgent and she felt her own answering his. Their hearts beat a pattern, and their needs quickly turned to lust. They groped each other's body, trying desperately to reclaim what they'd lost.

"Damn it, Mia," Damien said, pushing her away. "We're not kids. We're not doing this, not this way, in the car. We have a bed at home." He looked at her. "Are you ready to go home?"

"Yes," she answered and snuggled against him as his arms came around her.

"What's been going on, baby girl! What happened?"

"Not now, no talking, just us. I don't want to think about anything but now."

In a matter of minutes they had returned home, were undressed, and Damien was kissing Mia hard, clutching her to him. "Last chance," he moaned. "If we make love now we're not going back to what it was before."

"I don't want it like it was before."

Before the words had completely left her mouth she felt Damien plunge into her hot and heavy. She felt the same stab of pain as she had the first time and tensed a moment before forcing her body to relax. She threw her arms around him and arched her hips to meet his thrusts. It surprised her when after several grunts Damien growled and stiffened.

They were going to be okay, she thought. She'd not seen any pictures. She hadn't felt the unwanted comparison to her mother. Then again, there hadn't been time. It had happened so quickly. A tear of gratitude slid beneath her lashes. They would get better together. For now she'd gotten through the hard part. She and Damien were in their bed.

Damien opened his eyes in time to see the tear on Mia's face. He'd thought she'd wanted him. A horrible thought struck him. She had wanted him. He'd just failed to satisfy her. He wiped the tear away from her face. "So this is what pity sex feels like?" And he got up and walked away.

Mia's eyes opened wide and she stared in disbelief at her husband's retreating back and cried in earnest. This time she couldn't blame images of her mother. It was her. Damien wasn't satisfied with her.

For the next few weeks they continued in that fashion, Damien turning to Mia at night, her hoping this would be the night that he'd hold her afterwards, but he never did. In fact, it seemed to her that the time he was in her became shorter, as if he couldn't stand the thought of making love to her. Now there were no longer even the hungry kisses before or any attempts at caresses. He just entered her, did what he had to do, got up and left the room, leaving her in tears. Inadvertently, Mia had begun cringing when he came near her, afraid that if he touched her, he would move away. She couldn't bear that. Having him move away from her in bed was bad enough.

Damien's key entered the lock and Mia looked at the clock. Two a.m. He was staying longer and longer at the club. They couldn't continue like this. She knew it. They had to talk, had to make it right.

Mia sat on the edge of the bed waiting for her husband to come into the bedroom. "You're awake," Damien said to her as he came in and saw her perched there.

"Yeah, I am," she answered.

"Why?" She looked up at him, her look speaking to him of the vulnerability and pain in his heart. Usually Mia was asleep when he came home or at least lying in the bed in the dark. Then Damien could come to her, enter her body and not witness the sadness in his wife's face. Then he could pretend for a few minutes at a time that things were as they should be with them. But with her sitting there facing him, he couldn't pretend. He headed to the kitchen, then thought better of it. Damien turned back and walked to Mia, dropping to his knees. He encircled her waist with his hands.

"Don't look at me like that, Mia. I'm not going to hurt you." He pulled at her, his pulling bringing her closer to the edge of the bed, closer to him.

"What happened to us, Mia? I don't understand. You loved me when you said *I do*." He closed his eyes and lowered his head to her lap.

"I still love you."

"You keep saying that you love me, but I gotta tell you, baby girl, you sure have a hell of a way of showing it. And frankly I don't believe that you do. I think I deserve a truthful answer. What happened? What did I do?"

He felt the shudder that claimed her body but he didn't move from his position. Then her hands were on his head and she was caressing him.

"You have to believe me. I didn't stop loving you, Damien, not even for a second. How could I? You're a part of my soul."

"Then what?" He raised his head and looked into her eyes. "We were so damn good together, so hot for each other." He winced. "Now you can't stand my touch."

"That's not true."

"Yes, it is," he insisted. "You cringe whenever I come near. I've done my best to make it quick for you. I know you hate it."

"I don't."

"Don't lie to me, Mia."

Mia looked down. "I don't hate your touching me."

"You don't like it."

"I do," Mia said again and Damien's mouth dropped in surprise. He glared at her before getting up. He strode angrily about the room, returning to glare at her once more. "Please don't lie to me. I've been with enough…" He stopped himself. "You've never had an orgasm, Mia. Don't lie and tell me that you have."

"That doesn't mean that I don't enjoy it." She looked away from him. "What little there is."

Damien stared at his wife. If he went crazy she would be the cause. "Mia, what's going on? How about telling me? I'm sure you've told your brother and I don't like that your brother knows more about what's going on in our bed than I do."

"Keefe doesn't know."

Hope flared in his chest. "Then you're telling me that there is a reason?" God, what he wouldn't give to know why Mia had suddenly turned cold. At least with a reason he stood a chance. He shook his head and blinked. He had to stop glaring at her.

"Are you going to tell me what's going on, Mia?"

"I want to. I tried to."

"Then try again. I'm tired of living like this. This is not how I envisioned our life together." He saw her cringe. "Are you afraid of me? What the hell did I do to bring this on?"

"It's not you, Damien. It's me. We both know it. She shook her head and closed her eyes. "I've studied about it. I've counseled people with similar symptoms, but couldn't cure myself." She gazed at him. "I know you're tired of this, of the way I've been acting and you have every right to be. I don't blame you if you want to leave me. I know I haven't done anything to make you want to stay. To tell you the truth, I'm pretty tired of our living like this myself."

Her voice was so sad but it was her words that struck fear in his heart. "Leave you? Hell, Mia, I never thought about leaving you for a minute."

"You didn't?"

"Of course I didn't. Why would you even think that?"

"My mother...she always left."

"I'm not Lillian, baby. I'm not going anywhere, I promise," Damien said. "I'm in this for the long haul." He reached out his hand and pulled it back. "I just want to fix the problem. But I need to know what the problem is."

"I've wanted to tell you for weeks. I'm so ashamed of what happened. I thought if I told you, you would laugh at me or think that I was crazy. I didn't think you would understand what was happening. I barely understand it myself."

He pulled her by the hand to the bed and sat beside her. "Talk to me, Mia. I promise I won't laugh and I won't think you're crazy. Tell me what happened."

"In Vegas when we made love..."

"I definitely want to know what happened in Vegas, but what happened started before we got there. There was something wrong with you the day of our wedding. As much as I want to hear what happened when we made love I think I need to hear it all. Start at the beginning and tell me everything. I know whatever it is happened on our wedding day and if I did do something to you, something that I don't remember, I want to know what it was."

She laid her head on his cheek before she began. "Remember before we married and you wanted to make love, I told you I wasn't a slut? I never told you why not being one was so important to me." She sniffled. "You told me that our making love once we were married was fine. But I never told you why I was so worried about that."

"Honestly, I thought you were just kidding. You know…just wanting to make me stop. I never believed you really thought that. Are you saying making love with me made you feel like a slut?"

"Yes," Mia whispered.

"Why?"

"My mother. I didn't want to be like her ever."

Damien blinked before rubbing a finger gently down Mia's cheek. "Explain, baby."

"You saw how she behaved, how she was always trying to touch you, how she flirted with your father and Jerry. I've told you how many men she's had. What else do I need to say?"

"A lot more than that."

"I'm doing as you asked, Damien. I'm telling you from the beginning, but it's really the reverse of what happened. It was our making love that made me think of all the other things that had happened that day."

"The sequence doesn't matter. I just need you to tell me everything that happened that day." Mia started sobbing and Damien wanted to stop her, tell her she didn't have to say any more. But that wouldn't do either of them any good. She needed to get it out and he needed to hear it.

"During our reception when I went looking for you it was because of some awful things I heard my mother saying. I heard her telling Jerry that you were going to dump me. She said that she wished she could see your face when you tried to make love to me."

"I'm sorry about all that, baby, but your mother, she's not quite right. She has a problem, it's so obvious. The stuff she told you was garbage. I told you that. I thought we'd put it all behind us."

"So did I. She just has a way of getting to me that no one else has. I overheard her say you were dancing with her and you got an erection." Mia's eyes closed. "I knew in my heart it wasn't true, so I went looking for you and found you with Ashleigh. You didn't even see me. I stood there watching you and you didn't even look my way." She sniffled some more and looked away.

Damien was beginning to understand. Things were at last beginning to make some sense. "That's why you were in the bathroom crying and why Keefe was so damn angry?" He frowned. "There has to be something else. Granted you were upset then, but we went and cut the cake and you were smiling. I can't remember everything but I do remember you were happy when we first went up to the room. I can see your face perfectly and when you went into the bathroom to change you were happy. What happened then?"

"Nothing. It was just that when I came out you were sleeping. I tried to wake you. I couldn't believe it was our wedding night and you'd gone to sleep."

"I passed out."

"But it was like I couldn't hold your interest long enough for you to...to...and on our wedding night."

"It wasn't you, baby. I was tired and you were taking so damn long in that bathroom that I just passed out, that's all. Believe me, I wanted you."

"It didn't feel like it. Then there was the gift, the wedding gift you gave me. I couldn't believe it, a porno tape, *Fifty Ways to Please Your Lover.*"

"Mia, it was a joke."

"I think I knew that but I was...I was...doubting myself. I was so afraid and I didn't know of what. I was so mean to you, that stunt I pulled, my virgin sacrifice. I just needed you to hold me. When you wanted to do what we'd both been waiting for, I just got angry. It kind of felt like you did marry me only to have sex."

"Was it because of the tape?"

"No, I had decided to forgive you for that. It just wasn't the gift I had in mind."

"What did you have in mind?"

"Jewelry, sexy lingerie," she smiled, then shrugged. "I was mostly disappointed."

He stared hard at her. "Okay, that brings us to Vegas, just the two of us. After we fought and I came back to the room we were fine. You wanted me to make love to you, Mia, didn't you?"

She looked deep into his eyes before answering. "Yes, I wanted it as much as you did."

"Then it seems the real problem has something to do with me. I was making love to you. You pushed me off and ran crying into the bathroom. I have to tell you, baby girl, that's definitely not a confidence builder. Then on top of that, we get home and you sleep in a separate room. Every time I've tried to figure it out, it all comes down to my making love to you. Tell me what happened while I was making love to you." His voice was hoarse and he was hurting, but determined to hear the truth.

"You said I was a natural. That was the worst thing you could have said to me. My entire life, I've struggled not to become like my mother, and on the most important day of my life you practically said that I was her."

"Mia, I did no such thing."

"Like I said, Damien, it wasn't you. It was me. That's what I heard. We both know what my mother is, why pretend? Only a slut would try to hit on her daughter's man." Mia held her hand up to stop any protest from Damien.

"I was enjoying everything we were doing, Damien, really I was. I think maybe I was enjoying it too much. When you said what you did, all at once I felt I was like her…a slut. I was trying so hard to handle it but the more I enjoyed it the worst I felt. When I looked at you, in my mind I saw every man my mother had been with. And I knew I had turned into her. I couldn't look at you, so I closed my eyes. I tried to block the pictures out but I couldn't."

"You had a vision?" He shook his head a little.

"It wasn't a vision, Damien, it was a mental picture. Once the images started, my fear took over. It snowballed and got out of control. The only thing I could think to make it stop, was to make you stop."

"Why didn't you tell me that then, when I was going crazy thinking I had hurt you, that you hated me, that you thought…that you thought." He swallowed. "That you thought I'd raped you."

"I never thought that, but I couldn't tell you because I felt so dirty. And despite my feelings I wanted to do it again. I was so afraid that if you came near me I would give in to those feeling and I would be even more like her."

"Mia, there was nothing wrong with us making love. I'm overjoyed to know that you were enjoying it. All this time I thought you hated it, hated my touching you."

"No, Damien. I never hated it. Besides, I managed to work most of it out in my head, and with the help of my therapist. I knew our being intimate wasn't dirty, that it was normal, but by the time I came to that conclusion we had another problem. When we started back to…to doing it, I thought you hated making love to me. You did it so fast, never caressing me, none of the passion was there. And you got up so quickly and left the room that I thought you were disappointed in me. I thought I couldn't compete with all the women you'd had."

A lump was trying to work its way to her throat. She refused to allow it to stop her from finally telling Damien, what she should have told him weeks before.

"I've been trying to work through this also. But I kept thinking of all the things you'd said to me before we got married, how you kept saying you wanted me. And now that you had me, now that I wasn't a virgin anymore, you didn't seem to want me. Everything came flooding at me, including all the things my mother had said. It was all more than I could handle."

She began crying in earnest and Damien allowed her to cry it out. He hugged her to him, thankful to have her in his arms, tears and all.

"Mia, do you still think I married you just so I can sleep with you?"

She didn't answer.

"Mia, I love you."

Still she didn't answer."

"Mia, why did you marry me?"

"Because you complete me. You're the other part of my soul."

"And that's why I married you, baby girl. You complete me."

"But I don't make you happy."

"You're talking about in bed?"

"Yeah. I can tell. You always look so sad when you leave the room."

"And you thought that was because…" Damien sighed. "We should have talked. Every time I've…" He hated to say 'made love' because he didn't feel that he ever had.

"Mia, I thought you were only sleeping with me because you felt sorry for me, for the things my mother said. As much as I wanted you, I thought that you didn't really want me."

He held her gaze for a long time. "I just wanted to do it as quickly as possible. Then when I was done, I couldn't stand the thought of your not wanting me. That was the reason I left the room. You were always crying afterwards."

He took in a couple of deep breaths, then let them out in relief as he held Mia close to him. "Baby, you weren't the only one fighting demons. Hell, my mother said a lot of stuff to me just the same as she did to you, but I didn't believe it for a second. But I would have had to be a fool not to see that you didn't want me. Knowing that, knowing I couldn't satisfy you, do you know what that was doing to me? I never in a million years expected us to have such a problem."

Damien ran his hands through his hair, tugging on the long braids. "So neither of us has been satisfied with our relationship. Is that a fair statement?"

"Yes, I'd say it's a fair statement," Mia answered.

Damien stroked her cheeks, his love for her overwhelming him. "Do you want to know why I wasn't satisfied?" He waited while Mia nodded her head and looked down. He lifted her chin so that she was looking at him. "It's because I wasn't truly making love to you. All the passion we had for each other appeared to have evaporated somewhere along the line. Did I get off? Yes, but that wasn't all that I wanted. I wanted to soar to the clouds and I wanted to take you with me."

"And I wanted to go," Mia answered. "That first day in Vegas when you were touching me, I'd wanted it for so long. I loved your touching me, until…"

"Until you became afraid, until you thought I was comparing you with your mother, until you thought you were a slut. I never thought that Mia, never for a fraction of a second"

"But you stopped acting as though you think I'm special," she whispered. "I didn't know how to make you touch me again. I've been thinking, even though you meant it as a joke, maybe I should watch the tape, maybe it would help."

"Where is that tape I gave you, Mia? We need to clear that up now."

"In my suitcase."

"Go get it. I have a feeling you didn't even take it out of the box."

Mia went for the tape and Damien went to the kitchen and splashed cold water on his face. He couldn't believe it. He and Mia had talked about everything before they were married but this. The most important thing and they'd both clammed up. He remembered her saying once that she didn't want to be a slut, but he hadn't taken it seriously. How could he? She was a virgin for God's sake. He flexed his hands and walked to the sofa to wait for his bride. Okay, he could handle this. Together they would fix it. At least she still loved him. Mia handed over the still partially wrapped box.

"Take the tape out, Mia."

He waited while she looked at the envelope that was there. The surprise on her face told him that she'd never seen it before.

"Read it," he said.

Fifty Ways to Please Your Lover: Mia, you've covered every one of them by marrying me. I love you, baby girl, and I promise to try and use all fifty ways to please you. We have nothing to worry about, Mia. Our love will see us though any problems.

"Why didn't you tell me?" Mia whispered.

"Why didn't you read it?" Damien countered. I never meant for you to think you were lacking, I only meant the tape as a joke. I was stupid for not taking your worries more seriously." He stared at his bride for a moment, realizing what this meant. "Come here." He saw her trembling. "Why are you trembling? What's that about?"

"I've missed you so much," she answered and threw her arms around him.

And he was holding her close to his heart. "God, I've missed you too." He pulled back, traced her lips with the pad of one finger. Then he dipped her and kissed her. Damien kissed his wife with all the hunger that was in him, like a man denied food for so long who was suddenly presented with a banquet. He didn't think he would ever get his fill of her.

When he finally came up for air, he knew they would be okay. His wife loved him as he loved her. She always had. She was still trembling and so was he. With passion.

CHAPTER SIXTEEN

Damien felt as if a two ton Mack truck had been lifted from his shoulders. For months he hadn't been able to believe the path his marriage had taken. It had been like a bad dream, one he was praying constantly to wake from. And now that the dream was over Damien was ready for all the hard work ahead. He would give his all into rebuilding their relationship into what it should be.

He started laughing and Mia joined in. They danced around hugging each other, not stopping until they collapsed on the floor. Then and only then did Damien pull her into his lap. "Baby girl, we've got a lot of talking to do." He kissed her lightly at first, then deepened it until he felt the shiver of desire from Mia. Her response erased any lingering uncertainty. She wanted him still. He stared at her. "Wow!"

"Now do you believe me?" Mia said softly. "You've always had that effect on me." She attempted to pull him toward the bedroom. "I think we need to make up for lost time."

As much as Damien wanted to, he knew they needed to talk, to get everything said and put it behind them.

"Mia, you said you tried to cure yourself. How?"

"I knew I had to let go of the pictures in my mind. I knew you had nothing to do with that. Still, I had to work through it. I wanted you to make love to me."

"It was going to be pretty damn hard to do that in separate rooms."

"I know. I was secretly glad that you made me come into our bed. I loved lying next to you." She smiled shyly. "I'd lie on you when you slept."

Damien surprised her. "I know. All the times I wasn't asleep. Since you wouldn't touch me any other way, I took what I could get. You said you couldn't cure yourself. What did you do?"

"I started seeing a therapist."

"It helped?"

"I got rid of the pictures. And I know that what we were doing wasn't dirty."

He stared. "So, how come?"

"I thought it was too late. I didn't know. Like I said, I thought you couldn't stand making love to me," she whispered.

"Is that why you didn't want to go out with me? I could understand not wanting to go out to dinner with my pops, but you stopped coming to the club to hear me sing. I didn't know what the hell was going on."

"Damien, I kept thinking about what your father said the morning after our wedding when he asked if I was worth the wait. I knew I wasn't worth the wait and I couldn't stand having anyone know that I wasn't, not your parents, not mine and not my brother." She paused, making sure Damien understood. "I never told Keefe everything."

"You were worth the wait, baby. Believe me, you were always worth the wait."

She looked down. "Are you sure?"

"I'm sure." For once he wished that he didn't get an immediate erection around Mia, but that couldn't be helped. Still he could control it. As much as he wanted to take his wife into the bedroom and make love to her, they still had unfinished business.

"Mia, between the two of us, we're pretty well screwed up. My entire life I've been doing the same thing you tried doing with your brother and your mother. Be the peacemaker. And it didn't really work in either of our cases. My father molded me after himself. He doesn't hate you, Mia, it's what you represent in my life. He knows how much you mean to me. He knows that I don't want to live without you and he's trying to ruin it."

"Why?" Mia asked, then remembered she already knew that. "Don't answer that. I already know."

"From the time I could talk I think my pops started training me how to mack. Hell, it was fun. I'm not going to lie and tell you I didn't enjoy it or the power I seemed to have over women. I'm not even going to try and tell you that I didn't enjoy the sex because I did. For most of my life I didn't give a damn. I didn't expect to ever give a damn. Before you the only woman I truly loved was my mother. But things did start to change with Ashleigh. I cared about her. I wasn't in love with her but she was a good friend to me and it bothered me that I was treating her like crap. Not enough to stop, but enough that I noticed. That's when I really started seeing just how unhappy my mother was and I knew it was due largely to my pops, but I had a little to do with that too. I was hurting her when I hurt women. I'm not going to tell you that I had some big ass plans the day I met you. I was just out on the streets and I wanted Ashleigh to take me back, at least until I could find someplace to go."

"But you moved home."

"And do you really think I wanted to do that? I took a lot from my old man for making that move. And I had to put up with hearing what my mother had to say."

"Then why did you do it?"

"Because of you. When I met you I knew my life had changed. I wanted so much for you to stay in my life, and it wasn't just to sleep with you. You were the first person who ever told me that I was special. You knew I was a dog and you still said I was special. I wanted to become that for you."

"You didn't have to become special, Damien. You were when I met you."

"No, I wasn't. My mom was right. I was like my pops. I wanted to be the man you saw. That's what kept me going, that's what kept me faithful. That was what I was counting on when we finally came together. I wanted to prove to you that I was worth your time. Baby, you weren't the one my father should have asked that question of. He should have asked you if I was worth the wait. You would have told him, '*Hell no, the brother passed out on me.*'" Damien laughed and hugged Mia close. "I wish we had talked about this sooner," he said.

"So do I," Mia answered. "Now that we have, don't you think we should make up for lost time?" She touched his face, felt his jaw stiffen, felt his flesh beneath her jerk. "We've solved all our problems. Now I want the feel of your hands on my body. I want to feel what I've been missing all these weeks."

Damien groaned and shut his eyes tightly. He held onto Mia with strength that was slowing giving away to hunger. He couldn't believe the thought that was formulating in his mind, what he was about to suggest.

"Mia, I don't want you to have any doubts about us, about me."

"I don't, not anymore," she answered.

"I think we should wait."

"Wait?" Mia shrieked. "We've waited so long already. We know what the problems are."

Damien buried his lips in Mia's soft flesh and moaned, holding on to her ever tighter, his erection painful and growing more massive with each throb.

"I want to help you banish all your ghosts, baby, for good. If we make love now, you may still doubt. I don't want you to ever doubt my reasons for marrying you again."

"But I don't."

He couldn't help laughing. "You're horny, baby girl, so am I." He groaned again as Mia moved against his erection. He closed his eyes as feelings of pleasure flooded him. "This isn't about lust. This is about love and I need to prove to you that for me there is a difference."

"You don't have to. I don't care. I want you and I want to make love with you."

Damien groaned and pulled Mia to him again. "God, I'm glad we're finally talking. How about if we call this my wedding gift to you, to make up for the one that you hated?"

"I hate this one too."

"Hell, so do I."

"Then why do it?"

"I need to prove to you that it's you."

"You sure you're not trying to prove it to yourself?"

"Maybe just a little. Come on, I can't possibly do this without your help."

"Damien, I've waited so long to feel all the things you promised me I would feel. I don't want to help, not in this."

She was killing him. "Mia," he licked her neck, biting it just at the hollow. "What if I can guarantee you that after this, no matter what your mother or my mother or father or anyone says you'll be able to smile and never doubt our love ever again? What if I tell you that you will never think anything the two of us do in our bed is dirty? Would it be worth it to wait?"

She shivered in his arms, not wanting to answer.

"Come on, baby girl, would it be worth the wait?" He moaned and captured her lips, slaving them with his tongue. "Help me, baby girl."

"I want to help you," Mia answered. "But you won't let me." She rotated her hip and ground herself into his erection and felt her husband shudder. His hands went down to her hips, holding her there, helping with the movements, prolonging the contact. She twisted her head and contented herself with sucking on his tongue. Her entire body was on fire. Damien had to be crazy. "Let me help you, Damien," she whispered into his mouth. "Let me help both of us." She felt his hand go beneath her gown. His shudder moved into her body and enveloped her. His head quickly followed the path of his hand. His lips closed over her nipple and spasms of red hot desire coursed through her veins. "Make love to me, Damien."

"Stop, Mia," Damien ground out between clenched teeth, moving his head from underneath her gown and shaking it. "Believe it or not, we need to wait more than we need this."

"I don't believe you."

"God, you've got me so damn crazy, I don't know if I believe me." But somewhere in the back of his brain rational thought was taking place. "Please, Mia," he moaned. Please stop. I can't take much more of this. Come on, you're a professional. Help me. If we were patients of yours, what would you advise?"

She laughed. "I don't know."

"Yeah, you do. Think about it."

"I guess I would agree that if there was even the hint of a trust issue it has to be resolved."

"And?"

"And I'd say marriage was a lot more than sex, that maybe they should work on their emotions without the sex clouding things up."

"That's true. Wanting you has made me blind to everything. If I hadn't wasted so much time thinking that you didn't want me, maybe I would have seen why it was that you didn't."

He held her still on his lap and whispered in her ear, "Stop moving. What else?"

"I'd tell them to trust in their love, that if it is true love, it will be there when they're ready for it."

"Good," Damien said. "Go on."

"I would probably say something like, 'Learn to please each other. Touch first, let it go from there." Mia answered reluctantly, knowing what Damien was going to do with the information.

"I like that idea," he said.

She couldn't believe her ears. "You're saying you want to go back to not making love?"

"Remember, we haven't been making love, Mia." She blushed and he kissed her forehead. "Why don't we do that? Why don't we find out what touches make each other happy? Want to give it a try?"

She smiled at him. "Yeah, let's try." She reached for his hand but he ignored it and lifted her into his arms.

"We'll start slow." He kissed her deeply, feeling the heat shoot through his loins, wondering what the hell he was getting himself into now. For the first time in weeks Mia was in his arms willingly. He knew she loved him, wanted his touch, and he'd been fool enough to tell her that he was willing to take it slow. Damn.

He carried her to the bed, knowing Mia needed the reassurance of knowing that he wanted more from her. He needed it too, needed to know that his worth to his wife had nothing or at least little to do with his abilities to please her in bed. That could come in time. He'd put so much emphasis on it that, hell, it was a wonder he'd even been able to get it up.

No wonder his bride had worried after all of his boasting. He must have been crazy thinking his telling her of his prior conquests would ease her mind. He was damned lucky that she wanted him at all. There was only one woman he really wanted to please and that was Mia. He wanted to please her in bed and out. He would take it as slow as he had to.

"What do you want the first thing to be?" Damien asked. He laid her on the bed and felt her tremble.

"You okay?" he asked.

"Better than okay," she answered. "I want to touch you, she said softly, "with nothing on, no clothes."

Damien's flesh jerked and he bit his lips. Her hands touching him… Oh yeah, that was definitely not the way to take it slow.

"First I think we should get undressed," he countered, smiling just from the thought of her wanting him. A war waged within him, the same war he'd fought for almost a year of wanting Mia. Now they were married and she wanted him and still he was willing to wait. Too much was at stake.

He stroked Mia's cheek, loving the fact that he knew he could still make her tremble with wanting him. She was the reason he would find the strength to wait, because as powerful as his orgasms had been, the fact that he'd had them alone had diminished the pleasure.

Damien breathed in his wife's scent, loving the slight hint of vanilla she preferred. He made a vow that his wife would have an orgasm very soon, maybe several. He smiled at her, thinking about it. After all, she was behind and he definitely wanted to even the score. He looked at her. "You still okay with this?"

"I'm okay with this," she answered and pulled his shirt off his shoulders. She could barely breathe as his hands unbuttoned each button of her blouse, slowly.

"Mia." Damien groaned and kissed her, the heat flaring up between them. She trembled in his arms and he pulled away. "Who are you seeing?"

"Just you," she answered.

He undid her bra, his hand unsteady. Damien closed his eyes. "Mia, how long are patients usually advised to wait before actual penetration?"

"It depends on the couple. We try to get them to go through a couple of weeks of just touching."

"God, I don't know if I can."

"You don't have to." Mia pulled on his lips. There is no need for us to do this."

"Yeah, I do have to, baby. I want to." She laughed at him. "Okay, I don't want to, but for you I'm more than willing to do this, if it will let you know without a doubt that it's not about the sex."

He licked his lips. "My God, Mia, you're so beautiful, so soft." Without meaning to, he ran his tongue across the tender flesh above her breasts. He saw the fire light in her brown eyes and the haze as they clouded over with lust. Damien shook his head slightly to clear his own lust and a tremble of desire shook him to the core. Damn, this was going to be hard.

"It looks like you're the one getting to do all the touching," Mia chided gently. "Don't I get to participate in this game?"

"Yeah, you get to lie down and let me undress you completely."

She did and he did, and when he lay there naked, with her looking at him, he thought he would come right then and there.

"Mia, you're going to have to stop looking at me that way, okay?"

"What way?"

"That way." He smiled at her. "The look that's telling me that you want me."

"I do."

"I know," Damien groaned.

"Then forget this nonsense and make love to me."

He groaned again. "God, Mia, do you know how long I've waited to hear you say that?" He groaned again, closing his eyes as his entire body trembled. "I think this is a really good idea. If we can get through a couple of weeks of this, we'll have a lifetime of loving. And I meant it when I said I wanted to help you banish all the ghosts." He switched positions, trailing kisses down her body. He paid particular attention to the hollow of her neck, sinking his lips into her soft, sweet-smelling brown flesh. He glanced at her. Her eyes were closed and a slight shiver was evident.

"Open your eyes, Mia. I don't want you seeing anyone but me."

"Turn off the lights," she whispered.

Damien glanced at the light, then back at her, at the way she was avoiding looking at him. "I know what our first lesson will be."

"What?" she asked, still not looking directly at him. "Well, for starters, as much as I want to do other things, I think we're just going to look at each other until you can look at me and have me looking at you without feeling embarrassed. There is no need for shame, baby. We're married."

"I'm not…" She closed her eyes. "I'm not embarrassed."

He laughed softly. "You can't even say that with a straight face unless your eyes are closed. Now come on, open your eyes, look at me."

She reached her hand out to touch his chest and he moved away just a little bit. "You're trying to distract me. No more touching, baby girl, just look at me." He watched as she smiled and did as he asked.

"My turn." His eyes traveled from her face and rested on her breasts and Mia's eyes slid to the side.

"No, Mia, I want you to watch me. I want you to see how beautiful I think you are."

Damien continued until his eyes fell on the "V" between her thighs and a long sigh of longing filled him and he allowed it to escape. Then he fell down on the bed beside Mia and held her.

"That was good, baby," he moaned as he held her tighter. His arousal, having a mind of its own, pulsed and surged, touching any spot on her that it could. They were both trembling by now.

"Damien."

"Don't say anything, baby girl, or there's no way in hell we're going to be able to go through with this."

"Maybe we shouldn't."

"We should stop talking now and just go to sleep. I've been wanting this almost as much. I've waited a year to have you fall asleep in my arms."

Damien couldn't believe it, but they both fell asleep and when they woke in each other's arms, only an actual orgasm would have felt better.

Mia reached for the ham from the fridge and placed it on the counter. She took out the lettuce and tomatoes and every condiment that was there. She was going to make lunch and take it to Damien at Brookfield zoo. She was going to surprise him.

Baby steps, Mia, baby steps. Her hands shook as she attempted to concentrate on the sandwich. She kept smiling as she cut the bread and wrapped it in plastic and put it in a bag. She reached into the fridge again for a soda and hurried down the stairs before she could change her mind.

Mia walked around the zoo, enjoying it as she hadn't since she was a child. She glanced at her watch, not knowing when Damien would be taking a lunch break and wondering if she should have called him.

The hair on the nape of her neck stood on end and she smiled before turning around. Only Damien had that effect on her.

"Mia, baby, is anything wrong?"

"I made you lunch."

"How long have you been here?" Damien asked, moving closer to kiss her. "You may not want to get too close to me. Why didn't you call?"

"I've been here a couple of hours. I wanted to surprise you."

"You did."

"Are you on lunch break now?"

"Yeah, you picked the right time. What did you bring me?" he asked, taking her hand and leading her to a table under a grove of trees.

"Ham."

"I'm starved," Damien said, reaching into the bag and tearing into the plastic. "Mia, I think you forgot the ham." He opened the bread slices to show her, laughing at her embarrassment.

"I'm sorry. Where were you going to eat? We can get you something."

"I wouldn't dare. This is the best sandwich I've ever eaten." Damien kept swatting Mia's hand away as she tried to take the bread from him. But he refused, ate every dry crumb and rinsed it down with the soda that was now hot. He laughed every second. And finally Mia laughed with him. For the first time in weeks he saw the tension ease from her face. This was more like it. This was what he'd expected marriage to Mia to be like.

When they were done, he walked with Mia, giving her a personal introduction to some of his favorite animals, yelling for her to duck when one of the more aggressive monkeys decided to throw his droppings at them.

"You like it here, don't you?" Mia asked, moving out of firing range of another volley of droppings.

"Yeah, I do."

"More than singing?"

"No, but equally. I've been toying around with the idea of going back to school, becoming a vet."

"You're going to stop working at the club?"

"School will take years. Besides, singing is the fulfillment of a dream. I won't give it up but something more solid will be a good investment in our future."

"I like the sound of that, *our* future."

"You're okay with it?"

"I'm okay with anything that makes you happy, just as long as I'm in the picture."

"You are the picture," Damien said, taking her in his arms, forgetting about his dirty clothes or the monkey taking his aim.

CHAPTER SEVENTEEN

"Mia, you're positively glowing. What happened? Did you finally stop repressing and tell that brand new husband of yours what was going on in your head?"

Mia laughed. "You'll never believe what happened. It was Damien who really initiated the conversation. We started talking and it was all a big misunderstanding. Even the gift."

"What gift?" Dr. Grey asked.

Mia could feel her face getting red and was grateful that her skin tone was not as light as Damien's. She'd be forever blushing and then having to feel embarrassed about it.

"Damien gave me a tape, a porn tape. He left it on the nightstand on our wedding night."

"The tape upset you?"

"Of course it did. I was expecting something a bit more romantic."

"Did you tell him that."

"I didn't then but I did once we talked."

"Good."

Mia smiled and began licking her top lip with the tip of her tongue.

"What's up, Mia," Dr. Grey asked.

"Why do you think something is up?"

"You're licking your lip. For you that's a dead give-away, so go ahead and tell me what's on your mind."

"You didn't comment on the tape Damien gave me. Wouldn't it upset you if your husband had given you one?"

"No. And my husband has given me a bunch of porn tapes. So what? I've given him all kinds of kinky stuff, but, Mia, that's me. I was never repressed sexually."

"What are you talking about? I wasn't repressed, not sexually."

"Mia, come off it. Your brother had you so afraid of turning out to be like your mother that he put the fear of himself, God, sex and everything into your head and you were the good little girl. You played along."

Mia was getting angry. She always did when Dr. Grey ventured into the area of her brother. "I think you keep forgetting my brother was a kid. He had no business being saddled with me. He should have had someone taking care of him, not the other way around."

"I know that, Mia, and I'm not criticizing your brother. I'm merely saying that because of the way you were raised, you learned to survive by suppressing your emotions."

"Nothing I did was Keefe's fault. What I did was my fault alone."

"Who raised you, Mia? You said yourself your mother didn't."

"Would you get over trying to blame my brother? We were talking about my husband, not Keefe."

Mia stormed out of the room and went into the small vending area to blow off steam. She heard the click of heels and knew her therapist had followed her.

She stood glaring at Dr. Grey as she fed quarters into a machine. "Why are you following me?" Mia blurted.

"I'm not. I wanted something cold to drink." Dr. Grey retrieved her drink, then peered at Mia. "I've been reviewing your session tapes. You're doing an excellent job with the patients. They all love you."

Mia chewed on her lips. "Thanks. I guess it's myself I have to work on." She sighed. "I'm sorry I ran out like that."

"No problem. I still run out of my own therapy sessions when it gets too personal."

Mia laughed and moved in closer to Dr. Grey. "Tell me something. Why is it that all therapists are in therapy? It's seems a bit ironic don't you think?"

Dr. Grey laughed too. "When you think about it, it is. But, Mia, think about this. We're only human. And in our line of work we're like a human garbage dump. What do you think would happen if we never had a chance to get rid of all our refuse? No, I don't think I'd trust a therapist who wasn't seeing someone. First, getting therapy puts the therapist at the same level as their patients and they're better able to empathize." She took a long drink. "Ready to go back?"

Mia shrugged her shoulders. "Are we talking about Keefe or Damien?"

"I don't see how we can talk about one without the other. But I promise for today we'll concentrate on you and your marriage. That is what you want to work on, isn't it?"

Once Mia had settled comfortably in her chair she gazed around the room at the hot pink and blue colors that appeared to bleed into each other. Mia thought it was an ugly room and knew she wouldn't choose those colors for her own office. No, she'd choose pale greens and yellows, soothing colors, something more dignified.

"What are you thinking about, Mia?"

"Nothing." Mia turned toward Dr. Grey.

"Suppressing again, are we?"

"We're not, since you're asking. You're not in my body or my mind and if you really want to know what I was thinking… I was wondering why you painted your room such God-awful colors?"

Dr. Grey started laughing and Mia laughed too. "Okay, I suppress," Mia admitted. "But please don't ever refer to what I do as 'we.' I hate it."

"Good. Breakthrough!"

For a long moment the two women smiled at each other, each feeling genuine affection for the other.

"Why do you think you have to hold everything in, Mia? It's okay to say what you really think."

"I know that."

"I know you know that, but you don't practice it, even about something as silly as this damn paint."

"I don't like conflict."

"No one does."

"That's not true," Mia said, a half smile pulling at her lips. "My mother thrives on conflict and also, so it seems, my father-in-law."

"Touché. I meant most sane people."

"I'm in here seeing you. You call that sane?"

"Do you think all the patients that come to see you are insane?"

"Of course not. I was kidding."

"I think there might be some truth in what you're saying. You think it makes you weak to need help, yet you chose a profession where you will be forced to work with people you feel are weak."

Mia cringed, and twisted her lips.

"You may as well say it or I will," Dr. Grey smiled.

Mia refused to speak.

"Okay, then I'll say it. You think your patients are nuts, wacko, looney. Hell, Mia, I thought the same thing myself when I started twenty years ago."

Mia's eyes opened wide and she was perched on the edge of her chair, ready to bolt.

"Sit back down, Mia. That was a long time ago, before I discovered that all humans are flawed, including me, and that it didn't make a person weak to engage in therapy, but that it made them strong. Their desire to get better made them strong. And that's always what you wanted to be. I know that, Mia, you've always wanted to be strong. No names, but you were taught to be strong and to do that you started suppressing your emotions."

"Listen," Mia said softly. "You've got it all wrong. I keep telling you that and you keep insisting on putting labels on me."

"I'm not putting a label on you. If I am, I'm sorry. Why don't you tell me what started it?"

"I did it in the beginning when I was very little because I was afraid. My mom would leave us and I would be scared. My aunts or cousins would come over and I'd pretend that nothing was wrong. Keefe used to tell me that Mom would get in trouble if we didn't pretend that we were alright, that she was at the store."

"I thought you didn't want to talk about your brother?"

"I don't want you talking about him."

"Fair enough, go ahead."

"You already know about foster care."

"I know that you went and something happened and you landed in the hospital and shortly after your brother cooked up a scheme to get you out. I don't know anything that happened while you were there."

"Neither do I," Mia answered truthfully. "Most of the time I was so afraid and wanting my brother that I wasn't able to focus. I wasn't able to repress, suppress, take your pick. I couldn't do it. That time I did go a bit nuts. I'll admit it. I couldn't cope."

"Mia, you're much too hard on yourself. You were a little girl. You should never have had to cope with the things that happened to you."

Mia glared. "Stop pressing. I've told you a thousand times, I'm not holding back anything from that time."

"I didn't say anything."

"You didn't have to. Your look always says it for you," Mia fumed. "Do you want me to continue this or not?"

Dr. Grey shrugged her own shoulders. "I don't much care really, Mia. You're one of my most difficult patients. It's always harder treating a colleague."

Mia smiled despite her anger. "You think of me as a colleague?"

"Of course I do. You are a very good therapist with or without a license. And I think all the things you've been through in your life are going to make you even better. Now wipe that grin off your face and continue."

As hard as she tried, Mia couldn't erase the grin, but she did continue talking. "It took a lot of suppressing to not tell my friends that Keefe and I were living alone. I felt special, like we were so much braver than anyone else. I thought they were babies, that they had to have mothers and fathers taking care of them."

"Did you really?"

"Yeah, in a way I did. Keefe made things so much fun for me. He made it an adventure that I sat in fast food restaurants doing my homework for hours each night, waiting for him to get off. He bought me a ton of books, took me to the library every week for more, and quizzed me on each book I read. He made learning fun for me. I rarely whined about it."

"Didn't you ever do anything besides study while you waited for him?"

"Of course. Keefe got me a CD player and headphones.

"How about television?"

"Neither of us watched much television. We didn't have time for that. Keefe…" Mia hesitated. "Keefe was preparing us both to make it, to become successful. It worked." She smiled. "He did a good job and he was always there making sure I was safe."

"I agree." Dr. Grey smiled at Mia. "Your brother did a good job."

"He did," Mia said with pride. "And I'm grateful to him," she said more aggressively. "If it hadn't been for him, I would have been crying every time I wasn't invited to a party or something."

"Did that happen a lot?" Dr. Grey asked softly.

"Enough," Mia answered. "Keefe told me not to let them see that I wanted to come, that if they knew that they would use it to hurt me. So I learned to hold it in and I'd talk to myself in my head and work it out. That was my process."

"You taught yourself to do that?"

"No, my brother taught me, but I'm glad that I learned how. Whenever any of the kids at school thought they were bothering me, that I cared that I wasn't invited to their parties, I'd always smile and tell them about the things I was doing with my brother. They were all jealous that I got to stay up so late at night, that I was always eating out. None of their big brothers would take them any place and Keefe was always taking me to the movies, to parks. Wherever they went, he would find a way to make sure I had as good a time as any of them. And when we went home we would laugh. I knew that it worked because all the kids at school started asking if my brother would take them to the movies with me if they came to my house."

"Did he?"

"A few times, but after I almost told that we were living alone I started not wanting to be around too many people. I was afraid I would tell someone."

"You were afraid of being sent back to foster care."

"Of course, Mia answered. "If I hadn't been, then I really would have been crazy." She was getting annoyed again. "Listen, what does any of this have to do with Damien?"

"It all does, Mia. Don't you see if you had not been such an expert at repressing your feelings you would have told your mother off at the wedding? The next morning when Damien's father asked about your personal life, you would have told him to go to hell. You would have thrown that tape in your husband's face and told him you didn't like that garbage. Mia, you would have told him that his actions and the actions of others had caused you to imagine him with the tons of women he'd had. You would have told him he'd screwed up, that you were looking for something romantic and he'd better get it. Hell, if you'd told all the people off that you should have, you probably never would have seen those pictures. And then you would have never gone through the dry spell with no sex. And you wouldn't be sitting here with me right now getting angry because you don't want to talk about it."

Mia laughed. She looked at Dr. Grey's surprised expression and laughed even harder, laughing until tears rolled down her cheeks.

"You're yelling at me, telling me I'm repressed and telling me that I'm repressing. Well, duhh. No wonder you need a therapist." Mia laughed and Dr. Grey joined in.

"Good morning, baby girl."

"Good morning, how did you sleep?" Mia rolled over and looked into her husband's eyes.

"Better than I have in a long, long time. How about you?" "To be honest I've being sleeping better since we started sleeping in the same bed." She grinned. "I never knew how much fun sleeping with a man could be."

"Sleeping with a man?" Damien asked, grabbing for Mia.

"Sleeping with the most handsome, adorable, sensitive man in the world who also just happens to be my husband."

"That's better." Damien ran his hands down the side of her body, caressing her behind, then bringing his fingers back to rest on the twin mounds. "Ready to continue our lesson," he asked as his usual visitor poked its head, tenting the sheet. It had been established that he couldn't control that. So he didn't even attempt to try.

"What do you have in mind?" Mia asked.

"Would you like to join me in the shower?"

"Are we allowed to touch?"

"Maybe we could help with soaping each other up but anything else should be saved for an advanced lesson which we'll get to as soon as you're ready."

"Dr. Grey thinks you're a saint," Mia said as she bounced from the bed. She felt her husband's eyes on her naked body and turned back, smiling at him. "I know better," she cracked. "She also thinks you're very smart. She thinks you would make an excellent therapist."

Damien laughed. "We'll see. Come on." He pulled Mia behind him into the bathroom. "You know, I don't even know how you like your water. We've never showered together." He looked at her. "How do you like your water?"

"Hot. How about you?"

"Not so hot," Damien replied. "Let's see if we can find a happy medium." He adjusted the spray and waited while Mia put her fingers into the water. "That'll do," she answered and they both climbed in and lathered each other.

Damien couldn't resist when Mia's arms wrapped around him and she slid her tongue into his mouth. Maybe kissing shouldn't be counted as touching, he thought.

MISTY BLUE

Wet, soapy, hot and wanting him. Oh this was what he'd always thought they would be like together. Only he'd given his word to take it slow. Damn.

CHAPTER EIGHTEEN

Mia rushed into the restaurant, racing for the table she knew her brother had gotten for them. She was over twenty minutes late, but it couldn't be helped.

"Hey," Mia said quickly, hugging her brother tightly and kissing him. He was staring at her. "What are you looking at?" she asked, feeling embarrassed for some unknown reason.

"No reason. I just haven't seen much of you in the past two months and I wanted to see if marriage was agreeing with you."

There was something more to Keefe's statement than met the eye but she ignored it. "Oh, it's beginning to. It was a little rocky there in the beginning but we're working things out."

Keefe didn't say anything and Mia smiled to herself and waited. They had yet to talk about the hysterical call she'd made to her brother on her honeymoon, or his offer to fly out and get her.

"I'm okay, I promise." He was looking uncomfortable and Mia knew he wanted to ask her why she'd called. She toyed with the idea of not telling him but the continued look of fear on her brother's face changed her mind. So she said, "I started back to seeing Dr. Grey again."

"You did?" Keefe asked, genuine surprise tinting his voice. "Why?"

"I needed someone to talk to." Mia saw the brief flash of hurt. "Someone who wouldn't be embarrassed to talk with me about sex and someone who didn't want to save me, or go and kill my husband without even knowing what the problem was."

Keefe laughed. "Kicking your husband's ass if he gets out of line is my job. I'm your big brother, remember?"

"I remember. But hurting my husband is not your job. If he gets out of line I can take care of him myself."

Keefe smiled. "You sound awfully confident." He looked down, too curious not to ask. "What happened, Mia? Why did you call me sobbing as if your heart were breaking?"

"It was at the time," Mia answered, looking her brother in the eye. "Every horrible thing that I had imagined, that I had asked you about, that I had talked with Damien about, happened."

"You thought about him with Ashleigh?"

"Worse."

"With all the women he'd been with?"

Mia stared for a moment at her brother. "Are you sure you can hear this without running out of the restaurant?"

"I'll try my best."

"It wasn't pictures of Damien and other women that got to me, Keefe. I liked making love with my husband. I thought that liking it so much made me like mom, that I was a slut."

"Mia, I'm so sorry. I should have talked with you more."

"You have nothing to be sorry for."

"I think I do. If I hadn't harped so much on your not being like her—"

"Don't do this, Kee. If I hadn't been afraid I would probably have made love with James, a man I didn't even love. I'm happy I saved myself for Damien. If anything, I want to thank you for that. Besides, I'm not telling you for you to start feeling guilty over something you couldn't control. I know you've been worrying about me and I want to tell you what happened. Do you want me to continue?"

He ran his hand over his head, looked away then back at his sister. "Yes, tell me."

"Well, after I thought I had turned into her, God forbid, the images came and they wouldn't stop."

"You couldn't control it?"

"No, I tried. You have no idea how hard I tried. My process failed me."

For a moment, Mia felt weak admitting it to her brother, but then she smiled. "I tried to be strong, only being strong was pushing my husband away. He had no idea what was going on. I know I scared the bejesus out of him. He tried to help, he really did. But I was so scared of…of it happening again that I wouldn't let him near me, not even when we came home," she added.

"You didn't tell me that."

"I know. I didn't want you to know, but I wouldn't sleep in the bed with Damien." She looked down. "I was trying hard to work it out, to use my process. But it wasn't working. That's why I called Dr. Grey. I didn't want to lose my husband."

"Are you sleeping together now?"

"Yeah."

"So Dr. Grey helped?"

"Not with that. One night Damien came home, came into my room, picked me up and took me to our bedroom. He told me he wasn't sleeping alone."

"You didn't object?"

"God, I was glad.

"Did the pictures continue?"

Mia felt her face getting hot, wondering how she was going to tell her brother that for weeks Damien climbed on her, entered her, did what he had to do and left. She smiled. There was no way to tell her brother that bit of information. Besides, it wasn't important. "No," she answered at last. "No more pictures."

"So things really are okay with you?"

"Like I said, they're getting there." She took in a deep breath. "We're learning how to," she looked away, then shrugged her shoulder, "we're learning how to please each other."

There was a puzzled look on Keefe's face and Mia laughed. "Damien would kill me if he knew I was telling you all of this."

"Then why are you?"

"You don't want to know?" Mia teased.

"I'm not sure," Keefe answered. "I just wanted to make sure you weren't being forced to do things you didn't want to do."

Mia laughed again. "You really owe my husband an apology, Kee. Not only isn't he forcing me to do things that I don't want, but he's…we're not—"

"You're not making love?" Keefe gasped, wanting to put Mia and his own torture at her trying to tell him, behind them.

"No, we're not." Mia looked away. "It was Damien's idea. We're learning about each other, what works and what doesn't."

"Why?"

"I thought you weren't quite sure you wanted to know."

"I guess I changed my mind. I'm curious."

"He's doing it to prove to me that he didn't marry me just so he could sleep with me."

"Where did a crazy notion like that come from? Oh, let me guess, Mom."

"And his mother."

"Mia."

"I know."

"I told you to talk to him before the wedding."

"I did."

"Then?"

"Keefe, It's over. We're on the right track, believe me."

"So why are you still seeing Dr. Grey?"

"I still have a few issues that I'm working on. I need a new process," she told her brother. "Sticking to the old one nearly wrecked my marriage. I need to learn not to hide all of my feelings, no more repressing. I have to tell Damien what's bothering me."

Keefe rested his elbows on the table and propped his head between them. "Between me and Mom I'm surprised you ever got married. I'm sorry that I had anything to do with messing things up for you, Mia. I didn't know there would be repercussions later for you."

Mia took her brother's hands. "Don't, Kee. If it hadn't been for you I really would have gone nuts for good. You taught me how to deal with the pain. You were the only one I ever let in. Now I have to learn how to let Damien in." She smiled. "It's not as hard as I thought it would be. He's a darn good listener."

"You really are okay, aren't you?"

"Yeah, I am."

to let Damien in." She smiled. "It's not as hard as I thought it would be. He's a darn good listener."

"How is this? Tell me if you like it."

Mia had to force herself to concentrate as the slight pressure from Damien's mouth covered her breast. The touch was soft, as though a butterfly were kissing her. It was pleasant but nothing really special.

"It's nice," she answered smiling.

"Liar," Damien laughed. "If this is going to work you have to tell the truth."

"Really?" she asked.

"Really."

"In that case, it's no big deal."

She watched the look on Damien's face change to a mischievous glint as he applied more pressure and pulled her nipple into his mouth. A shot of desire sprung throughout her loins and she moaned.

"Still no big deal?" Damien asked.

Mia closed her eyes to enjoy the sensation. This was definitely a big deal.

"Your eyes are closed."

"I know."

"Open them."

"Damien."

"Come on, baby. I get nervous when you have your eyes closed."

Mia opened her eyes, complying with her husband's request. "What you were doing, it felt so good that my eyes closed automatically." She saw the desire that filled him had made his eyes turn a deep amber color. "Damien, make love to me."

She slid her hand toward the side of his muscular body before slowly inching her fingers toward his center. She felt for him, touched his warmth. Her eyes never leaving his face, her fingers curled around him and she smiled as his flesh danced in her hand. "Make love to me."

"Oh, God," Damien said aloud. "Mia, this is too damn hard. I want you so much. I want to make love to you more than I've ever wanted anything in my life," he groaned, "except for proving to you how very much you mean me."

His eyes closed of their own volition and he sucked in a breath, enjoying Mia's touch yet trying to find the strength to follow through with their plan. A rush of lust claimed him and he groaned, gritting his teeth. How the hell had he found himself in this situation? Mia wanting him, touching him and him saying no.

He had two choices: to thrust himself deeply into Mia and relieve the ache, or push her away. He did neither. He couldn't push Mia away, no matter how much it was killing him to have her hands on him and not do as she asked. He had to find the strength for both of them. He had to.

"I don't know how I'm ever going to make it," Damien said softly as he ran his hands possessively over Mia's body.

"It shouldn't be so hard for you." She blew on his tiny pebbled nipple. "You did it for almost a year before we were married." She dipped her head and tasted the pebble. "Surely you can go a few more days," she challenged wickedly.

"Yeah, but that was before I knew just how good it felt to be inside you. Now that I know…," he pressed Mia closer and moaned. "It seems like forever since I felt release and I might just combust."

"Technically, Damien, this is harder on me than you." She saw him arch one brow and give her a suspicious look that smacked of let's-get-real.

"How?" he finally said.

"Well, it's only been a few days since you had release," Mia finally said and looked straight at him.

"I don't believe you actually said that," Damien laughed.

"You said you wanted sharing, you didn't want me to hold anything back, so hey, I'm just fulfilling your request."

Damien laughed again. "I do have to tell you that I like what you have to say."

"So what's our lesson tonight?" Mia asked as she continued raining kisses on Damien's chest.

"What do you think it should be?"

Mia gave her husband a meaningful look that told him much more than her words could have.

"No, we're going the full two weeks." he said to her softly as he began caressing Mia and doing more kissing than anything.

Mia's skin burned where Damien's lips touched her. She lay in his arms, content for the moment to just feel his heat. He began stroking her cheeks.

"Mia, I've been thinking about what you said and you're right. You've been cheated. I think tonight we need to even the score."

"But I thought you said—"

"There are other ways besides penetration, baby girl, and tonight you're going to have your first orgasm."

"But I want us to be together…I mean I want you making love to me."

"I will be."

"Damien." Mia was becoming flustered. "You know what I mean. When I have my first orgasm I want you inside me like I've always imagined it."

"Trust me, baby girl, when it happens you won't give a damn about your plans. I am going to make love to you, baby. I want you to have an orgasm and I want to watch you as you come." He saw her eyes dart to the side and knew she was mortified. He grinned and kissed her forehead. "Don't worry, I won't watch tonight. Tonight I have something else in mind."

He saw that she was still ill at ease. "When it happens, I guarantee you're not going to be embarrassed."

Damien kissed his way down Mia's body, pulling on the tender brown flesh, running his tongue lovingly over her abdomen, twirling it in the indentation of her navel. He felt his wife shiver with delight and smiled to himself. She was so hot and her heat was making him hot, hot and rock hard. He smelled her scent rising to meet him, and knew without touching her that she was flowing. She was ready and damn if he wasn't ready himself. He pushed her hands away, knowing her protests were feeble. She needed this and he was going to give it to her. Only heaven help him as to how he would avoid completing the act. He chanted inwardly, *This is for Mia, you're doing it for Mia.*

Damien moved into position between his wife's thighs his arousal throbbing, and he thought to himself, *Down boy, that's not where you're heading.* For a long moment he buried his head in the soft flesh of Mia's thigh. He had to steady himself. When he thought he had his emotions under control, he began kissing her flesh. Changing his direction he kissed gently at her entrance and felt his flesh jerk forward. He needed more time, he knew it, or he'd never be able to just give to his bride without receiving in kind.

He slowly reversed his path, kissing his way back up Mia's body and suckling her breast until he felt her trembling in desire and need. This time when her eyes closed he didn't ask her to open them. He only smiled as he once again worked his way down her abdomen, loving the feel of her soft skin stretched taut over her slim frame. He paid special attention to her belly, thinking of the day that it would swell with their babies, and he shivered himself.

He continued with his kisses moving down, down, and then her hand reached out once more, trying to push him away. He heard her voice, soft, wanting, embarrassed as hell.

"Damien, I don't know if I want you to do that."

"If you don't like it, I'll never do it again," he promised as he looked into her eyes and kissed her inner thigh. His body was trembling so hard that he almost missed Mia's body tensing. Would it kill either of them for him to give her what she wanted, to give both of them what they wanted? Hell, they were married. Why was he playing games? Why didn't he just make love to his wife, bury himself in her?

"I love you," came Mia's sweet, sweet voice giving him his answer. That was the reason he was taking it so damn slow. Above everything else he wanted his wife to know how much he treasured her. She didn't think he could hold out. Hell, he didn't think he could but he needed to. He needed to prove to both of them that it wasn't just sex.

He tasted her and groaned. He'd known she would taste the way that she did. She attempted to pull away and he reached his hand around her hip and pulled her closer as he breathed in the essence of his wife. And he did as he'd promised. He made love to his wife in the only way he was allowing himself. He wanted so much to see her face when she came. But that would wait until later.

He tasted her secrets, thoroughly enjoying the reactions of her body. When he felt the tell-tale sign of her impending release he increased his efforts, smiling inside. He heard her cries, her moans of pleasure, heard her calling his name, but he didn't stop until she was finished. Then and only then did he allow himself to come to her side, to take her in his arms and hug her to him.

"Why are you crying, baby? Didn't you like it?" For a few moments she didn't answer, only held him even tighter.

"That was your first orgasm, baby girl. How did you like it?" She didn't answer. She buried her lips into his neck and he could feel her smile. "So you liked it?" he teased.

"Damien, I never knew it would be like this. If I had, I don't think I would have waited," she laughed.

"I'm glad you waited for me to find you, baby girl." And he was. It was worth the wait. She was worth the wait.

They lay together for the longest time until Mia raised her head and gazed down at her husband, saw the contentment in his eyes from the pleasure he'd given her. But she saw something else there, unfulfilled need. And it didn't matter about their two week plan. She had a plan of her own.

"Damien, school's out for tonight, right?"

"Yeah," he whispered, attempting to bring her head back to his chest. "Why?"

"Because I have something I want to do. And I swear if you give me one word of instruction I will castrate you."

215

Before Damien could ask, Mia was showing him as she rolled over on him and began kissing her way south.

"Mia."

"Don't stop me, Damien. This is my show and I know what I'm doing. I watched the tape," she whispered before she took him in her mouth.

When she was done her husband's unfulfilled needs had been fulfilled.

And so had Mia's. She knew for her there was no going back. She could no longer repress her needs.

Within moments Mia was sleeping in Damien's arms and he laughed to himself. Tonight they had skipped ahead in their lessons. He felt the sensations of pleasure that continued to swirl in his blood. He couldn't believe the gift Mia had given him. And he damn sure couldn't believe he was still spouting nonsense about holding out for two weeks. Oh yes, he'd changed, he thought as his hands touched Mia, caressing her sleeping body. Well, even though he'd changed, he wasn't dead.

Damien was dishing up the cheese and eggs he'd made for them. "Guess what? I got the honeymoon suite at Stavro's, the same room we had on our wedding night."

Mia smiled. "That's so romantic."

"I figured we should go back there and start over. Four more days and it's no more waiting."

"Ten days seems like a lifetime, doesn't it?" Mia asked.

Damien glanced toward her. She was biting her nails and had a dreamy expression on her face. There was something going on and he was going crazy wondering what it was. "What are you thinking about?" he asked.

Mia sucked on her lips, wanting to laugh, feeling embarrassed but wanting to know. "How was I?"

The fork stopped midway to his mouth and Damien stared at his bride. "Do you even have to ask?"

"Yes," she answered. "I have to ask. I want to know."

He dropped the fork, came to her side of the table and took her in his arms and gazed into her eyes. "Baby, you took me to heaven."

"Yeah?"

"Yeah," he answered. "And I want to take you someplace tonight."

"Where?" she grinned.

"Somewhere that requires clothes." he teased. "I want to take you out on a date. Can you make it? I know you have a class tonight. Do you think you can skip it?"

"That depends. Where are you taking me?"

"Skip class and I promise you'll be glad you did."

"Okay," she answered. "How should I dress?"

He smiled and kissed her lips. "Casual is good. Now eat up, we both need the protein."

Twenty minutes later he was reaching for the lunch Mia had made for him and heading for the door. "Does this one have meat or is it my favorite, bread on bread?" he asked, teasing her.

"It has meat."

"I'll see you tonight," he said as he kissed her and went out the door laughing, not telling Mia that tonight they were taking it back to the beginning, to their first meeting.

CHAPTER NINETEEN

"I can't believe you thought of this," Mia said smiling as she munched on a fry. "Of all the places to come, McDonald's. It's so romantic. I love it."

"I knew you would." Damien beamed. "It's where we fell in love."

"That happened in Ashleigh's apartment."

"I didn't think you wanted to go there. Besides this is where we sealed the deal. Where we acknowledged to ourselves what we'd felt there. This is where we fell in love," he insisted, and at last Mia agreed.

"Tonight I watch you," Damien promised Mia as they went through all the exercises they'd agreed on, touching, kissing and as he did, watching as his hands trailed down her body and his fingers made their home deep inside of her.

Her eyes glazed over but remained open and fixed on his face. Then her muscles tightened and her breathing deepened and so did her voice. "Damien." She was fighting it. "It's time. I want you."

She was right, it was time, but not until she came. He watched her face, saw her release and then he held her body trembling against his.

"I'm tired of waiting," Mia moaned.

"Me too."

They'd gone ten days. That was almost two weeks. "It's only four more days." He felt her hands touching him, caressing away his determination and he shuddered so violently that he worried about frightening her. "Mia, I wanted to do this for us."

"But you've proven it. We've graduated. This is the next logical step. Don't make me beg," Mia purred.

"You never have to beg me," Damien answered and before either of them could say another word he was buried inside her. A deep guttural moan ripped from his throat and he vaguely heard the tinkling sound of her laughter as she wrapped her legs around him and whispered in his ear.

Finally Damien made love to his wife and watched her face as she soared with him, glad for having gone through the past ten days. He knew her body, what she needed, and he knew without a doubt that she wasn't faking. He was glad they'd waited when they hit the crescendo together. Then he held her in his arms, exhausted.

Hours later he asked, "No more demons, Mia?"

"No more demons."

Keefe sat across from his sister and her husband and he knew instantly that they were no longer waiting. She had a glow on her face and Damien was bouncing off the walls. The looks he was giving his wife were as though they were making love right there at the table. He watched them for a while, content to know that Mia was finally happy, content to know that their mother had not destroyed his sister's marriage.

"You two sure look happy," he said.

"How can you tell?" Mia quipped.

"Oh, maybe that stupid smile on your face." He glanced at Damien. "And that same stupid smile on your husband's face gave me a clue."

"We're in love," Mia sang, "And we're newlyweds."

Keefe shook his head and stared for a moment at his new brother-in-law. "Damien, thanks for making Mia happy. I'm sorry that our mother made things so tough for you. I never would have believed that she would grope you right there at the wedding, right under Mia's nose. That's a new low, even for her."

Keefe was smiling but stopped when he saw the silly grin Damien had been sporting all night slide off his face. He turned just in time to see the grin leave Mia's face. God, she hadn't known. He glanced toward Ashleigh, who was giving him a knowing look of pity.

"Damien, I'm sorry. I thought you told her."

"Told me what?" Mia asked, the knowing in her voice as she looked from her brother to Ashleigh. Then her gaze landed and stayed on her husband. "Did all of you know?"

"Mia, it was no big deal."

"Then why did the three of you try so hard to keep it from me?"

"How the hell was I supposed to tell you that?" Damien asked quietly.

"Maybe the same way that you told Ashleigh or the way you told my brother."

"I didn't tell Keefe."

"But you told Ashleigh?"

"Mia, I was asking her advice. I just wanted to know if she thought I should tell you."

"And she said no." Mia glared at Damien, then Ashleigh, then her brother. "You knew this, Kee?"

She felt a stab of pain in her chest and closed her eyes, willing the pain and the image of her mother groping her husband to go away. Then she blinked and opened her eyes. That was her old process. She was tired of burying her feelings.

"I want to know exactly what happened," she insisted.

"Not now, baby girl. I'll tell you when we get home. We're having a good time. There's no need to spoil the evening."

"I'd say that ship has sailed. I want to discuss it now." Mia refused to acquiesce. "Aren't you the one who said we won't lie? Did you mean me or both of us?" She saw Damien's jaw clench and knew he was getting annoyed. And she didn't care, not one little bit.

"The three of you have a hell of a lot of nerve."

"Mia, there's no need for you to swear," Keefe admonished.

She turned and stared at her brother. "I'm an adult, big brother, a married woman. I can say what I please. And I meant what I just said. How dare any of you try to decide what's best for me. What did you do? Have a meeting, take a vote? Did you all decide that Mia was too weak, too looney to handle the fact that her mother felt her husband up at her wedding?"

She began shaking. "God, I hate her!" she spit out. "I'll never forgive her for that, ever."

Keefe touched his sister's hand, surprised that she was making a scene at the table. She really was changing. Still, he attempted to calm her down. "Mia, you're upset now. You'll get over it."

"I don't think so," she answered, then glared at Damien. "Is that why she told Jerry that you got an erection?"

Damien's mouth opened. "I didn't encourage her, Mia."

"I believe him, Mia," Keefe interjected."

"So do I," Ashleigh added.

"Who asked you, either of you?" Mia almost screamed. "It's none of your business. I didn't ask for your opinions. I asked my husband. Damien, I can't believe that you kept something like this from me. When were you going to tell me?" She blinked rapidly to keep back the tears. "Were you ever going to tell me?"

"I don't know," Damien answered truthfully. "Probably not. I didn't think it would serve any purpose."

"And what purpose do you think not telling me has served other than to let me know that I can't trust either my husband or my brother. Thank you for helping me learn that lesson."

"Mia," Damien interrupted. "You know that's not true."

She turned her hand to him. "Don't talk to me, or I'm going to scream right here."

She cut into her steak and began eating, ignoring the three people at the table. Her new process was frightening but at least her stomach wasn't tied in knots.

When she was done eating, she looked up at the three of them staring at her. "I can't remember ever being this angry and in time I'll more than likely forgive all of you. Just not tonight. I'm not in the mood for forgiving so easily. As for Mom, I meant it when I said I'm never forgiving her. I hate her and she's not my problem any longer. When she comes to town, you deal with her, Keefe. She calls, you answer. I don't want anything to do with her, not ever again."

"You know I won't go to her aid without your coercion."

"Then she won't be receiving any more aid because I won't be coercing you."

"This isn't like you, Mia."

"You mean it wasn't like me, Kee. This is the new me. Get used to it."

She saw the hurt in her brother's eyes, the simmering anger in her husband's and the confusion in Ashleigh's. Okay, she was changing too rapidly for them to keep up with. She sighed to herself, then smiled to take away the sting of her words.

"How do any of you expect to know if I'm unhappy if I don't tell you? I'm ticked at all of you. I don't want any of you wondering if I'm really angry. I want you to know for sure. I am angry."

Mia couldn't believe how liberating it felt to admit that she was angry. She still wasn't done and as she walked behind Damien into their apartment, she intended to show him just how not through she was. She wanted to know the details, all of it.

"Okay," she said and sat on the sofa. "Tell me when, what and where."

"Why?"

"Because all of you know and I think I should also. I'm your wife."

"Are you blaming me for this?"

"Just tell me."

"On the dance floor." Damien sighed. "Right before I walked away from her. She had been doing things all day but I looked over them. I didn't want to upset you. I mean, after all, she's your mother. I figured most of it was because she'd had a few drinks. I thought, what the heck, humor her a little, maybe it would be enough to make her back off. Besides, I was teasing you, remember? I wanted to make you leave. I thought my dancing with her would do it." He shrugged his shoulders and took a second before continuing.

"I'll admit I knew she pushed your buttons and you were a bit jealous. I was going to use it to make you leave the reception. I take full responsibility for that, baby. I'm sorry. Please forgive me. I was wrong to try and manipulate you like that."

"What happened?" Mia questioned, with not a trace of emotion in her voice.

"She ran her hand down the front of my pants, then she cupped me."

"Why didn't you push her hand away when she first touched you?"

"It all happened so fast." He looked sadly at her. "You are blaming me?"

"I'm only after the facts. Between touching you and cupping you, you couldn't push her away?"

Damien didn't answer.

"Did you have an erection?"

"Yes."

"Is that why you didn't push her hand away?"

Damien folded his hands across his chest and sat back. "This is your story. Suppose you tell me. Did I want your mother? Did I get a hard-on because she touched me? Did I not push her hand away because I liked her touching me? I'm the one on trial here, you tell me what your verdict is."

Mia looked at him for a moment. He was glaring at her. It would be nice if some of the blame for her mother's behavior could be apportioned to someone else, but not to her husband. That she wouldn't do. She knew in her heart Damien wasn't guilty of the crime.

She leaned back and tucked her legs underneath her body, her gaze locked with her husband's. "I know it wasn't your fault. I just hate that my own mother would do that. I'm sorry."

"You have nothing to feel sorry for, Mia. You didn't do it, your mother did."

"Yeah, but do you have any idea how that makes me feel?"

"Responsible. I know, but we both have to learn that we can't control others' behavior. We can barely control our own. Will you forgive me for trying to use your mother to make you jealous? I should have known better."

"Yes, I forgive you, just don't ever do it again."

Damien stretched his legs out in front of him. "That was some performance you pulled back in the restaurant. I thought you were going to kill either Keefe or me, or both. Your poor brother," Damien laughed. "He looked totally flabbergasted. I've never seen him speechless. He didn't know what to make of you."

"I know," Mia grinned. "Screaming and yelling is not part of my process."

"You know he's going to blame me for your changing?"

"I know." Mia grinned again.

"And you're okay with that?"

"It serves you right for hiding things from me." She cocked her head to the side. "Damien, I'm serious. Don't do it again," she said in a sterner voice.

"I suppose you want me to stay on my side of the bed tonight?" he asked, looking down at her.

"No, that would be punishing me," Mia replied. "And I'm not a masochist." She smiled, then grinned when Damien lifted her, then carried her off to the bedroom.

Mia couldn't believe how quickly the time was passing. In just a couple of weeks they would be celebrating their six month anniversary. She had less than a year before she earned her Ph.D. and Damien had surprised her just a month before saying that he wanted to be a veterinarian.

Mia looked over the list that she still had to finish, ignoring the comment Damien had made.

"Are you ignoring me?" Damien asked.

"Yes, this is our first Christmas together and I want us to spend the day together."

"We will," he argued, "but they need me to work at the club. They're willing to pay me double."

Mia's hip jutted out and she leveled her husband with a glare meant to stop him in his tracks and it did. "This is important," she said. "I spent Thanksgiving in the club sitting at a table alone while you sang. I'm not spending Christmas like that. You're just going to have to tell them that you're not working."

"What if I get fired?"

"Then you get fired." She turned away from him. She was sounding bossy and a bit like a shrew and she didn't like it.

"You're being unreasonable."

"I don't think so." She kept working on her list, the memory of the first holiday in her life she'd not spent with her brother on her mind. He'd gone with Ashleigh to spend the Thanksgiving holiday with her parents and Mia had felt alone. Mia had no plans to put a damper on her brother's love life but at the same time he was the only blood relative that she was claiming and she didn't want to start a habit of them going their separate ways on the holidays. She'd talked to him, told him just how she felt. And together the two of them had decided that no matter what, they would spend two of the major holidays together, even if it was for only part of the day. Christmas was the first holiday dinner that she would be fixing for her new husband and her brother. It was their opportunity to bond as a family.

"Mia, how are we going to pay all our bills if I lose my job? Singing pays three times what I make at the zoo. We've already taken a chunk out of our savings to pay my tuition. Do you want me to drop out before I even start?" he asked.

"You know I want you to go back to school."

"Then we need the money."

"There are some things more important than money and I think spending our first Christmas together is one of those things."

"You're not giving an inch on this?"

"I can't, it's too important."

"Mia, you're stubborn," he said, coming up to her. "But if it's that important to you, I won't fight you on it. Hopefully I'll have a job singing the day after Christmas, but like you said, there are some things more important than money. And without a doubt you are the most important thing in my life."

"Don't worry about the money for your classes. I'll pay for them."

"Before I met you if a woman had made that offer I would have taken her up on it without a thought. But no thanks, baby. I'll pay for this on my own." Damien whispered in her ear.

"And before you, I would have never made the offer," Mia answered. "Keefe would have killed me. I have a compromise," she said. "We can pay for it together, just include it as a household expense and pay for it from our joint account."

"We'll see, baby girl. Hopefully it won't come to that. This is really something I want to take care of on my own. It means a lot to me." He pulled her tighter. "I'd say it's as important for me to do it myself as my staying home for Christmas is for you."

"That sounds like blackmail. Okay, I understand, just know that you don't have to worry about the money. What's mine is yours. Okay?"

"Okay, thanks, baby."

He held her from behind and nibbled on her neck. "That's an awfully long list that you have there."

"I know," Mia answered. "I want to make at least one special thing for everyone that's coming. For Keefe I just have to make mashed potatoes and he's set. Ashleigh wants fresh cranberry orange sauce. I haven't asked your mother yet what she would like."

"You asked my mom to come?"

"Of course I did. I want this to be a family dinner."

He rubbed the back of her neck with his thumb. "Do you mean that?" he asked and smiled as she turned in his arms. He could tell from the look of panic on her face that she knew where he was heading.

"Do you mind if I invite my pops?" he said, not looking at her. When she didn't answer, he brought his gaze to hers. "What do you say, baby girl? Is my pops welcome in our home for Christmas dinner?"

"That wasn't what you asked before. There is a difference. Of course your father is welcome in your home. He's your father."

Damien twirled her around, her excitement finally infecting him. "I never thought the day would ever come when I'd have my parents in my own home, with my wife making dinner for everyone." He lifted her into the air. "I'm glad you fought me on this." He kissed her so deeply that he took her breath away.

CHAPTER TWENTY

"I love you, Mia," Damien said as he kissed his way down the side of Mia's neck. "Merry Christmas." He held her so tightly that she pushed him away.

"Damien, what's wrong?"

"I say I love you and you ask me what's wrong?"

"You can't fool me. I could feel it in your touch and I heard it in your voice. What's wrong?"

"Nothing." He shrugged his shoulders. "I'm happy, baby, that's all."

Mia's hand went up and stroked his cheek, her eyes holding his. "Even with the deep voice, Damien, I can tell something's wrong. What is it?"

"Today," Damien said, attempting to make light of what he was about to say. "You've given me today."

She was waiting for him to say more. He'd hoped just those words would tell her but they hadn't, so he smiled at her. "I never knew how much I wanted this until this moment. I've never spent a holiday with both of my parents."

He saw Mia's expression change and the sudden sparkle of tears in her eyes. "Thank you for making it happen." He closed his eyes and hugged his wife to him again and this time when he held her even tighter she didn't push him away.

Tears seeped beneath Mia's lids as she held on to her husband. She felt ashamed for the thoughts she'd been having, wishing that something would happen, that Charles would be his usual selfish self and not show up to ruin their day. Now for her husband's sake she was praying that he'd come. And she'd do her part to make the day pleasant.

For the last several weeks, in her sessions with Dr. Grey, Mia had spent a lot of time reliving the things she'd missed having, not ending the thoughts when she left the session. She'd been so occupied with her own raw deal that she'd never considered that the man she loved with all her heart had had an even worse life than hers.

She'd had joy in her life. She'd had Keefe. And a couple of those years she'd had Jerry. She'd even had a mother for several of her Christmases. She hugged Damien tighter, knowing now that was the reason he'd fought her about working. He hadn't thought he could have this family day. Now Mia was glad she'd fought with him, glad that he wanted his father.

"I made the pecan pie," Mia said into the flesh of her husband's neck.

"You did?" he said, pulling away and looking at her as if she'd created a miracle.

"You said your dad loves pecan pie and I promised that I would make one special thing for everyone. Just wait until you see what I made for you."

"I only want dessert," Damien leered, "and I don't think it goes in your oven."

"You're bad," Mia grinned. "But I really do have a surprise. Come on into the living room." She pressed the button on the CD player.

"'It's been such a long, long time.'"

Damien started laughing. "Gladys Knight." He held out his arms and danced with Mia, singing the words to her.

When the song was over, Mia pushed away and went to the CD player and pushed another button. Another version of "Misty Blue" came on. Damien frowned slightly. "That almost sounds like Gladys but it's not. Who is it?"

"Dorothy Moore. Now I want my black card reinstated."

Damien burst out laughing, "'Just the thought of you.'"

"'Turns my whole world, misty blue,'" Mia sang.

"Now about that dessert."

"You can have dessert," Mia said, meaning it, "Any time you want."

"Even now?"

"Even now."

"Do we have time?"

"We'll make time. There is nothing more important than us. And if dessert is what you…what we want, then dessert it is."

They sank to the floor and made love to what was now their song. After they were done with their special dessert, they showered quickly and Damien went out to the kitchen to help.

"I never knew I was getting such a great cook in the bargain. How did you learn?" He laughed, "Don't tell me your brother taught you?"

"Sort of. He made me take cooking classes in school, then whenever the college or park district had a cooking class, he'd enroll me."

"He wanted you to make a great wife?"

"He wanted me to cook food he could eat and he hated cooking. Besides, he said it was time I learned how to eat healthy. Remember, we ate out a lot for a lot of years. So he was right. One of us needed to cook."

"And for that, I'm saying, hooray, hooray, to your brother."

Mia turned from the oven. "You like him, don't you?"

"Yeah, I do. I never thought the day would come, but we get along and we're becoming friends."

Mia smiled. "Good, we're becoming family. I like your mom too." She saw Damien's raised brow and the grin on his face. "It's going to be fine."

"I don't know about that. Your brother hates my pops, and with good reason, I might add. I'm thinking it might get to be a little tense in here. Actually, I'm surprised Keefe's coming, knowing my pops going to be here."

Mia turned her attention back to the turkey and basted it.

"You didn't tell him, did you?"

"No."

Damien sighed. "This is going to be an interesting day."

"An interesting family day and remember, there is no such thing as a perfect family. They're all dysfunctional and we're not a bit different."

"You're sounding more and more like an expert," Damien teased, then went to open the door for their first guest.

"Merry Christmas." Damien kissed Ashleigh's cheek and shook hands with Keefe, clapping him on the shoulder.

"Umm, it smells good in here," Keefe said and made his way to the kitchen. "Mia, he said as soon as he saw her, "you're really going all out, aren't you?" He gave her a hug before peeping into the covered containers. "It looks like you're cooking every dish you ever learned how to make."

"I am," she answered. "I want this day to be special, a new tradition, the start of our new, blended family."

She looked away and decided to get it over quickly. "Charles is coming."

She walked closer to her brother. "Please be nice. Damien has never had his parents together for a holiday. Neither have we," she added. She saw the muscle twitch in her brother's jaw. They never spoke of their own father. There was no reason. They didn't know who he was or where he was. But Mia knew her brother would understand what having his parents together for Christmas meant to Damien.

"I don't know how long we can stay," he shrugged.

"You will stay until dinner is over and an hour or so of conversation after that," Mia ordered. "And if you're hating it, at that time you can leave."

She picked up a tray of canapés, ordered Keefe to pick up the platter of shrimp she'd prepared from the refrigerator, and went out to begin serving. The bell rang again and it was Kathy.

"Mom, where's pops?" Damien asked.

"I didn't come with your father. I have to leave no later than eight. I have a date."

Everyone in the room turned to look at her with the exception of Mia.

"You have a date?" Damien's face held the surprise that his voice relayed. The bell rang again and Damien answered it, hugged his father and returned to question his mother. "You have a date?" He noticed his father was listening.

"Yes."

"Where did you meet this man?"

"Mia introduced us."

All eyes were on Mia and she knew it but pretended that they weren't as she went from person to person, holding the tray of delicacies out for them to sample. Charles stared at her for a moment.

"Merry Christmas, Charles. You remember my brother, don't you?"

Charles and Keefe looked toward each other and nodded. Mia had not expected them to shake hands and the nods of acknowledgement were enough for now. Charles' eyes had quickly swung back to her. Mia could tell he was evaluating her. He smiled and she knew he'd found her a worthy adversary. But that wasn't what she wanted to be today. Mia didn't want to fight with him. She wanted to give her husband something he'd never dared hoped for. A family. She wanted to give that to all of them.

"Damien, how long has it been now that you've been on lockdown, six months?"

Mia walked toward the kitchen, leaving her husband to deal with his father's question. When she returned, she walked directly up to Charles and held her peace offering out to him. "This is for you to take home." She handed Charles the pecan pie. "I have another one for us to eat here." She stared at him until his smirk turned into a genuine smile. She'd called a truce and he'd agreed.

"This pie looks good, Mia. Thanks."

Damien grinned. "Wait until you taste her cooking." Then he looked at the paper saucer of goodies his father was munching on. "Those are homemade, by the way, not store bought."

Everyone watched in anticipation as Charles bit into first one, then another hors d'oeuvre, and sighed. He didn't comment but the fact that he continued eating was all the answer that was needed.

Mia went to stand beside Damien and felt his arm slide around her. He was beaming.

"Wait until you taste Mia's mashed potatoes," Keefe piped in. "She does things with potatoes that no one has ever thought of." He looked at the pecan pie that Charles had put to the side with a bit of envy. "I didn't know she'd learned to make pecan pie as well."

Mia smiled up at her husband, knowing that everyone was trying, even her brother.

With the last morsel of food either eaten or wrapped for someone to take home and the gifts exchanged, Mia knew the day had been a success. They were a patchwork family with plenty of warts and never for one moment did she believe they would always get along so well. Still, Mia knew they had taken a small step toward becoming a family.

"It's over." Damien smiled up at Mia. "Thanks again, baby girl."

"You're welcome." She smiled back as she heard the beep from their answering machine in their bedroom. I guess it's time to get that."

They had not allowed anything to interrupt the day, not even the ringing phone. They had let the answering machine pick up. Only when Keefe and Ashleigh left did Mia even hear the constant beeping sound.

"It was a very good day, baby girl. Are you sure you want to get that now?"

"We might as well," Mia said and pushed the play button. Let's see who called."

"Mia, hi, Merry Christmas. I figured you're probably still in your little snit since I didn't get a gift from you. But I know you can't stay mad. You feel too guilty for that. Hey, you sure didn't get that from me. Listen, since you're married, and by the way tell that handsome husband of yours I said hi, you can afford a better gift now. Don't buy me anything you pick out. God knows you have atrocious taste. There is this bracelet that I want. It's a little over a thousand dollars. Oh, just make it twelve hundred. Send me

the money and I'll get it myself and while you're at it, tell your brother that I saw a necklace to go with that bracelet. Tell him to give you a thousand dollars to send me. That shouldn't put him out too much. Okay, Mia, I'll be looking for the check. Merry Christmas

Mia closed her eyes for a long moment, then felt her husband's arms coming around her and the feel of his lips on her neck as she whispered to herself, "Baby steps, Mia, baby steps."

CHAPTER TWENTY-ONE

"I want to have a baby?"

"Why?"

Mia stared into Damien's dark eyes. She had not expected this, his questioning. She had expected his acquiescence.

"Why do I have to have a reason?" she asked.

"Because I don't think we're ready."

Pain sliced into her. Mia winced. It was her. Damien didn't think she was ready.

"I want a baby," she repeated, holding his gaze.

"Why?"

Couldn't he think of a different word? *Did he really want her to say it?* She wanted to give a child what neither of them had had, two loving parents, a stable home. Mia was becoming annoyed. It shouldn't be this hard. Damien should be kissing her, making love to her, giving her the baby she desperately wanted.

"Mia, a baby won't change our pasts."

"I didn't say that it would," she answered testily. "I just said that I wanted to have one."

"A baby's not an experiment. I don't think we're ready."

"You mean you don't think I'm ready," she lashed out at him. "Look, Damien, you're my husband, not my father, so stop trying to fill that role. And don't bother throwing Keefe's name into this."

"Why not? I was going to let that one go, but since you're the one that brought it up, we both know I couldn't act like your father if I tried," he replied, rising to the bait. "Like you said, your brother has that one covered."

Mia forgot the plans she had as her annoyance turned to anger. "I think it's better that my brother thinks he's my father than your father thinking he's your pimp." She regretted the words the moment they were out. The look of pain that crossed Damien's eyes darkened his features and relayed his feelings.

"I don't want to fight with you, Mia, not about this. You're dumping on me because of the phone call your psycho mother made to you. That was two weeks ago, Mia, deal with it."

"This has nothing to do with my mother." She knew she was lying and what was worse, she knew that he knew it. "Sometimes it's just you, Damien, that makes me angry. Believe it or not, you're not perfect."

"Why don't we stop before we say things we don't mean? Like I said, I don't want to fight with you."

"No, of course not," she sneered, unable to stop the hateful words. "Mia's too delicate, she might snap or worse yet, she might stop sleeping with me. That's your real worry, isn't it?"

She shoved aside her memories of their passion just a few hours before. She wanted him to understand how important it was to her to have a child and she didn't want to explain or beg him to impregnate her.

"I'm not going to fight with you," Damien repeated again. This is stupid."

"So now you think I'm stupid."

Damien shook his head and stared at her for a moment. "Is it your time?"

"What are you talking about?" Mia looked at Damien as if he'd taken leave of his senses, watching as he marched toward the calendar.

"No, you have another week and a half. So what's the problem?"

Mia watched Damien in fascination, feeling insulted that he'd thought her wanting a baby had anything whatsoever to do with PMS. At that moment she was relieved that there was no more time to debate the issue. She simply glared at Damien.

"You are still taking the pill, aren't you?" he asked.

"If I'm not taking them it's my choice. It's my body."

"You're right," he agreed. It is your choice," he said as he kissed her goodbye and walked out the door shaking his head as though to say, Women, who needs them?

⚘

"I'm thinking of having a baby," Mia announced to Dr. Grey the moment she was seated. She watched the older woman carefully, studying her reaction. When the therapist didn't speak, Mia became slightly annoyed.

"I know what you're thinking, so go ahead and say it."

"If you know what I'm thinking," Dr. Grey began, "then there is no need in my saying it."

Mia got up from her chair and walked around the room. "You really should repaint your office. It's really ugly."

"Thank you for your critique, Mia. Did you come here to discuss my décor?"

Mia turned and smiled, feeling that she'd just had a bit of the stuffing knocked out of her. "What do you think about what I said?"

"About your phrasing, or the subject matter?"

"Both," Mia answered.

"This one's for free, Mia, and only because you're a friend. You're wondering if I noticed that you said *you* were thinking of having a baby, not you and Damien, just *you*. Of course I noticed. I would be a fool not to and a very bad therapist to boot. So now if you want to stop playing games and testing me, why don't you tell me what's going on."

Mia exhaled noisily and returned to her seat. "I told Damien that I wanted to have a baby."

"And?"

"And he said no, that we weren't ready."

"Do you think you are, Mia?"

"I think I'll make a wonderful mother and I know Damien would make a wonderful dad."

"I agree. Any child that the two of you have will be very lucky to have the two of you as parents."

"But?" Mia asked.

"No buts. It's just in a very short time you'll have your Ph.D. You will have accomplished your goal. Have you considered what having a family is going to mean and how it's going to impact your career?"

"You have a family," Mia countered.

"And my family has suffered, Mia. What do you think I talk about with my therapist?"

Mia cocked her head to the side and waited.

"I tell him how I've screwed up my kids' lives, how I wasn't there raising them and I know they're more than likely in therapy somewhere or they will be, telling someone what an awful mother I was."

Mia looked thoughtfully at her therapist who was acting as her friend. "I think you had to have done a good job, you were so good with me when I was young."

"I was good at giving to my patients, Mia. I forgot to give to my family."

Mia swallowed and looked away. She'd seen the glint of tears in her friend's eyes and it saddened her.

"Mia, don't you dare feel guilty for what I just said. I know you. You carry the weight of the world on your shoulders. Not everything that happens is your fault. Your mother being a bad mother is not your fault, your brother not having a childhood is not your fault, his ex taking him for a bundle of money is not your fault. And the fact that I was a bad mother and could more easily bond with you than my own kids is not your fault."

Tears slid beneath Mia's lashes as her friend came toward her with tears on her own cheeks.

"I am so proud of you, Mia, and all that you have become. Whatever choices I made in my life were mine to make. You were such a lovely child. And I loved you instantly. It's been a pleasure watching you grow and the idea that I influenced you in some way to help others is thrilling."

The two women embraced for a long moment until Mia pulled away and wiped her face with the back of her hand. "I think we both know I don't need to come to you anymore."

"You haven't needed to come to me for a long time, Mia."

"I know. I just like talking to you. I guess it's time to look for a new therapist. You're too close to me and I like it that way. I like that you're my friend."

Mia gave her friend another quick hug and headed for the door.

"So what are you going to do about the baby, Mia?"

"I'm not sure. I think Damien and I need to talk about it a bit more, but I'll keep in mind the cost to both the baby and my career."

Mia sat at the table alone, listening to her husband sing, watching the women scream. She smiled as the women flirted with Damien, knowing that at the end of the show he would sing the love song he'd written to and about her. Damien smiled at her with no hint that he still remembered her angry words from the morning.

Mia smiled back. Part of her knew the time wasn't right to be thinking of having a baby. She and Damien had not spent enough time together. They needed time for themselves before they became a family. Still, there was an empty spot in Mia's heart that craved the love of a baby. And by the time the show was over she still hadn't reached a decision.

When they reached home she'd pretty much decided to put it on hold when Damien began kissing her and carried her to their bed. At that moment the only thing on Mia's mind was making love with her husband. He smiled down at her and she smiled back. Then his hand reached out toward the nightstand on his side of the bed and he opened the drawer. A shiver of anticipation curled Mia's toes as she wondered what he was up to. She saw the foil wrapped paper and watched in horror as his gaze locked with hers, never wavering. He slid the condom on and entered her, his gaze still locked with hers.

MISTY BLUE

Before Mia could utter a complaint, she was quickly rolling toward the edge, her desire mixed with her husband's heat pushing her objections away for the moment. Afterward, she lay trembling in her husband's arms, sated in spite of the anger that lay low in her belly. Mia turned away and lay on her side of the bed. And when Damien curled his muscular body around hers, she moved away.

"Mia," Damien whispered, pulling her back and wrapping his body around her again, this time even tighter. "Our bed will not become out battleground. Remember?" he asked. "We both promised." He sucked her earlobe into his mouth and licked it. "Goodnight, baby girl," he whispered.

"Goodnight," she said and closed her eyes.

Mia had been up cleaning for over two hours when she felt her husband's presence. She paused in her work.

"Did you make coffee yet?"

"No."

"Do you want me to put it on?"

Nothing.

"Mia?"

Again she didn't answer but she did go into the kitchen. She started the coffee, made toast and eggs and put the plates on the table. All without speaking to her husband.

"We're not doing this, Mia."

Mia didn't even spare a glance in Damien's direction.

"I mean it, baby girl."

This time Mia looked up, still not answering him.

"You're giving me the silent treatment. And I'm telling you now we're not doing it."

Still nothing.

"Remember what you said to me before we married, Mia?"

She glared at him. She'd said a lot of things.

"You said no divorce."

Mia blinked, her heart thudding. He now had her attention. "It's things like this, nonsense that couples allow to fester until they stop trying, that cause divorce." He smiled slightly. "We're not going to let that happen. You're pissed at me, but you will talk to me."

"How do you plan on accomplishing that?"

Damien's smile grew bigger until Mia let go of her anger, realizing he was right. She was talking to him.

"A condom? Do you know how insulting that is? As if I'm a child. Or you think I'll try and trap you with a child you don't want."

"It was nasty," Damien conceded. "But I had to make you understand just how serious I am. As far as you're concerned, I may be whipped, baby girl, but only to a point. We're not having a baby to prove a point. A kid's not a toy. You don't get to take it back if you don't want it." He saw Mia wince and softened his tone. "We're not ready, Mia."

"Why are you the one who gets to make the decision?"

Damien didn't answer and she'd not expected that he would. "Tell me it's because you're the man and I'll slug you."

"I don't have a death wish," Damien answered at last. "I'd never say anything that crazy to a woman. That's suicidal."

"So tell me," Mia insisted. "Why do you get to make a decision that affects both of our lives?"

"What made you think it was your decision to make?" Damien countered. "Like you said, it's a decision that affects both of our lives."

Mia bit into the cinnamon toast. "I just want a baby."

"No, you don't, Mia, you want someone to mother. You want to see if it was really that hard for your mom. You don't know whether to forgive her or forget her, so you want to try it and see if you can do a better job."

Mia dropped the half-eaten toast back onto the plate. "Stop psychoanalyzing me," she snapped and pushed her chair back, intending to head back into the bedroom. In an instant Damien was standing in front of her.

"Like I said, baby girl, we can slug this out, but you're not running to the bedroom to close me out. Never again. It's a fight we're having, Mia. We'll live through it and we'll fight again. There is nothing you can do or say to push me away." He paused, his voice dropping an octave. "Tell me, why are you trying so hard to push me away?"

Mia's eyes closed and a ragged breath forced its way past her lungs. She shuddered, not backing away from Damien's open arms. He tightened his hold on her and she lay on his chest.

"Don't worry, Mia, when the time is right we'll have plenty of babies."

"No more condoms," Mia said softly. "Trust me to do the right thing."

He tilted her chin with the tip of his finger. "Listen to me, Mia. I'm happy that you're not repressing your feelings anymore. I know how hard all the changes you've been going through have been on you, but I won't be your punching bag." He smiled. "Its not that I can't take it, I don't want to take it. When you're angry at me, hell yes, yell at me. I'll deserve it. But you're not going to abuse me because you're angry at someone else. I'm not going to let you tear away at our marriage."

When she didn't answer, he lifted her chin even higher. "Are you listening to me, baby girl?"

"I'm listening," Mia answered.

"And?"

"And I think you're right. There are a couple of things I need to do. I need to talk to my brother and I need to talk to my mother."

"You're going to give her a call?"

"No, I'm going to Phoenix."

"Do you want me to go with you?"

Mia smiled. "No, this time I won't need a knight riding in to save the day. This is something I have to do on my own."

"I never thought of myself as your knight, more like your Prince Charming and you were my Sleeping Beauty." He leered at her. "And baby, I enjoyed awakening your passions."

His tongue slid into her mouth and a sense of urgency filled his kiss and his arousal pressed against her. Damien's muscles bunched with the swiftness of his hunger. He lifted her into his arms and carried her back into their bedroom. He entered her unsheathed, and Mia accepted that that was her husband's way of sealing the bargain. Just as he would not brook closed doors or her silence, she had a right to a few demands of her own. She wanted him without the feel of latex.

⚜

"You don't think I'm wrong to hate my sister, Dr. Terrell?"

Mia had given up trying to tell the patient that she wasn't a doctor, not yet. She wore a name badge that spelled out plainly that she was an assistant, little more than a student really. But for the past several months she'd been on her own more and more. And this patient had become one of her primary charges, going so far as to ask for her visits to be scheduled with Mia. While exhilarating, it was also scary.

"Doctor, did you hear me?"

"I heard you," Mia answered.

"Well, what do you think? Should I be angry after all this time that my sister slept with my husband and had his baby? After all, the child is my niece. My pastor told me I have to forgive her for my peace of mind. What do you think?"

"Tell her to go to hell," Mia blurted out without thinking. "You don't need her in your life." It wasn't until the patient stared at her open-mouthed that Mia realized what she'd said.

"Are you saying I'm right?" the patient asked.

"I'm saying your feelings on this are valid." Mia thought momentarily of the consequences of what she was about to say and wondered who would be reviewing the taped conversation.

"My parents told me to be strong, to be heroic and keep the pain inside. I've been trying to be heroic, doctor, but I'm losing the battle. I don't think I know how to be a heroine."

"My idea of being heroic is living through the pain, making mistakes, not knowing what to do, yet not giving up. You're here, you're talking, you're not giving up. You're trying to get better, trying to accept your own role in your life. And I find that heroic. You could just say forget it, but you haven't," Mia said.

"But doctor, all the women in romance novels, they're always so strong."

"That's fiction. In the world I live in there is no such thing as perfection. No one is strong all the time, trust me."

"How about you? You always seem in control. You seem like one of those romance heroines. Are you?"

Mia smiled. "I'm human." She stood then. "So are you. Yes, we professionals advocate forgiveness and it's because its healthy for your own spirit."

"What do you think I should do?"

"You know I can't tell you what to do." Mia sighed, then decided to do a little more than book protocol psychology, aware that when she did she might very well lose her rights to treat patients until she became a full-fledged psychologist. Right now she didn't care. Her patient needed help now, not in a year when she was done with school.

"I'll tell you what I'd do." Mia saw the hope surge through the woman and knew she was doing the right thing.

"I would confront the person who'd hurt me and I would tell her that she'd hurt me. I wouldn't worry so much about the forgiving. I'd opt for baby steps, first things first," Mia finished.

She smiled, knowing she'd just solved her own dilemma. She was planning to implement the things she was telling the patient. She too would confront her own demons. It was past time she put an end to the ghosts that had chased her for most of her life.

"I've wanted to tell my sister how I've felt for a long time. I really thought that I should do that, but everyone told me not to."

"It's your life," Mia advised, "not theirs."

"I'm going to do it." The woman smiled at Mia.

"Then that makes you heroic," Mia said and hugged the patient, giving her strength and receiving it as well.

Twenty minutes later when the patient had gone, Dr. Grey stuck her head in before Mia's next patient. "I was observing you with the patient today."

Mia waited.

"You did a good job."

"Thanks," Mia answered, not bothering to tell her friend that she was going to take her own advice. From the look on her face, Mia knew Dr. Grey was already aware of her decision.

"By the way, Mia, I forgot to tape today's session. I'm sorry we don't have a record of the session." She smiled at Mia and closed the door.

Mia had made her decision. She and Keefe both needed closure on their past. She was the only one who could give her brother what he needed so that he could have his future without having to worry about Mia.

"Hi," she said, hugging him when he entered the apartment.

"Hey, where's Damien?"

"He has a class tonight. I wanted us to have time to talk."

"Anything wrong?" Keefe asked.

Mia noticed that he looked away. "Kee, don't worry, Damien and I are very happy. I just wanted to tell you what I'm planning on doing. I also thought we needed to clear some things up." He was frowning at her, a puzzled look on his face. "Why haven't you asked Ashleigh to marry you?"

"What?" he sputtered.

"You heard me. You love her, don't you?"

"Yes."

"Then why haven't you asked her to marry you?"

"I don't know. I guess the time isn't right."

"I'll tell you why, because somewhere in the back of your mind you feel that you have to be there for me, that if something happens with Damien you want to make sure you don't have a wife who can object to your running to save me." She smiled. "Big brother, I don't need saving anymore."

"Mia, I didn't—"

"Yeah, you did, maybe not consciously but we've both been tied to our past, as hard as we've tried to get away from it. I'm going to do something about it."

Mia studied her brother for a moment. "I've ended my sessions with Doctor Grey."

"When?"

"Oh, a couple of weeks ago. I don't need them anymore, Keefe." She smiled. "I don't have any more ghosts. I remember everything." She saw the worried look that came into his eyes and she smiled again. "You can stop worrying, big brother, nothing happened."

She saw him swallow, saw the tears that came into his eyes, before he asked, "Really, Mia, nothing happened?"

"Nothing." She smiled at him. "I was just afraid and I wanted to be with you, but nothing happened."

Her brother gripped her in a bear hug and held her for the longest time. She felt his shudders of relief and knew she'd done the right thing. Mia still didn't remember what had happened or had not happened to her while in foster care, but she knew her brother needed to believe that nothing had happened to her. And who knew, maybe nothing had.

When he finally let her go, the look in his eyes was what she'd waited an entire lifetime to see, joy and a duty fulfilled. She'd rid her brother of the unnecessary guilt he'd carried and she'd rid herself of her guilt for robbing him of his childhood at the same time. It might be too late for her to give him back his childhood, but it definitely wasn't too late for her to give him what he needed to begin a real commitment with Ashleigh.

"You said you were going to do something," Keefe said, his voice still hoarse with tears and relief.

"I am. I'm going to Phoenix."

"Why, Mia? She'll only hurt you again."

"That's because in the past I gave her the power to hurt me, Kee. I'm going to go there and face her and take it back."

"Do you want me to go with you?"

"No, big brother, I'm going to go this one alone."

"I don't want her to hurt you again, Mia."

"I'm a big girl. If I get hurt I'll deal with it. It won't be your fault. But I don't think I'm going to get hurt, Keefe. She's a sick woman. All the jokes we said about her through the years, they weren't jokes. She does have a narcissistic personality. She won't care about anything that I have to say to her."

"Then why are you going?"

"Because I have to say the things I've held in my heart. I have to say them to her face, for me." She smiled, "And for you. I've been taking out my anger at her on Damien and I'm not going to do that anymore."

Keefe smiled. "So the new Mia pissed her husband off, huh?"

"Royally," Mia answered, laughing. "He told me in no uncertain terms that he wasn't taking my crap. He was right."

"You know, I'm liking that husband of yours more and more."

Mia hugged her brother again. "And he likes you, Kee."

"Seriously, Mia, when you…you know, when you and Damien…there are no images?"

"No, big brother. When my husband makes love to me, there are only the two of us in our bed." She saw her brother blush and she kissed his cheek. "I will always love you, Keefe Black. You were and are the best big brother that a girl could have."

Mia sat in the taxi for a moment, surveying her mother's home admiring the pale colors and the well-manicured lawn. It should be a nice house, Mia thought. After all, she'd gotten her brother to shell out a bundle in the last few years for its upkeep. She wondered what would happen now that the money would stop coming. For good.

"Miss, isn't this the address that you wanted?"

Mia glanced at the driver and noted that his attention had shifted and he was staring in the direction of her mother's home with a silly grin on his face. Immediately Mia's head snapped toward the porch. There stood her mother dressed in short black shorts and a black halter. She was smiling broadly and moving her body seductively. Mia knew neither the moves or the smile was for her. She glanced again at the driver.

"That's my mother," Mia said and saw the driver's eyes flick over her then back to her mother. "Listen, I won't be here very long. Do you think I could buy you dinner and then give you a call when I need you to come back?" When the driver didn't answer, Mia smiled. "I could introduce you to my mother when you return." *But I won't*, Mia thought to herself.

She had him. The man smiled at her and Mia handed over the money for the fare, along with money to treat the man to a meal. "I promise I'll make it worth your while."

"I may need to pick up another fare while I'm waiting If you take too long."

"A couple of hours should be more than enough time," Mia replied. "I'm thinking half of that time, you'll be eating." Mia glanced toward her mother, knowing that the driver would look also. "It won't be long," she said, then exited from the cab after getting the driver's number.

Mia walked toward her mother, shaking her head slightly at the attention her mother could still attract without trying. She almost laughed aloud at that crazy thought. What had she been thinking? Her mother tried all the time, constantly, in fact. She was beautiful and she knew it. And she used it for all it was worth.

When Mia got closer she saw something she'd never allowed herself to see before. Her mother was a middle-aged woman trying just a bit too hard to garner attention. She noticed the skin wasn't as taut as it had been and there was a thin sheen of foundation on her mother's face. Mia wondered if her mother had any idea how the desert heat would age her, but decided not to ask. She didn't care.

She glanced again at the too tight, too short clothing her mother wore and felt a moment of pity. She could imagine her mother at ninety in the same outfit, still thinking she was turning heads and all she would be getting more than likely would be laughs.

"Mia, you didn't have to bring the checks. Mailing them would have been fine."

Mia laughed out loud. "Nice to see you too." She then took a closer look around her mother's home, wondering how on earth the woman managed to pay for all the things in her house. She didn't work and there was no way either she or Keefe had shelled out all the money for the luxuries. Mia looked at the sixty-two inch plasma screen television. She didn't even know plasma screens came in that size. She wondered what would happen to all her mother's possessions when the money stopped. Mia shook the thought away. She didn't care.

"I didn't bring a check, Mom. I just came to talk."

"Then why didn't you use the phone? They do have those in Chicago. Right?"

"So if I had a check, you'd be happy to see me?"

"At least there would be a reason for you being here. Why are you here?"

"Who knows? This seems to be more of an exercise in futility now."

"What?"

Mia shook her head. "I know that you tried to seduce my husband at my wedding." She stuck her hand out when her mother attempted to protest. "Save it, Mom. I know you groped him. I came here to tell you what a despicable woman you are and that I hate you and will never forgive you. I came to tell you how much you've hurt me my entire life, to let you know how much pain you caused both your children. I came to tell you that because of you I worried about being a slut and almost screwed up my marriage because of the nonsense you told me"

Mia sighed. "But now that I'm here and see you, I pity you."

"Pity me?"

"Yes, I pity you because at least for most of my life I wanted you in it. I needed you. I don't need you any longer."

"You ungrateful little snot. I did everything I could for you and your brother. Where the hell do you think you would be without me? If it wasn't for the advice I gave you, you wouldn't be with that husband of yours right now. And your brother wouldn't be with Ashleigh. You were both too stupid to know how to go after them."

Mia started laughing. "That's why I pity you. You believe that. Listen, I am grateful to you for the one time in my life when you helped me. That was more than I expected of you, so thank you for that. But your telling me that your life is my fault, that won't work anymore, Mom. I'm over it. I've let go of the guilt that I never should have had in the first place. Your life and your choices were never my fault."

"Well, I know what was your fault. You could have kept your ass in foster care and allowed your brother a chance to have a life free from you. Have you let go of the guilt for making your brother responsible for you, for him not having a life because of your needs coming first? He had to take care of poor crazy Mia before she wound up in the looney bin."

"Yes, that's over too," Mia answered calmly as she watched the shock come across her mother's face. She'd played her trump card and lost. Mia was not crumbling into tears as her mother had imagined.

"You see, Mom," Mia began, "it wasn't my fault that Keefe's childhood was taken. It was yours. It wasn't his job to take care of me. That was yours also. Neither of us asked to come into this world, so the things that happened to us fall on your head. Am I grateful that my big brother didn't abandon me as you did? Yes. Do I feel guilty that he did it? Not any longer."

"And you had to come here to tell me this. You could have done this on the phone."

"I didn't want to. I needed to tell you this to your face. I needed to let go of the hurt. I've allowed you to hurt me for too long now. It's over. You can't hurt me anymore."

"I hope you didn't think I was going to get all teary and tell you I'm sorry. As far as your husband goes, are you sure it wasn't him trying to seduce me? His father was trying hard enough. The one thing I've never had to do as far as men are concerned is try to get them, Mia. They all want me. They always have. So if you're having problems with your husband, don't come here dumping it at my doorstep. It's not my fault if you can't satisfy your husband. Don't blame me if he sees you and thinks of me. That's also not my fault."

Mia grinned. "Mom, if you had been able to satisfy even one of your husbands half as well as I please mine, you'd still be married. I can guarantee you that when he's with me he's not thinking of you. He sees me, Mom, and only me."

Mia pulled out her cell and dialed the number of the taxi she had asked to wait for her. She had somehow known it wasn't going to be a very long visit. "By the way, I've decided to call you Lillian. Calling you Mom never felt right, since you never behaved as one.

"Good. I'd rather both you and your brother call me Lillian. I don't want anyone to know I have kids as old as the two of you." She patted her hair. I look far too young. Did your brother send a check?"

Mia looked around at her mother's home, barely able to believe the woman would still ask for money. Then Mia remembered what she'd told Keefe was the truth. Their mother was unable to care for anyone other than herself. She was her main concern.

"You look like you're doing pretty well to me without Keefe's help."

"I need money."

"Get a job."

"Can't you give me a loan?"

"I could. But I won't. You're not my responsibility. You're young, you're healthy, you're an adult. Get a job!"

"I'll call your brother for the money."

"Go ahead. We both know Keefe is not going to give you a dime."

"He will if you ask him to."

Mia couldn't help laughing even though she felt sorrier than ever for her mother. Mia knew she didn't get it and she never would. Mia was done wasting her breath.

"Mia, please?"

"Lillian, no. There is no way I'm ever again going to ask Keefe to hand over money to you. The gravy train is over. You can't blackmail either of us any longer. You won't love us no matter what we give to you. You couldn't if you tried, and frankly, we just don't care anymore. Either of us."

Mia heard the honk of the horn. "By the way, I'm changing my number," she said as she walked out the door. "If I were you and I really needed money, I'd think about trying to find a new job. The old one of getting paid for making me feel guilty for ruining your life is over."

Mia climbed back into the waiting taxi for the ride back to the airport. "The introduction isn't going to happen," she explained to the driver. "But the tip will make up for it. Thanks."

She sat back with a sigh. Mia didn't feel what she thought she would when she'd made the journey out. There was no jubilation, no sorrow and no tears. Only the sense of accomplishment, the quiet closing of the door on her past.

She leaned back into the cushion and felt the weight she'd carried for more than half of her life lift from her shoulders. For the first time in her life she truly did feel free. She consciously thought of all the things in the past that had brought a surge of guilt, now nothing. The guilt was where it belonged, in the past. As for her, she was heading home to be with her husband. Damien was her present and her future.

Mia lay in bed in her husband's arms, telling him of the visit with her mother. "It's over," she said when she was done. "It really is over."

"Did she admit to what she had done?" Damien asked.

"Of course not," Mia replied. She said it was you, that I didn't satisfy you."

"And?"

"And I laughed in her face. Like you said, all that waiting, it really did help. I have no doubts about us. I know better."

Damien grinned. "I'm happy to her that, Mrs. Terrell, because I could use with some satisfaction right about now." Mia grinned and gave in to her husband's needs and her own, amazed that she'd ever allowed anything to come between them. She closed her eyes, enjoying the feel of his hands on her body, his fingers inside her, and her hands on him. She moaned.

"Open your eyes, Mia."

Mia opened her eyes slowly and smiled at the love she saw reflected in her husband's eyes.

"Tell me, Mia, what do you see?"

"I see you, Damien, my beautiful, wonderful husband. I see you."

She felt him sheathe himself deeply inside her body and again her eyes closed involuntarily. An internal explosion rocked her as she screamed her husband's name. Mia clung to Damien as the feeling intensified and built again and they soared high above the clouds together. His shudders became her own as she fought to take him even deeper than he was. Tears of joy washed away everything but the two of them and rivulets tunneled down her cheek as the earthquake of her soul tapered off.

"Mia, Damien moaned. "What did you see?"

"Only you, my love," she replied. "Eyes closed or eyes open, I see only you. All of the ghosts have been banished for good."

EPILOGUE

"Mia Terrell."

Mia was beaming as she walked across the stage. It was official. She was receiving her Ph.D. She smiled as she stopped in front of Dr. Grey, her friend, her ex-therapist. She'd chosen her to do the honors of giving her her newest degree. When it was done, Mia looked down into the audience and smiled at her husband. Damien was beaming also, his love for her apparent in his eyes. Keefe was wiping away tears and Ashleigh was trying to steady her hands to get a picture. Mia posed for a moment, then moved from the stage.

It had been a long road to her destination. When she walked to the group of people clustered around to greet her, Damien lifted her from the floor and kissed her before releasing her to her brother. Keefe, speechless, hugged her tightly, then released her to Ashleigh, whose hug was almost as tight as his had been. Mia couldn't help noticing the glow on Ashleigh's face. It was almost as bright as the diamond engagement ring Keefe had placed on Ashleigh's finger.

Mia turned and saw Kathy coming toward her with Mark, the man Mia had introduced her to, at her side. Mia smiled at them, and hugged them both. Out of the corner of her eye she saw Charles walk up and look longingly at Kathy. Mia wondered if he'd waited too late. But that wasn't her problem. It was their lives and they would have to work it out.

"Damien Terrell."

Mia kissed Damien. "Go ahead, baby, that's you." Damien ran onto the stage to collect his bachelor's degree. Mia's heart was bursting with pride. She was glad that they'd done this together, glad that both ceremonies had been combined. It hadn't mattered whose name was called first. It was a thrill that they could celebrate their individual victories together. Damien had had more college credits than they'd thought and in the year she'd worked on her Ph.D. he'd worked on his own degree. He'd already been accepted at a top veterinarian college and they would manage to pay for it together.

As for the baby, Mia had put that on hold. Right now she was plenty busy showing her husband just how much she loved him.

ABOUT THE AUTHOR

Award winning author **Dyanne Davis** lives in a Chicago suburb with her husband Bill and their son Bill Jr. She retired from nursing several years ago to pursue her lifelong dream of becoming a published author. She was able to accomplish this with her husband's blessing and financial support.

Her first novel, *The Color of Trouble*, was released July of 2003. The novel was received with high praise and several awards. Dyanne won an Emma for Favorite New Author of the Year and was presented with the award in NYC in April of 2004.

Her second novel, *The Wedding Gown*, was released in February 2004 and has also received much praise. The book was chosen by Blackexpressions, a subsidiary of Doubleday Book club as a monthly club pick. The book was an Emma finalist in March 2005 for Steamiest Romance and for Book of the Year.

You can reach Dyanne at her website. **www.dyannedavis.com** She also has an on-line blog where readers can post questions and photos. http://dyannedavis.blogspot.com.

Excerpt from

THROUGH THE FIRE

BY

SERESSIA GLASS

Release Date: March 2006

CHAPTER ONE

Brandt Hughes sat in the shadows of his living room, searching for a reason not to die.

Photos lay scattered among the wood shavings of his carvings. Photos he didn't have to see to recall, snapshots of the life he'd once had. In the last four years memories had deteriorated into nightmares that haunted him and sapped at the innate instinct to survive.

Brady… He hung his head as his son's name echoed through the remnants of his heart. His son would have been eight years old tomorrow. Which meant Brandt would have to endure a day of phone calls and visits from his parents, brothers, and sisters. Maya would want to go with him to Brady's grave, his mother would concoct some home repair emergency to get him to visit, even though his father owned half of Brandt's construction business.

It had been bearable the year before, the year before that. But now the grief sat like a stone on his chest as it had those first few days, weeks, months after Brady, after Sarah. It weighed him down, threatening to sink him. Grief and anger. Always the anger.

He couldn't face his family tomorrow. Couldn't face his parents and siblings staring at him, pitying him, accusing him. No, he'd have to do something today.

The phone shrieked. He grabbed for it, clutching it like the lifeline it was. Probably Maya, probably worried. He had to convince her that she needed to look after her new family, not her sorry excuse for a brother. "Yeah?"

"It's Mack."

Brandt forced his muscles to relax as he heard his best friend's voice. "What's up?"

"I need a favor," Mack said in that same no-nonsense voice he'd used when leading their unit. Mackenzie "Mack" Zane had never been one for beating around bushes or tolerating fools. Why he still bothered with Brandt, the latter had no idea. "Can you come down to Serena Bay?"

Serena Bay. Brandt remembered that Mack had described it as a small lazy town on the east coast of Florida. He considered it for half a moment. Spending time in a small town during a Florida summer might do him some good. Anything would be better than where he was, what he was doing. "When?"

"As soon as you can," his friend answered, "but don't you want to know what the favor is?"

"Don't need to know." Brandt would do anything for Mack, especially since the commander had saved his ass on more than one occasion. Still, curiosity made him ask, "You out of deputies or something?"

He still couldn't believe that Mack had traded in his general issue uniform for small-town sheriff brown. Being brass in Miami, maybe, but Sheriff Andy? On the other hand, if Mack had gotten as tired of the bloodshed as he had, Miami wasn't the place to go for law enforcement.

"Nothing like that, though you know the offer will always be on the table," Mack replied. "An old Spanish mission on the coast is getting renovated, but no one's got the skills to restore the chapel. I think you could do it."

Brandt failed an attempt at a laugh. "Think they'll let me in the door?"

"I didn't get struck by lightning when I went inside," Mack informed him. "Besides, you didn't do anything I didn't order you to do."

"I've gotten more blood on my hands since then." Brady. Sarah.

"You know my opinion on that, so I won't waste my breath," his former commanding officer said evenly. "But I won't lie to you about the mission. The place would probably be better off if they razed it and started over. It's definitely a challenge. This building's just waiting for you to bring it back to life."

"A challenge, huh?" Why not? Getting away would probably do him some good. And maybe, just maybe, restoring the chapel would earn him some brownie points with the man upstairs.

"I've done work in St. Augustine, so I'm good to go. Give me two days to clear things here and I'll be there."

"Excellent. Let me give you the address and directions. Got something to write on?" Brandt retrieved pen and paper, and then Mack rattled off the information.

Afterward, Brandt disconnected, then sat back in his chair. Relief swept through him. It didn't matter if the construction help Mack needed consisted of building a birdhouse or an outhouse. It would give him something to do and somewhere to go, somewhere where memories wouldn't stalk his every waking moment and sleepless night. Somewhere where no one knew or cared about his past, his sins.

He didn't need two days to get things in order, either. He'd had everything in his life settled for years, no loose ends, just in case.

Leaning to the left, he placed the cordless phone on the table. He hesitated a moment, then grabbed his M9 Beretta and popped the clip out.

Today wasn't the day.

2006 Publication Schedule

January

A Lover's Legacy	Love Lasts Forever	Under the Cherry
Veronica Parker	Dominiqua Douglas	Moon
1-58571-167-5	1-58571-187-X	Christal Jordan-Mims
$9.95	$9.95	1-58571-169-1
		$12.95

February

Second Chances at Love	Enchanted Desire	Caught Up
Cheris Hodges	Wanda Y. Thomas	Deatri King Bey
1-58571-188-8	1-58571-176-4	1-58571-178-0
$9.95	$9.95	$12.95

March

I'm Gonna Make You	Through the Fire	Notes When Summer
Love Me	Seressia Glass	Ends
Gwyneth Bolton	1-58571-173-X	Beverly Lauderdale
1-58571-181-0	$9.95	1-58571-180-2
$9.95		$12.95

April

Sin and Surrender	Unearthing Passions	Between Tears
J.M. Jeffries	Elaine Sims	Pamela Ridley
1-58571-189-6	1-58571-184-5	1-58571-179-9
$9.95	$9.95	$12.95

May

Misty Blue	Ironic	Cricket's Serenade
Dyanne Davis	Pamela Leigh Starr	Carolita Blythe
1-58571-186-1	1-58571-168-3	1-58571-183-7
$9.95	$9.95	$12.95

June

Cupid	Havana Sunrise
Barbara Keaton	Kymberly Hunt
1-58571-174-8	1-58571-182-9
$9.95	$9.95

2006 Publication Schedule (continued)

July

Love Me Carefully
A.C. Arthur
1-58571-177-2
$9.95

No Ordinary Love
Angela Weaver
1-58571-198-5
$9.95

Rehoboth Road
Anita Ballard-Jones
1-58571-196-9
$12.95

August

Scent of Rain
Annetta P. Lee
158571-199-3
$9.95

Love in High Gear
Charlotte Roy
158571-185-3
$9.95

Rise of the Phoenix
Kenneth Whetstone
1-58571-197-7
$12.95

September

The Business of Love
Cheris Hodges
1-58571-193-4
$9.95

Rock Star
Rosyln Hardy Holcomb
1-58571-200-0
$9.95

A Dead Man Speaks
Lisa Jones Johnson
1-58571-203-5
$12.95

October

Rivers of the Soul-Part 1
Leslie Esdaile
1-58571-223-X
$9.95

A Dangerous Woman
J.M. Jeffries
1-58571-195-0
$9.95

Sinful Intentions
Crystal Rhodes
1-58571-201-9
$12.95

November

Only You
Crystal Hubbard
1-58571-208-6
$9.95

Ebony Eyes
Kei Swanson
1-58571-194-2
$9.95

Still Waters Run Deep –
Part 2
Leslie Esdaile
1-58571-224-8
$9.95

December

Let's Get It On
Dyanne Davis
1-58571-210-8
$9.95

Nights Over Egypt
Barbara Keaton
1-58571-192-6
$9.95

A Pefect Place to Pray
I.L. Goodwin
1-58571-202-7
$12.95

Other Genesis Press, Inc. Titles

A Dangerous Deception	J.M. Jeffries	$8.95
A Dangerous Love	J.M. Jeffries	$8.95
A Dangerous Obsession	J.M. Jeffries	$8.95
A Drummer's Beat to Mend	Kei Swanson	$9.95
A Happy Life	Charlotte Harris	$9.95
A Heart's Awakening	Veronica Parker	$9.95
A Lark on the Wing	Phyliss Hamilton	$9.95
A Love of Her Own	Cheris F. Hodges	$9.95
A Love to Cherish	Beverly Clark	$8.95
A Risk of Rain	Dar Tomlinson	$8.95
A Twist of Fate	Beverly Clark	$8.95
A Will to Love	Angie Daniels	$9.95
Acquisitions	Kimberley White	$8.95
Across	Carol Payne	$12.95
After the Vows	Leslie Esdaile	$10.95
(Summer Anthology)	T.T. Henderson	
	Jacqueline Thomas	
Again My Love	Kayla Perrin	$10.95
Against the Wind	Gwynne Forster	$8.95
All I Ask	Barbara Keaton	$8.95
Ambrosia	T.T. Henderson	$8.95
An Unfinished Love Affair	Barbara Keaton	$8.95
And Then Came You	Dorothy Elizabeth Love	$8.95
Angel's Paradise	Janice Angelique	$9.95
At Last	Lisa G. Riley	$8.95
Best of Friends	Natalie Dunbar	$8.95
Beyond the Rapture	Beverly Clark	$9.95
Blaze	Barbara Keaton	$9.95
Blood Lust	J. M. Jeffries	$9.95
Bodyguard	Andrea Jackson	$9.95
Boss of Me	Diana Nyad	$8.95
Bound by Love	Beverly Clark	$8.95
Breeze	Robin Hampton Allen	$10.95

Other Genesis Press, Inc. Titles (continued)

Broken	Dar Tomlinson	$24.95
By Design	Barbara Keaton	$8.95
Cajun Heat	Charlene Berry	$8.95
Careless Whispers	Rochelle Alers	$8.95
Cats & Other Tales	Marilyn Wagner	$8.95
Caught in a Trap	Andre Michelle	$8.95
Caught Up In the Rapture	Lisa G. Riley	$9.95
Cautious Heart	Cheris F Hodges	$8.95
Chances	Pamela Leigh Starr	$8.95
Cherish the Flame	Beverly Clark	$8.95
Class Reunion	Irma Jenkins/John Brown	$12.95
Code Name: Diva	J.M. Jeffries	$9.95
Conquering Dr. Wexler's Heart	Kimberley White	$9.95
Crossing Paths, Tempting Memories	Dorothy Elizabeth Love	$9.95
Cypress Whisperings	Phyllis Hamilton	$8.95
Dark Embrace	Crystal Wilson Harris	$8.95
Dark Storm Rising	Chinelu Moore	$10.95
Daughter of the Wind	Joan Xian	$8.95
Deadly Sacrifice	Jack Kean	$22.95
Designer Passion	Dar Tomlinson	$8.95
Dreamtective	Liz Swados	$5.95
Ebony Butterfly II	Delilah Dawson	$14.95
Echoes of Yesterday	Beverly Clark	$9.95
Eden's Garden	Elizabeth Rose	$8.95
Everlastin' Love	Gay G. Gunn	$8.95
Everlasting Moments	Dorothy Elizabeth Love	$8.95
Everything and More	Sinclair Lebeau	$8.95
Everything but Love	Natalie Dunbar	$8.95
Eve's Prescription	Edwina Martin Arnold	$8.95
Falling	Natalie Dunbar	$9.95
Fate	Pamela Leigh Starr	$8.95
Finding Isabella	A.J. Garrotto	$8.95

Other Genesis Press, Inc. Titles (continued)

Forbidden Quest	Dar Tomlinson	$10.95
Forever Love	Wanda Thomas	$8.95
From the Ashes	Kathleen Suzanne	$8.95
	Jeanne Sumerix	
Gentle Yearning	Rochelle Alers	$10.95
Glory of Love	Sinclair LeBeau	$10.95
Go Gentle into that Good Night	Malcom Boyd	$12.95
Goldengroove	Mary Beth Craft	$16.95
Groove, Bang, and Jive	Steve Cannon	$8.99
Hand in Glove	Andrea Jackson	$9.95
Hard to Love	Kimberley White	$9.95
Hart & Soul	Angie Daniels	$8.95
Heartbeat	Stephanie Bedwell-Grime	$8.95
Hearts Remember	M. Loui Quezada	$8.95
Hidden Memories	Robin Allen	$10.95
Higher Ground	Leah Latimer	$19.95
Hitler, the War, and the Pope	Ronald Rychiak	$26.95
How to Write a Romance	Kathryn Falk	$18.95
I Married a Reclining Chair	Lisa M. Fuhs	$8.95
Indigo After Dark Vol. I	Nia Dixon/Angelique	$10.95
Indigo After Dark Vol. II	Dolores Bundy/Cole Riley	$10.95
Indigo After Dark Vol. III	Montana Blue/Coco Morena	$10.95
Indigo After Dark Vol. IV	Cassandra Colt/	$14.95
	Diana Richeaux	
Indigo After Dark Vol. V	Delilah Dawson	$14.95
Icie	Pamela Leigh Starr	$8.95
I'll Be Your Shelter	Giselle Carmichael	$8.95
I'll Paint a Sun	A.J. Garrotto	$9.95
Illusions	Pamela Leigh Starr	$8.95
Indiscretions	Donna Hill	$8.95
Intentional Mistakes	Michele Sudler	$9.95
Interlude	Donna Hill	$8.95
Intimate Intentions	Angie Daniels	$8.95

Other Genesis Press, Inc. Titles (continued)

Jolie's Surrender	Edwina Martin-Arnold	$8.95
Kiss or Keep	Debra Phillips	$8.95
Lace	Giselle Carmichael	$9.95
Last Train to Memphis	Elsa Cook	$12.95
Lasting Valor	Ken Olsen	$24.95
Let Us Prey	Hunter Lundy	$25.95
Life Is Never As It Seems	J.J. Michael	$12.95
Lighter Shade of Brown	Vicki Andrews	$8.95
Love Always	Mildred E. Riley	$10.95
Love Doesn't Come Easy	Charlyne Dickerson	$8.95
Love Unveiled	Gloria Greene	$10.95
Love's Deception	Charlene Berry	$10.95
Love's Destiny	M. Loui Quezada	$8.95
Mae's Promise	Melody Walcott	$8.95
Magnolia Sunset	Giselle Carmichael	$8.95
Matters of Life and Death	Lesego Malepe, Ph.D.	$15.95
Meant to Be	Jeanne Sumerix	$8.95
Midnight Clear	Leslie Esdaile	$10.95
(Anthology)	Gwynne Forster	
	Carmen Green	
	Monica Jackson	
Midnight Magic	Gwynne Forster	$8.95
Midnight Peril	Vicki Andrews	$10.95
Misconceptions	Pamela Leigh Starr	$9.95
Montgomery's Children	Richard Perry	$14.95
My Buffalo Soldier	Barbara B. K. Reeves	$8.95
Naked Soul	Gwynne Forster	$8.95
Next to Last Chance	Louisa Dixon	$24.95
No Apologies	Seressia Glass	$8.95
No Commitment Required	Seressia Glass	$8.95
No Regrets	Mildred E. Riley	$8.95
Nowhere to Run	Gay G. Gunn	$10.95
O Bed! O Breakfast!	Rob Kuehnle	$14.95

Other Genesis Press, Inc. Titles (continued)

Object of His Desire	A. C. Arthur	$8.95
Office Policy	A. C. Arthur	$9.95
Once in a Blue Moon	Dorianne Cole	$9.95
One Day at a Time	Bella McFarland	$8.95
Outside Chance	Louisa Dixon	$24.95
Passion	T.T. Henderson	$10.95
Passion's Blood	Cherif Fortin	$22.95
Passion's Journey	Wanda Thomas	$8.95
Past Promises	Jahmel West	$8.95
Path of Fire	T.T. Henderson	$8.95
Path of Thorns	Annetta P. Lee	$9.95
Peace Be Still	Colette Haywood	$12.95
Picture Perfect	Reon Carter	$8.95
Playing for Keeps	Stephanie Salinas	$8.95
Pride & Joi	Gay G. Gunn	$15.95
Pride & Joi	Gay G. Gunn	$8.95
Promises to Keep	Alicia Wiggins	$8.95
Quiet Storm	Donna Hill	$10.95
Reckless Surrender	Rochelle Alers	$6.95
Red Polka Dot in a World of Plaid	Varian Johnson	$12.95
Reluctant Captive	Joyce Jackson	$8.95
Rendezvous with Fate	Jeanne Sumerix	$8.95
Revelations	Cheris F. Hodges	$8.95
Rivers of the Soul	Leslie Esdaile	$8.95
Rocky Mountain Romance	Kathleen Suzanne	$8.95
Rooms of the Heart	Donna Hill	$8.95
Rough on Rats and Tough on Cats	Chris Parker	$12.95
Secret Library Vol. 1	Nina Sheridan	$18.95
Secret Library Vol. 2	Cassandra Colt	$8.95
Shades of Brown	Denise Becker	$8.95
Shades of Desire	Monica White	$8.95

DYANNE DAVIS

Other Genesis Press, Inc. Titles (continued)

Shadows in the Moonlight	Jeanne Sumerix	$8.95
Sin	Crystal Rhodes	$8.95
So Amazing	Sinclair LeBeau	$8.95
Somebody's Someone	Sinclair LeBeau	$8.95
Someone to Love	Alicia Wiggins	$8.95
Song in the Park	Martin Brant	$15.95
Soul Eyes	Wayne L. Wilson	$12.95
Soul to Soul	Donna Hill	$8.95
Southern Comfort	J.M. Jeffries	$8.95
Still the Storm	Sharon Robinson	$8.95
Still Waters Run Deep	Leslie Esdaile	$8.95
Stories to Excite You	Anna Forrest/Divine	$14.95
Subtle Secrets	Wanda Y. Thomas	$8.95
Suddenly You	Crystal Hubbard	$9.95
Sweet Repercussions	Kimberley White	$9.95
Sweet Tomorrows	Kimberly White	$8.95
Taken by You	Dorothy Elizabeth Love	$9.95
Tattooed Tears	T. T. Henderson	$8.95
The Color Line	Lizzette Grayson Carter	$9.95
The Color of Trouble	Dyanne Davis	$8.95
The Disappearance of Allison Jones	Kayla Perrin	$5.95
The Honey Dipper's Legacy	Pannell-Allen	$14.95
The Joker's Love Tune	Sidney Rickman	$15.95
The Little Pretender	Barbara Cartland	$10.95
The Love We Had	Natalie Dunbar	$8.95
The Man Who Could Fly	Bob & Milana Beamon	$18.95
The Missing Link	Charlyne Dickerson	$8.95
The Price of Love	Sinclair LeBeau	$8.95
The Smoking Life	Ilene Barth	$29.95
The Words of the Pitcher	Kei Swanson	$8.95
Three Wishes	Seressia Glass	$8.95
Ties That Bind	Kathleen Suzanne	$8.95
Tiger Woods	Libby Hughes	$5.95

269

Other Genesis Press, Inc. Titles (continued)

Time is of the Essence	Angie Daniels	$9.95
Timeless Devotion	Bella McFarland	$9.95
Tomorrow's Promise	Leslie Esdaile	$8.95
Truly Inseparable	Wanda Y. Thomas	$8.95
Unbreak My Heart	Dar Tomlinson	$8.95
Uncommon Prayer	Kenneth Swanson	$9.95
Unconditional	A.C. Arthur	$9.95
Unconditional Love	Alicia Wiggins	$8.95
Until Death Do Us Part	Susan Paul	$8.95
Vows of Passion	Bella McFarland	$9.95
Wedding Gown	Dyanne Davis	$8.95
What's Under Benjamin's Bed	Sandra Schaffer	$8.95
When Dreams Float	Dorothy Elizabeth Love	$8.95
Whispers in the Night	Dorothy Elizabeth Love	$8.95
Whispers in the Sand	LaFlorya Gauthier	$10.95
Wild Ravens	Altonya Washington	$9.95
Yesterday Is Gone	Beverly Clark	$10.95
Yesterday's Dreams, Tomorrow's Promises	Reon Laudat	$8.95
Your Precious Love	Sinclair LeBeau	$8.95

Order Form

Mail to: Genesis Press, Inc.
P.O. Box 101
Columbus, MS 39703

Name _____
Address _____
City/State _____ Zip _____
Telephone _____

Ship to (if different from above)
Name _____
Address _____
City/State _____ Zip _____
Telephone _____

Credit Card Information
Credit Card # _____ ☐ Visa ☐ Mastercard
Expiration Date (mm/yy) _____ ☐ AmEx ☐ Discover

Qty.	Author	Title	Price	Total

Use this order form, or call 1-888-INDIGO-1

Total for books _____
Shipping and handling:
  $5 first two books,
  $1 each additional book _____
Total S & H _____
Total amount enclosed _____
Mississippi residents add 7% sales tax